AWAKENING

BEAUTIES FROM ASHES

BOOK 4

ENDORSEMENTS FOR AWAKENING— BEAUTIES FROM ASHES BOOK FOUR

The Beauties from Ashes series reaches beyond this world to the unseen spiritual battle waging around us. Captivating and at times disturbing. *Awakening* delivers the satisfying conclusion readers have been waiting for. A must-read for those who love page-turning teen drama.

—**Carol Alwood**, author, The Good Shadows series

Beckie Lindsey doesn't hold back, and I'm so glad she didn't! In this next installment of the Beauty from Ashes series, we learn that being a Christian doesn't let us off the hook in terms of spiritual warfare. In fact, sometimes it gets exponentially worse. Our beloved characters face issues such as teen pregnancy and adoption, bulimia, suicidal thoughts, and more. Laced with hope and healing, Lindsey engages readers authentically. We need more books like this.

—**Hope Bolinger,** author of the Blaze trilogy and the Dear Hero duology

Once again, Beckie Lindsey has crafted a wonderfully entertaining story. *Awakening*, the fourth book in the Beauties from Ashes series, is rich in the telling of God's mercy and unconditional love amidst life's spiritual battles to which today's teen will relate. Insights linger long after the book is read.

—**Marilyn King**, author of The Winds of Love Series

AWAKENING

BEAUTIES FROM ASHES

BOOK 4

BECKIE LINDSEY

Cover and Interior Design: Jeff Gifford, Gradient

Library Cataloging Data

Names: Lindsey, Beckie (Beckie Lindsey)

Awakening—Beauties from Ashes Book Four / Beckie Lindsey

354p. 23cm × 15cm (9in × 6 in.)

9781637971826 (HC) 9781637971864 (PB) | 9781637971901 (e-book)

Key Words: Demons, spiritual warfare, bulimia, teenage pregnancy, adoption, Christian, redemption

TRIGGER WARNING

Readers, please be advised that *Awakening*: Book Four of the Beauties from Ashes Series includes themes and events surrounding sexual trauma, depression, abortion, and suicide. Those of you who are experiencing these issues may find some of the content emotionally distressing and/or triggering. Triggering is defined as heightened feelings or memories associated with a traumatic experience when exposed to descriptions or similar events that are reminiscent of the experienced trauma. If this occurs, please stop reading and consult with a licensed mental health professional who specializes in the treatment of sexual trauma, depression or suicide.

If you have experienced sexual traumas or thought about suicide and have never talked about it with anyone, I encourage you to tell a trusted adult. I also encourage you to talk to a licensed mental health professional who can help you walk through the first steps of healing.

DEDICATION

For my bro and sis, Scott and Dawn

January 25, 2020

"I'll See You Soon"

ACKNOWLEDGMENTS

Jesus Christ, my Lord, and savior: I desire to live a life worthy of Your calling. I want everything I write to make you smile.

Scott, my husband: Thank you for your love, support, encouragement, and for always pointing me back to the Lord.

Charity, my daughter: You have been my greatest cheerleader. Thanks for the many hours you invested in this project and me. It is a true joy to share my writing dream with you.

Kevin, Chad, Katie, and Michelle, my other kiddos: Thanks for supporting your mom. I love you, family!

Krystal, Sue, Tammi, Jill, and Wendy: Thanks, dear friends for being my prayer partners, cheering me on when I felt unqualified, and for your love.

Patty, Rebekah, Kassidy, Karla, and Marilyn: Your critiques have helped make me a better writer. I could not have written these books without you all.

Carol Alwood and Martha Jane Orlando, my author pals: Thank you for taking the time to be another set of eyes on this project, and for your prayers.

The Beauties from Ashes Launch Team and book clubs: It truly takes a village to successfully publish and launch a book. I couldn't have done it without my amazing team.

Cyle Young, my agent: A huge shout out for your support and belief in these books.

Cristel Phelps, my editor: Thanks for going the extra mile to make these books shine. I also cannot tell you how much your kindness and gentle edits mean.

YOU, the reader! Thank you for reading the Beauties from Ashes series. It is my prayer that you are blessed richly.

CHAPTER 1

BRYCE needed to hit something. Hit it hard. He gripped the bat, waving it high over his shoulder, eye on the pitching machine. A white blur approached. SMACK! He sent it sailing several yards ahead of him. The machine fired another ball, which Bryce hit directly above his head, bouncing off the net, and landing behind him. Pitch, swing, smack. Pitch, swing, smack. It went like this until the machine timed out. Bryce tossed the bat aside with force. He removed his helmet and wiped his forehead with the back of his hand. It felt good to sweat. It felt good to have his mind focused on nothing but the ball for a while. But the feeling was short-lived. His thoughts were, once again, back on his pregnant girlfriend. She didn't even mention the flowers he sent, or more importantly, the card. What was it like to be in her place? Truth be told, there was part of him that understood why she listened to Dawn and was considering an abortion. He never told her, though. Better not to give her the idea termination was even an option.

A father and son walked toward Bryce's cage. "You 'bout done?" the man asked, yanking Bryce from his troubled thoughts.

Bryce nodded and shoved his gear into his bag. He opened the door to the chain-link fence, holding it ajar for the father and son. The gate clanged shut behind him as he walked away—sort of reminiscent of the door shutting on his childhood. He huffed, remembering when life was simple and his dad was proud of him. Now every time he looked into his dad's eyes, there was pain and disappointment.

His cleats crunched the red dirt as he walked past the bleachers. He paused and turned around, deciding to jog up the stairs for a bit more exercise. When Bryce reached the top, he grabbed ahold of the metal railing, his breath visible in the cool winter air. He eyed his gunmetal gray '67 Mustang in the parking lot below. He and his dad had spent a lot of hours working on that car together. It looked like a matchbox car from this vantage point. Things always look different and smaller from a higher vantage point. He wished this was the case with the seemingly insurmountable problems he faced.

God, I could use some help here.

A stream of early evening sunlight poked through an opening in the otherwise dismal cloudy sky. Silas emerged, his massive wings allowing him to hover just above Bryce. With outstretched arms, the angel spoke words of encouragement that fell over Bryce like a refreshing morning dew.

Bryce looked up at the sky, suddenly realizing there was one good thing in this whole mess—Krystal had turned to God … finally! What were the odds, when her mother had been a self-proclaimed atheist? But now, even her mom and brothers believed in God. Bryce's mouth turned upward in a lopsided grin. Yeah, things were going to be okay. He could sense it. Uplifted, he jogged down the bleachers and all the way to his car. He'd give

Krystal her space and call her tomorrow.

KRYSTAL pulled the blankets over her head to block the morning sunlight. Cheeto pawed to get inside the covers. Krystal lifted a small opening for him to slide in. She pulled him close, feeling his purr vibrate against her side. Why was life so complicated? Why couldn't she just be a cat? She found herself whispering an awkward prayer.

"God, it's me, Krystal." She paused, feeling dumb, but continued despite herself. "Pft! I guess you know that. I'm not really sure how to talk to you." She pulled Cheeto closer and tried again. "There's a lot going on, and I need your help. I really don't want to have this baby. I'm so scared. But it scares me even more to have an abortion. I feel like you want me to have the baby and let Grant and Lauren adopt it. They work for the church and they love kids. But Bryce says he wants to be a *family*. It seems like no matter what I do, someone will be hurt.

"And that's just *my* problems, God. I'm worried about my friends too—especially Sadie. I know she was lying through her teeth about Gary. I think she's slipping away from you. She didn't even care that we became Christians. That's not like her. Please help. Oh, and I'm worried about Mackenzie's mom too, and Tammi and my mom and—well, that's it for now. Thanks for listening. Uh, Amen."

Krystal forced herself up to face the day. At least, it was winter break and she didn't need to worry about those ridiculous packets from the independent study program. Maybe she would try calling Mackenzie and see if she wanted to bake cookies or do something festive like that. But first, she needed to get some coffee.

When Krystal entered the kitchen, she found Mom sitting at the breakfast nook reading the newspaper.

"Morning," Krystal said. She never said 'good' morning, because what's good about mornings?

Mom set down the newspaper. "Good morning. There're eggs, bacon, and coffee."

Krystal scooped some eggs and placed a few slices of turkey bacon onto her plate then plopped down across from her mom. Mom eyeballed Krystal over the rim of her steaming coffee. Krystal nibbled her bacon, trying to ignore Mom's obvious search for words. Saying they had a strained relationship was the understatement of the year. The tension between them had escalated when her dad walked out several months ago, and life had increased to Mach Five with Krystal's pregnancy.

Mom cleared her throat. "Sooo, what do you have planned for today?"

"I dunno."

"Well, I'm off work until after Christmas. Maybe we can do some shopping?"

Krystal's insides cringed at how awkward hanging out with Mom would be. "Um, I'm sort of worried about Mackenzie." *Well, it was the truth.* "I never heard from her yesterday. She was supposed to go see her mom. So, I kinda want to catch up with her today."

Although Mom's head nodded, her brevity and tone sent a different message. "Oh."

"And, I'm sort of worried about Sadie too." Krystal was hoping to have a bonding moment—opening up about her personal life—to somehow make up for not shopping, and possibly a lot more. She instantly regretted that tactic—Sadie and Bryce's moms were her mom's close friends from college.

"What's wrong with Sadie?" Mom's eyebrows practically jumped into her scalp.

"Um, you know. Just teenage drama stuff."

Now the brows lowered to a scowl, hovering just above her squint. If eyebrow gymnastics was an Olympic event, her mom would win a medal. "Uhhh! Don't get your panties in a wad. I know you're friends with her mom and all. *Please*, don't say anything. I promise to tell you if it's something serious."

This time, Mom only lifted one brow into a high arch. Yep, she'd win the gold, for sure! "I know," Krystal said softly. "After everything I've done lately, you probably don't believe me. But I have something else to tell you that might help. It's about God and stuff ..."

CHAPTER 2

MACKENZIE peered at herself in the mirror, noticing the dark circles beneath her eyes. She gently dabbed a bit of concealer around them, but the puffiness still showed. She finished her makeup and hair and was headed to the front door when Harper stopped her.

"'Kenzie, wait up." Harper looked as tired as Mackenzie.

"What's up, Sis? I'm late."

"Did you see Mom at the hospital yesterday? I wanted to talk to you, but you must've gotten home super late."

Mackenzie's gut tightened. That was such a loaded question. This conversation would require time and sensitivity, and she had neither at the moment.

"I did, but can we talk when I get home later? I'm supposed to meet up with Krystal right now." As the words came off her lips, she watched the usual sparkle diminish from Harper's dark eyes.

"Just tell me if she's okay. I need to know. I'm worried that she tried to …" Harper had the same concerns as Mackenzie about Mom's depression.

"Well, she came out to see Dad and me in the visiting room. So, that's a good sign, but—" Mackenzie searched for the right words. At nearly fourteen, Harper wasn't a baby, but Mackenzie always felt the need to protect her. "I'm still worried too. But I'm glad she's agreeing to stay at the hospital, at least for now." She reached for a strand of Harper's long black hair and gave it an affectionate tug. "We'll talk more about it tonight, okay?"

Harper nodded. "Thanks for being honest with me."

Mackenzie pulled Harper into her arms. "Love you," she whispered as she released her sister and headed for the door.

When Mackenzie arrived at Hank's Diner, Krystal was already seated at their usual booth in the back.

"Hey, sorry I'm late." She plopped down into the booth. "Harper stopped me to talk about my mom as I was leaving."

"Mm-hmm, I sorta wanted to talk about that too." Krystal took a sip of coffee, her eyes narrowing over the ridge of the mug. "I ordered us both cinnamon rolls."

"Thanks," Mackenzie said.

The waitress arrived with two piping hot cinnamon rolls, their spicy, sweet aroma making Mackenzie's mouth water. She flipped Mackenzie's mug right side up and poured coffee without asking. Maude, the perfect name for a middle-aged diner waitress, knew all her customers.

"Anything else, girls?" She raised her painted-on brows and snapped her gum.

Both girls shook their heads, simultaneously picking up their forks and cutting into the sweet pastries.

"So?" Krystal mumbled between bites. "Did she actually overdose again?"

Mackenzie set the fork down and wiped her mouth

with a napkin. "My dad says it's a—"

She raised her fingers in air quotes above her head—"'*mystery*.' I'm not so sure."

Krystal scowled. "You think he's lying?"

"No. I think that's what he *wants* to believe. He said the doctors told him they'd been adjusting her new medication, and the new dose was probably too much. Whatever …" she shrugged, fighting tears. "Mom said she wanted to come home and Dad couldn't make her stay there. When I told her we all miss her, but we don't want her to come home until she's better, she got up and left. My dad tried to go after her, and she told him not to. That was the end of the visit. Then I went to the track and ran until my lungs burned so bad I couldn't run anymore." Mackenzie didn't tell Krystal that after the run, she sat in her car crying for another two hours and after that, she fell asleep and didn't get home until 3:00 a.m.

"I'm sorry," Krystal said, her light brown eyes filled with compassion.

"Let's talk about you," Mackenzie said.

Krystal rolled her eyes. "Uh, well, I'm still pregnant. And Bryce sent me flowers the day after Bible study with a note saying something like, 'Welcome to the family of God. I want us to be a family—me, you, and our baby.'"

"That's really sweet. Why do you sound so snarky?"

Krystal huffed. "I dunno. I guess I'm just worried that eventually he'll realize I ruined his life and leave me."

"So, no more thoughts of having an abortion, right?"

"You know, it's kinda weird, but since we prayed the other night, I'm feeling different. I'm clearer about things." She leaned forward, her eyes wide. "I've been doing the math. I'll have the baby in June. I could give it up for adoption and in the fall, go back to school for our senior year. Who knows, maybe I'd still have a shot at a track scholarship. I just want my life back." She took a sip of coffee, shaking her head. "And I don't want to keep the baby, and Bryce does." She shrugged. "I'm not sure what to do about that part yet."

Mackenzie bobbed her head, unsure how to tell Krystal how relieved she felt.

"I don't even know if my mom or Bryce's family will like the idea of adoption either. But 'Kenzie," she leaned forward again. "I really think we are supposed to let Grant and Lauren adopt our baby. Lauren asked me to consider it that night before youth group. I know Grant talked to Bryce too."

"Wow. You've got to talk to him, K," Mackenzie said.

"I know. But after his flowers and card, I'm afraid of losing him. He won't have to do the right thing and he can go on with his life without the girl who messed everything up."

Mackenzie started to speak, but Krystal interrupted. "I'm scared of having the baby and losing him, and I'm afraid if I give up the baby, I'll lose him. I hate that I'm feeling all vulnerable and stupid."

"It's not stupid. But Krystal," Mackenzie reached across the table, touching her friend's arm. "I know that guy loves you. It's not just because you're pregnant. You need to talk to him. And for what it's worth, I'm so proud of you. I think your idea sounds amazing. Grant and Lauren would be the perfect parents, and you could still be in the kid's life."

Krystal leaned back against the booth, her eyes intense. "I guess I didn't think about that. That makes things complicated. I sort of just want to give the baby up and move on. You know, like it never happened. Grant and Lauren would be the kid's parents and that's it."

"What?" Mackenzie was shocked. How could Krystal not want to be a part of her own child's life?

"You *heard* me."

"Well, I think you need to give that more thought. You might regret it. And I bet Grant and Lauren would be just fine with you and Bryce being involved if that's what you're worried about."

Krystal grabbed her bangs in a fist and drew them back over the top of her head. "Look, I just want it over with. I want my life back. I'm not gonna get fat either." She shoved the plate with her half-eaten cinnamon roll to the middle of the table. "I went for a jog last night."

"Is that safe? I bet your mom won't like that."

Krystal huffed. Her face was rigid. "It's safe. I googled it. Jeez, I'm not stupid. And I don't need *another* mom, thank you."

Mackenzie's chest and neck were on fire. Sometimes Krystal could be the biggest jerk. She stood up. "I better go." She tossed a five-dollar bill on the table and walked to the door. Krystal called to her, but Mackenzie quickened her pace. She flopped into the seat of her car with force, jammed the key into the ignition and backed out just as Krystal was coming through the diner door. Welp, too bad. She had enough to deal with. Krystal could just stew for a while. Besides, it was best to leave before saying something she'd regret.

Mackenzie looked through her rearview window as she pulled out of the parking lot. Krystal was still standing near the door, hands at her sides, looking helpless. She felt a pang in her chest.

Oh, man. What did I just do?

CHAPTER 3

TAMMI gripped her jacket sleeves as she paced around Sadie's front porch before finally ringing the bell. She didn't have Krystal with her this time, and it felt wrong to just show up unannounced. But after she ran into Dawn, it became clear Sadie had lied to Tammi and Krystal yesterday about seeing Gary. Dawn's hazel eyes twinkled with fiendish delight when she shared how her dear cousin Gary asked to use her apartment again for another rendezvous with his "secret lover." Disgusting! And all the more reason to confront Sadie.

Tammi jumped back when the front door flew open.

"Oh!" Sadie squealed. "Tammi, you scared me."

Tammi glared up and down at Sadie slowly and deliberately. Sadie's usually naturally rosy face was packed with makeup like a runway model—thick foundation, black eyeliner, and red lipstick. She was wearing a form-fitting black top with a low neckline that revealed a hint of cleavage, no doubt from her padded push-up bra.

"We need to talk," Tammi said.

Sadie slouched forward on her crutches. "Um, I'm kind of in a hurry."

"Got a hot date with your *secret lover* at Dawn's apartment?"

Sadie straightened and jutted her narrow chin in the air. Her pupils dilated, making her blue eyes appear dark.

"Why are you here?" she snipped.

Tammi stood arms akimbo to mimic Sadie's tough-girl stance and took a few steps forward, scowling down at the top of the little pipsqueak's puffy blonde curls that reeked of hairspray. "You didn't answer me."

"Move back. Stop trying to intimidate me."

Tammi inched closer, the toe of her boot touching the toe of Sadie's shoe. "You lied."

"Okay. I did. But this—" she waved her hand— "is why."

"What? That people care about you?" Tammi's heart thudded. She didn't enjoy this.

Sadie turned and placed the crutches over the threshold. "Come in." She waved over her shoulder. "Let's go to my room and talk."

Tammi followed. Maybe this wasn't a good idea. She hated confrontation. And although Sadie was tiny, she was wiry and animated. This could get out of hand with Sadie yelling, or worse, dissolving into a puddle of tears. How would Tammi handle that?

Sadie edged into her bedroom, propping her crutches against the wall, and hopped on a fuzzy fuchsia moon chair. Tammi had never been in her room. She glanced around, taking in a dizzying sea of pink as if someone had splashed a giant bottle of Pepto-Bismol over everything. Tammi stepped over a fuzzy hot pink and white leopard-patterned throw rug and sat down on the matching comforter, leaning back into massive pillows and an array of stuffed animals. She eyed a few music posters—Twenty One Pilots, John Mayer, and ... *Dawn Rising*. What?

"When did they make a poster?" Tammi asked.

"I know. Isn't it cool? Gary says it was Dawn's idea. It's the same photo as the cover of their album, which, by the way, sounds sooo good."

Tammi's stomach seethed with a lake of acid as she glared at Dawn's gorgeous face and tawdry clothing— what there was of it. The rest of the band looked amazing too. Gary wore black, skin-tight jeans, platinum bangs over one eye, and was twirling his drumsticks. Gil and Ed both wore shades and stood back-to-back with guitars draped across the front of their black T-shirts. It looked legit. Trying to quell the storm raging inside, Tammi simply nodded.

"Did you hear the album yet?" Sadie's tone was annoyingly chipper.

"What the—? I'm not here to talk about that. Let's talk about you and Gary and how you've been lying to your best friends and sneaking around."

"Don't yell at me."

Oh no, here we go, Tammi thought. "Ugh. Do you think I like doing this? I'm really worried about you."

"You don't understand."

"Okay. Explain."

"Gary really cares about me *too*. And I like him so much. The only reason we are sneaking around is because of my parents' stupid no dating rule. Gary said he would gladly meet my parents. But there is no way that can happen. They would lock me in my room until I graduate *next year*." She folded bony arms across her chest and huffed, a blonde curl dancing across her forehead.

Tammi chuckled. "Seriously? What. A. Crock. How

about they don't want a twenty-year-old man in a rock band dating their adopted daughter in *high school* when she spent years being sexually abused in foster homes? Hmm? They are trying to protect you, Sadie. And so am I."

Sadie's chin lowered, and sobs began.

Oh, no. I've done it now.

"Hey, seriously. I'm not trying to make you cry," Tammi said. But she was too late.

Sadie grimaced, a streak of black mascara sliding down her cheek. She stood from the chair, hobbling on one leg to the bed and sat next to Tammi, draping her arms around Tammi's shoulders and sobbing into her neck. At first, Tammi sat stiffly with her hands in her lap, Sadie's tears rolling under her collar. Her heart constricted as she slowly raised her arms and squeezed Sadie tightly, feeling her small frame convulse.

The wretched demon, Incest, oozed from the floorboards, clawing its way up Tammi's back. *"Who are you to judge her?"* it hissed, sticking a forked blue tongue in Tammi's ear. *You had sex with your dad and probably fifty others. You are a dirty whore!*

A shiver twisted through Tammi as Lust, Shame, and a horde of other demons emanated in Sadie's room. Bat demons with leathery wings and distorted faces hung upside down from the ceiling, screeching curses.

And you think you are a Christian now? Shame draped its snot-green body over Tammi's shoulders with force. *You are too broken. Too dirty. Too messed up. You'll NEVER be clean!*

Tammi shuddered. Who did she think she was? *Please God, help me.*

The warrior angel, Silas, appeared beside the bed in a blasting blue light, sword raised. Demons hissed and yelped as the mighty angel slashed left and right. Incest quickly dropped to the floor, stubby lizard legs scratching wildly as it scurried beneath the bed while Silas sliced through the bats. Lust and Shame had already vanished. The cowards! Incest would wait patiently and resurface when the angel was gone. This way Incest would be the one to receive the praises of Duke Astaroth while the others would surely suffer the beast's wrath. The little brute hunched low, a devious sideways grin emerging as it planned the next attack.

CHAPTER 4

SADIE lifted her head and caught a glimpse of Tammi's misty gray eyes as she stood and turned her back to Sadie. Tammi was the closest thing to a best friend Sadie had ever had. Well, with the exception of Katerina from her foster care days. Their foster mom— *monster*—Isabel, used the bond between Sadie and Kat against them. Isabel knew it would crush Sadie to send in one of her clients to hurt little Kat who'd already been through much more than Sadie. As if that wasn't bad enough, Isabel had Kat sent away. Sadie could still hear Isabel's diabolical rasp. *"I make a better profit from you with your golden curls and blue eyes than from that ugly fence post."* she'd said, flicking her cigarette butt to the ground.

Sadie winced, recalling the loss of her friend. She'd tried with no luck to find out what happened to Kat. Sadie used to pray for her every night. But lately, praying had become difficult.

Sadie shoved those thoughts away as she brought her focus back to Tammi. They were opposite in pretty much everything but one … *abuse*. The worst kind. But Sadie had no doubt that Tammi and her other friends truly cared. She just needed to convince them that Gary wasn't a bad guy.

Crying always made her voice sound froggy. Sadie cleared her throat.

"Thank you, Tammi." She sniffed and continued, "I know you mean well. But I just don't think you understand. You have an attitude toward Gary because of Dawn. He's not like her. He likes me for who I am."

Tammi spun around, a scowl marring her perfect brown complexion. "What does that mean—for who you are?"

Sadie shrugged, eyeing her stump. She was broken inside *and* out. Gary wasn't embarrassed by her. An intelligent nurse who happened to be a cool, hunky drummer in a rock band wanted to be with *her*. She chewed her lip. Why *did* he want to be with her? He could have practically any girl he wanted. Sadie noticed the way girls gawked at him, flaunting themselves. It irked her to the core. But she'd convinced herself it didn't matter because Gary had chosen her. Sadie pictured his face centimeters from hers, as he began to slide his hand inside her shirt.

Stop! she told herself. *It wasn't right, and you know it.* Why couldn't she just relish her thoughts without a stupid twinge of guilt tarnishing the whole thing? She knew what it was. It was her parents' stupid religious rules.

"Well?" Tammi tapped her leather boot.

The doorbell rang and Sadie sprang from the bed. "Oh my gosh. That's him. Hand me my crutches."

"Get them yourself," Tammi said and stomped out of the bedroom in a hurry. She was on a mission and those long legs would get to Gary first.

"Tammi, wait!"

Sadie swiped at the mascara beneath her eyes, then grabbed her crutches. She strained, propelling her crutches forward in time to catch a glimpse of Tammi's long waves as she rounded the corner into the living room.

There were voices. Then a thud. And then, the front door slammed.

"Gary?" Sadie hollered, as she entered the living room.

"That girl hates my guts," Gary said.

"What happened?"

Gary blinked slowly. "The door opened, and I expected to see you." he paused, running a hand through his bangs. "Instead, it was like I was hit by a semi. She body-slammed me … and took off."

Sadie heard a squeal of tires outside. This wasn't good. Would Tammi tell her mom? No. She wouldn't do that. Sadie's stomach tightened. But she might tell her sister, Ming, or worse, Krystal.

"You look worried. I'm okay," Gary said. "It's no biggie."

Sadie frowned. "Uh, yeah, did she hurt you?"

"Nah." He rolled his eyes. "She was definitely sending a message."

"I know. I'm afraid she's going to tell. I mean, I don't think she'd tell my parents." Sadie stopped short. "Oh, no. But Krystal *would*. My mom and Krystal's mom are old friends."

Gary stepped close, placing his hand on the side of Sadie's jaw, pulling her face toward his. He leaned in and crushed his lips into hers. Sadie sighed. He drew back, but his face remained inches from hers.

"Let's just go. There's nothing we can do about this

now. Why ruin our time together? Who knows, it might be our last."

Sadie laid her forehead against his. "Don't say that," she whispered.

All at once, he scooped her into his arms. The crutches fell to the floor with a clang. Gary carried her to his car and sat her gently on the seat. She watched as he walked back inside, returning with her crutches. Her heart ached thinking this could be their last time together.

Anger moved in close. Its two misshapen heads lowered, one over either side of the headrest. *"It's all because of their stupid rules!"* the thing spewed in stereo in both of her ears. *"It won't be your last time. You will find a way."*

Sadie clenched her teeth then relaxed her jaw. She would find a way to make this work.

Gary opened the back door, gave her crutches a toss and hopped in the driver's seat. He sat still for a moment. She could tell he was contemplating. *No, Gary! Don't you dare!*

"Hmm," he rubbed the back of his neck then looked at her with a weak smile. "Sadie, I really like you. *A lot.* But I don't want to mess things up with your family and friends."

A fire from Sadie's belly blasted throughout her entire body, causing her to shake. "Gary, if you like me the way you say you do, then shouldn't we try to figure this out?"

"Trust me, I want to, baby." He touched her cheek softly.

"Let's go. I don't want to waste our time sitting in the driveway." She leaned in and pressed her lips to his.

She opened her mouth and allowed his tongue to mingle with hers, then gently pulled back and stared into his eyes while running her index finger down his neck.

Gary exhaled deeply, nodded and put the car in reverse. Sadie wondered if he planned to take her back to Dawn's apartment. Thinking about the last time made her queasy and excited all at the same time. She imagined his shirt off and running her hands over his toned abs.

Lust slithered from beneath the seat, its orange and black body winding up her leg until it was inches from the side of her face. *"Tell him to take you back to the apartment."* It coaxed, black beady eyes boring into her head.

Sadie reached across and set her hand on his Gary's thigh. "Where are we going?"

"We have reservations. It's a surprise."

She felt fluttery. "You're so romantic." She ran her finger down the length of his arm. "And are we going to the apartment after?"

"Well, uh." Gary smiled a bit. "You'll just have to wait and see." He winked.

CHAPTER 5

"I want a full report!" Duke Astaroth's voice reverberated off the cinderblock walls of the deserted hotel's basement. Exposed leaky ceiling pipes swayed as bat and raven demons struggled to remain perched. "Anger, Bulimia, Lust—come forward."

The troll, Anger, swung its long arms past the smaller demons, kicking the reptile Lust high in the air, its orange and black stripes flashing as it somersaulted into the rafters. Master Sergeant Terror moved in Anger's path and stood like an impenetrable wall. Anger stopped short, baring jagged teeth from both of its large jowls. No one wanted a confrontation with Terror.

Bulimia crawled on all fours past the greater demons. "I have a report, your grace." The potbellied varmint bowed its knotted head, approaching the great-horned man-beast.

Astaroth's orange eyes smoldered. "On with it then, idiot!"

"Although the new—" Bulimia swallowed in hesitation. "Uh, the new *convert*, Krystal, is still with child, she has succumbed to my influences, sir." Bulimia glanced up briefly, its deformed mouth curving upward. "She continues to stuff herself with food then vomit— even at the risk of losing the baby."

Astaroth drummed its claws on the lectern. "Hmm,

yeess. This could work." The beast lowered its head and glared at Bulimia. "I want that child dead! Carry on, soldier."

Bulimia rose from its crouched position, stood tall and gave a salute. "Permission to leave that I may continue with my orders, sir?"

"I SAID *CARRY ON*, YOU FOOL!"

Bulimia zipped upward in a tiny puff of smoke, barely missing a blow from Duke Astaroth.

Krystal checked her phone again as she shuffled into the kitchen for a snack. Two texts from Bryce about a "surprise" that she hadn't bothered responding to yet. Sometimes his kindness only made her more aware of what a jerk she was. She was hoping for a text or call from Mackenzie. Krystal was giving her some space to cool off after what happened at the diner. But now it was Saturday afternoon, and there was still not even a text from her best friend. Well, at least she had some of Grandma's fudge to take the edge off. Krystal removed the lid from a red tin container, the sweet aroma of chocolate filling her nostrils. She lifted the waxed paper and popped a piece in her mouth. She closed her eyes and let the fudge sit on her tongue for a moment before slowly chewing, savoring every bit. It was smooth and delectable. She swallowed and grabbed another piece. And another, and another. Feeling a bit nauseated, Krystal wiped her mouth and snapped the lid on the container, placing it clear to the back of the lower pantry shelf. As she walked out of the kitchen, she caught a glimpse of her reflection on the shiny refrigerator door.

Bulimia sat with its knobby legs dangling from the top of the refrigerator. *"Fat cow. Go get rid of it."*

"What a cow," Krystal whispered.

Bulimia hopped down, landing on Krystal's shoulder, clinging tightly as she trudged up the stairs and into the bathroom. *"Just do it. No one will know."*

Krystal locked the door, shut the lid of the toilet and sat down. She chewed her lip, twirling a strand of hair between her fingers. She thought about her counseling sessions with Pastor Dave and how to take control of the "urge to purge." But there was no way she could allow the bazillion calories she'd just consumed to remain. They'd most likely go straight to her thighs and butt. It was no use. She pulled hair into a ponytail, slid to her knees, lifted the lid back open and faced the porcelain god to give up her unholy offering.

Now that the deed was done, she scooted on her butt and sat against the bathroom door, a tear sliding down her cheek. A wave of cramps roiled across her abdomen, ushering a cold wash of fear. Could that have harmed the baby? She hugged herself tightly and waited for the cramps to subside. Feeling some relief, she leaned to one side and removed the phone from her back pocket. She began to type in the search bar: *cramps during pregnancy* when her phone vibrated in her hand. Bryce again. She'd better answer.

"Hey, Bry."

"Come outside."

Oh no! He was at her house. She should have texted

him back. Her chest fluttered as she hurried to the mirror. Not enough time to do much. She took a swig of mouthwash and swooshed it around, then spit in the sink. Next, she traced beneath her eyes with eyeliner and put on some lip gloss. She loosened her ponytail and ran a brush through her hair, then raced downstairs just as her brother Kasey was letting Bryce in the door. Bryce's sexy green eyes peered at her as she took the bottom step, flipping her hair in an attempt to look nonchalant.

He took her hand. "Come on," he said, using his other hand to grab her jacket from the coat rack behind her.

"What's going on?"

"Here, it's cold outside," he said and opened the front door, a frigid breeze quickly proving his point. "Come on. I told you I had a surprise."

"Um, yeah. But I didn't answer. Maybe I was sleeping in and never saw your texts."

Bryce kissed her cheek. "Looks like you did. Let's go."

Krystal rolled her eyes, trying not to smile, and followed. His excitement was contagious. Try as she might, she couldn't stop loving the guy, although she would never understand why he was still in love with her. Sure, they had history, but who actually ends up with their childhood sweetheart? Bryce opened the passenger door, and she sat down. His car smelled like Old Spice and leather. She breathed in deep. What was he up to? He was too good, too nice, too handsome, too *everything.*

Bryce flashed one of his gorgeous smiles before backing out of the driveway. "I just thought you needed a little Christmas outing. Ya know, something *festive and fun.*" His dimples were working overtime. "Can you guess where I'm taking you?"

"Um, festive? And no, ya goofball. I cannot *fathom* what you're up to."

Bryce laughed. "Come on, guess. I even gave you a hint." He reached over and tickled her ribs.

She giggled. Bryce brought out the best in her, and come to think of it, she was good for him too. A yin to his yang. Or maybe she was the yang and he was the yin. Whatever … somehow, they worked. "Not a clue," she said, shaking her head.

As they continued to drive, Krystal noticed he was heading away from town and out toward County Line Road which wound up the hills. And then it hit her—he was taking her ice skating at Santa's Village. They used to go all the time when they were kids. That was back when her dad still lived at home. She sighed, a flood of painful memories clouding her short-lived joy.

Bryce put on some music, which was a relief. Now she didn't need to pretend. She could just lose herself in the music without feeling the pressure to hold a conversation. But then again, that was another thing that *worked* between them. They could just sit and listen to music and not have to talk. He knew her better than almost anyone. Her chest was heavy with how much she loved him and how afraid she was of losing him. But at least the cramps had stopped. She willed herself to forget about that and began singing as Bryce kept the drumbeat on the steering wheel, seemingly clueless of her inner turmoil.

Several songs later, a billboard with giant candy canes on either side peeked over the top of the pine trees in the distance. Bryce glanced at her, a grin taking over his face.

She rolled her eyes. "Yeah, I saw it." Krystal slugged him in the arm.

A twinge of excitement fluttered in Krystal's belly as they entered the parking lot. Bryce parked and came around to open her door. She'd barely stepped out when Bryce tugged her into his arms and pressed his warm lips against hers.

He pulled a few inches from her face, staring into her eyes. "I love you. Everything is going to be okay. I promise."

For a moment, Krystal almost believed him.

CHAPTER 6

MACKENZIE tugged the comforter tighter around her shoulders. She squinted at the clock on the nightstand. It was past noon, and no one had disturbed her. That was strange. Usually one of her three siblings would have come in by now. She listened. The house was quiet as a tomb. Oh well. She decided not to bother checking. Besides, she didn't have the energy to deal with people today.

The demon, Depression, sensed Mackenzie's vulnerable state and edged from the foot of the bed. Its yellow cat eyes glared at Mackenzie's body curled pathetically on her side. Depression grabbed hold of the blanket, clutching tightly with its talons and hoisted itself on top of her, pressing down firmly with all its weight. The thing stretched out its stubby legs and covered her like a scaly blanket.

Pity landed on her head, grasping strands of her hair for balance. The ragged bird pecked its beak into her temple, tapping like a Woodpecker. *Oh, poor me.* Tap. *My mom is suicidal. My family is a mess.* Tap, tap. *My best friend probably hates me now.* Tap. *No guy will ever like me.* Tap, tap, tap, tap.

Mackenzie squeezed her eyes closed, hoping to shut out her negative thoughts and foul mood. *I hate feeling this way. I need help. God, I gave my life to you, so why am I feeling even worse than ever?*

Silas stood unnoticed beside Mackenzie's bed. He prayed, singing holy Scriptures in a heavenly language, his voice echoing as if it was coming from a deep cavern. A pure white dove fluttered gracefully to her side, causing the evil spirits to halt their harassment. They twisted and shrieked as they shot out of the room in an obsidian streak.

The brawny angel touched Mackenzie's shoulder with the tip of his sword. "Rise and take courage, princess of the King," he said, then disappeared as quickly as he'd arrived.

Mackenzie tossed the comforter from her shoulders and rolled out of bed. *I'm not giving in to these thoughts. I need to think about good things.* Her eyes landed on a roll of wrapping paper in the corner. *Yeah, good things like Christmas!*

A noise came from outside her room, causing Mackenzie to jump. Someone *was* home. She opened her door slowly, catching a glimpse of Harper from behind as she shut the bathroom door. From the look of her sister's matted hair, she'd just woken up too.

Mackenzie knocked on the bathroom door. "Hey, Harp?"

Harper's voice was groggy, "Just a minute."

"Come to my room when you're out."

Mackenzie hurried to Dad's bathroom so she could take care of business before Harper came out. She paused, sucking in a shallow breath as she entered her parents' dark empty bedroom, imagining her mother's small frame curled in a fetal position beneath the covers. She shook the image away and continued to the bathroom, once again smacked with another gruesome memory—a bottle of pink and white pills strewn across the tile and her mother's lifeless body being carried away on a stretcher while the entire neighborhood gawked.

With the angel of God now gone, Suicide slid across the floor in a winding motion, its tongue licking the air with pleasure. *You'll end up just like her,* it hissed.

Mackenzie's heart jumped to her throat.

"I don't want to end up like her," a voice whispered from over her shoulder.

Mackenzie spun around, nearly smacking into her sister. "Oh!" she grabbed her chest. "It's just you. Wait, what did you say?"

"I get scared sometimes that I could go crazy like Mom."

"Yeah, I've had those kinds of thoughts." Mackenzie took Harper's wrist. "Let's go to my room and talk."

"Good idea."

"Uh, I'll meet you there in a minute," Mackenzie said, opening the bathroom door. "I nearly peed my pants." She forced a shaky laugh before shutting the door.

When Mackenzie walked in her bedroom, Harper was sitting cross-legged on the bed, twirling a strand of dark hair between her fingers. Mackenzie wanted to initiate a conversation about how their mother's mental health had affected her, but the words wouldn't come out. Instead, she sat next to Harper, laying her head on her sister's shoulder.

"So, you have thoughts like that too?" Harper asked, staring at the wall.

Mackenzie lifted her head. "Yeah. I hate it."

Harper faced Mackenzie. "Me too." Her dark eyes

were barren, her mouth a straight line. She looked away again. "I thought it would feel different now. Ya know, after Bible study the other night?"

"I have an idea," Mackenzie said. "Let's see if Lauren can meet with us."

"Couldn't hurt, I guess."

"Okay, I'll text her. But … before I do that … I have a question." Mackenzie's heart skipped a beat then began to flutter violently. "Um, I saw some marks on your arm. Are you cutting?"

Harper's bottom lip dropped. "What?"

Mackenzie touched Harper's arm and gently rolled up the sleeve of her SpongeBob pajama top. Harper instantly yanked her arm away and stood—looking half-angry, half-frightened. Her eyes were as wild as her bedhead. She began to pace the bedroom without speaking. Mackenzie watched and waited, afraid to say anything. Harper finally stopped pacing and stood in front of Mackenzie, rolling up her sleeves to reveal several red linear cuts resembling railroad ties on her forearms. Her right arm had what appeared to be the letter "C" etched into her pale skin.

"Why?" Mackenzie asked, feeling a bit sick to her stomach.

Harper's lips quivered. "I don't know," she whispered. "I'm crazy, right?"

"Is that what the 'C' stands for?"

Harper nodded.

Mackenzie's mind was a blank page. She didn't know what to say or how to help. *Say something. Do something. God help me!* She pulled her phone out. "I'm going to text

Lauren."

"No! I don't want anyone to know."

"Harper, you need help."

"You think I'm crazy like Mom."

"No, I don't. I *do* think it would be crazy not to get help."

Harper's shoulders hunched, and she shriveled to the ground like a worn-out piece of clothing. Mackenzie kneeled, placing an arm over her sister's back. "It's going to be okay. Lauren is great. I'm sure you could tell from youth group. We can trust her." Mackenzie put her hand around Harper's waist, lifting her to her feet and leading her to the bed. "Come on. Lay down."

Mackenzie began to text, but her shaking fingers wouldn't work. She took a deep breath and called Lauren instead. "Hey, Lauren? It's Mackenzie. Are you busy?"

The sound of Lauren's voice filled her with hope as she squeezed her sister's hand. For some reason, Mackenzie had the feeling things were going to be okay.

CHAPTER 7

TAMMI peeled around the corner with a squeal. She was too angry to go home. All she'd do is sit and stew over the situation with Sadie and Gary. Going to see Krystal or Mackenzie was an idea, but she dismissed it. Why was she so angry, anyway? Was it because she didn't want her friend to get into trouble with a loser the way she had in the past? Or was this more about Dawn? What Tammi wanted to do was punch Dawn in the face. She whipped the car around in a quick not-so-legal U-turn and was headed toward the Grind in a fury when she heard a siren and saw red flashing lights in her rearview mirror. Tammi cursed under her breath and pulled her car safely to the nearest curb. Her hands began to shake, and she gripped the steering wheel harder. Did she have her seatbelt on? Check. Did she have her wallet with driver's license? Check. Proof of registration and insurance? Better to sit tight and wait for the officer she saw approaching from her side mirror.

She rolled down the window. "H-h-hi, officer," her voice barely croaked.

"Do you know why I pulled you over, Miss?"

Tammi gulped and tried to respond, but the words were stuck in her throat. She nodded, noticing how young the officer looked. He had on the typical aviator sunglasses and was cleanly shaven. The muscles in his forearms bulged, making the sleeves of his uniform look a size too small.

"Have you been drinking?" he asked.

Tammi shook her head profusely, but still couldn't speak.

"Step out of the car, please."

Tammi unbuckled her seatbelt and opened the door. But when she got out of the car, she nervously lost her balance and fell into the officer. She could smell his cologne wafting into her nostrils as he reached out to steady her.

"Oh my gosh. I'm so sorry." She finally found her voice again. "I know what this looks like, but I promise you, I have *not* been drinking. I don't even drink. I mean it. Not even a beer. Not even when my friends drink. I mean, my dad is an alcoholic. Like, I don't want to end up like him, ya know?" Her stomach felt like it had dropped to the pavement. She sounded like a raving lunatic.

The officer's dark brows rose above his sunglasses. "Okay, okay. What's your name, Miss?"

"Tammi Gerard, sir."

He pulled a pen from his pocket, then removed his shades, revealing striking light brown eyes. He tucked the shades in his pocket and held his pen in front of Tammi's face.

"Follow the pen, please," he said as he slowly moved it to the left, to the right, and then up and down.

Tammi did her best to follow but was sure he thought she was either hopped up on something or nuts. The fact that he was so attractive and young caused her insides to roll like she was on a boat in the ocean.

A deep crease etched between his eyes. He took a deep breath. "All right, so you don't appear to be impaired," he said. "Step back in the car and get your license, please."

Tammi quickly handed him the license and sat tapping her hand on her bouncing leg.

"You wanna tell me why you were driving so erratically?"

Tammi rubbed her temple. Where to begin? "My life has been one big suck for like the last month." She huffed. "Well, even longer. It started with a car accident. Oh, but it wasn't my fault, though." She paused, noticing him raise an eyebrow. Why did she even mention that to a cop? For whatever reason, the words seemed to spill out of her uncontrollably. "And then one of my friends got pregnant and tried to have an abortion. My best friend who's only sixteen and supposed to be a Christian is seeing this guy who's twenty and using her. My abusive, alcoholic dad has cancer. Oh yeah, and my other friend's mom tried to commit suicide, and …"

This was turning into a long tirade that sounded a lot like Sadie. What the heck was she doing? Tammi paused for a breath, swiping a tear from her cheek, as she took notice of the officer's eyes. She saw in them a kindness just like Lauren's. In fact, he resembled her. He seriously looked like he could be her brother. She glanced at his name badge—Hughes. Not the same last name. Then again, Lauren was married.

Officer Hughes spoke, jarring her from her thoughts. "Tammi, you mentioned a friend who's a Christian. Are *you* a Christian?"

"What? Uh, well, yeah. I actually just made that

decision only a few days ago." Why was he asking her this? Maybe he *was* related to Lauren. Wouldn't that be crazy?

He smiled, revealing a row of perfect white teeth. "Best decision of your life."

Tammi tilted her head. Come to think of it, she'd seen this guy before. At church. "Um, do you go to Sunrise Church?"

"Sure do," he said.

"Well, me too. I mean sorta. I guess."

His smile went crooked. "You guess?"

"Um, my grandparents have been going there for years. I just recently started going ... *sometimes*. And I go to the youth group. That's where I accepted Christ."

"At Grant and Lauren's, right?" he asked, but didn't wait for her to answer. "Yeah, that's my big sis."

"Mm-hm, I thought you looked kinda familiar. That is, after I got over the shock of being pulled over." Tammi swallowed. "Are you writing a ticket?"

Officer Hughes tilted his head. "No. But I need to caution you. Don't drive when you're this upset." He rested a hand on her shoulder for a moment, his touch making her head spin. "You know, Tammi, I don't think it's a coincidence that we met. I sense the Lord is trying to get your attention. My name is Jason, by the way." He extended his hand to shake hers.

Tammi reached out tentatively. His grip sent a shock buzzing through her arm. He was the cutest, sexiest, kindest man she'd ever laid eyes on. She wondered how old he was. He said Lauren was his *big* sister. Still too old for *her* being a high school student. Instantly, her thoughts turned to Sadie with a pang of guilt when she thought of body-slamming Gary. And now here she was pining over a cop that she could never be with.

She blinked slowly. "Nice to meet you, Officer Jason Hughes." Did I just flirt with him?

"You made a wild U-turn. Where are you off to in such a hurry?" he asked. Guess he didn't pick up on her attempt at flirting. Well, good, it was stupid! Pull it together and answer this fine man.

Tammi sighed.

"I wasn't sure. I just knew I didn't want to go home and deal with all my thoughts."

Jason nodded his head. "This is a bit unusual, since I'm on the job and all. But do you mind if I pray for you? It sounds like you could use it."

This was unreal. What were the odds? It had to be God. "Yeah, I'd really appreciate it."

Jason closed his eyes and cleared his throat. Tammi stared at him as he lowered his head and began to pray. At first, it was hard to concentrate on his words, because he was so flipping beautiful. But after a few words from his gorgeous lips, Tammi closed her eyes and let his prayer fall over her like a comforting blanket. When he said "amen," Tammi kept her eyes closed a moment longer, allowing the timbre in his voice to linger. She bet he was a singer like Lauren. When she looked up, he was smiling down at her like a father would upon his daughter. Maybe he was married. She tried to see if he was wearing a ring.

"Okay, Miss Tammi Gerard. Carry on. Be safe out there and see you at church Sunday," he said, taking a step back. "Oh, and Merry Christmas."

"Thanks for … for not giving me a ticket. And for praying. It helped," she said. "And I'll look for you at church."

"Sounds good," he said as a voice crackled from his radio. "Gotta go."

Tammi tilted her head, watching his left hand.

Warmth spread through her chest.

No ring.

She smiled and started the car, her mood now lifted despite her Sadie-like behavior.

CHAPTER 8

SADIE gazed in her closet looking for an outfit to wear to church. She tugged a baby blue sweater dress from the shelf and slipped it over her head. Tights and her gray tall boots would go nicely—well, *one* boot anyway. Sometimes she forgot about her stump. It had been almost four months since the accident and yet sometimes she still felt like her leg was still there—"phantom limb sensations" they called it. She'd be glad when her recent injury was healed, and she was back to wearing her prosthetic. The crutches sucked. She grasped the wall for balance and made her way to the full-length mirror. She pulled her hair up. Maybe a bun or a ponytail? As she messed with her hair, there was a knock at the door.

Ming slowly peeked her head in. "Good, you're almost ready. Can we talk while you finish?" she plopped down on the bed, scooting back into the pillows.

Sadie's gut tightened. Did Tammi tell her about Gary? Had Ming suspected something when Bryce dropped her off last night? He was the only one she could think of to call and pick her up at the Grind after her date with Gary. Sadie purposely avoided Bryce's questions by keeping him talking about Krystal and the baby. He rambled on about taking Krystal ice skating and how he was so relieved she seemed better. When it was time to drop Sadie off, he forgot about asking her why she needed a ride. Out of habit, she told him she'd pray for him and Krystal. But she didn't pray. It used to come so naturally for her, but lately, she found herself out of the regular routine. If she did remember to pray, her guilty conscience prevented her from staying focused. And if she wasn't careful, the guilt would eat its way through her ever-growing facade. What a phony she was! How was she going to make it through church?

"Sure, we can talk. What's up, sis?" Sadie asked Ming in her best happy voice, still fixing her hair and looking at her sister through the mirror.

"Um, how are you?"

Uh-oh. Ming knew something. Sadie avoided looking at her and continued wrapping her ponytail into a bun. "I'm great! It's Christmastime." She smirked and went into a chorus of "It's Beginning to Look a Lot Like Christmas," bobbing her head from side to side.

"Yeah, I love this time of year," Ming said. "But," she hesitated. "I can't put my finger on it, Sadie. Something seems off with you. Are you sure everything is okay?"

Sadie's mind scrambled to come up with something on the fly to keep her sister from nosing into her private life. "Well," Sadie turned and hobbled to the bed, scooting next to Ming. "It's just been so much to take in lately, ya know? With the accident, losing my leg, Krystal and Bryce, Mackenzie's mom ..." She squeezed her eyes shut, forcing a tiny tear that slid gracefully down her cheek.

What an actress! She should consider Broadway. But truly, all Sadie wanted was to dance again once she had her new prosthetic and more exciting, the pointe ballet prosthetic! Sadie couldn't wait to start more advanced dancing again. All she'd been able to do lately was work on Mom's ballet barre in the garage and strengthening exercises with a dancer's TheraBand.

"Oooh. You poor thing," Ming put her arm around Sadie's shoulders and gave her a tight hug. "It has been a lot to process. But you're right. It's Christmastime and we have lots to be happy about despite how rough the last few months have been."

Sadie sniffed. "I know, you're right. Thanks for caring about me, Ming. You are such a great sister." Sadie meant that part. Ming *was* a great sister. But she was also *n.o.s.y*! She had an uncanny ability to read people. Sadie would have to be extra careful as long as Ming was around for winter break.

"Well, you better finish getting ready. It's almost time to leave. You can ride with me if you want," Ming said. "Need any help?"

"I'm good. Just trying to decide between leggings or tights. Sheesh! I'll be glad to get my new prosthetic."

Ming headed to the door, turning as she opened it. "Okay, hurry up and maybe we'll have time to grab a coffee. I'm taking my own car because I have shopping to do later. You can come if you want."

"Yes, and yes! See ya downstairs in a few," Sadie chirped.

Ming and Sadie arrived at church with ten minutes to spare despite Sadie's procrastination at the coffee shop. Sure enough, Sadie caught a glimpse of Tammi speaking with Krystal and Bryce on the patio in front of the entryway. *Oh, great!*

"Oooh, looks like there's still donuts left. Let's stop before going in," Ming said.

"Uh, you go ahead. I gotta pee. I'll meet you inside," Sadie said. "Get us a seat near Mom and Dad." She was thinking quick. Usually Ming would sit up with Sadie and her friends. But that was too risky.

"Why?"

Sadie rolled her eyes. "Um, it's Christmastime. You know Mom will love it." She winked then hurried inside before Ming had a chance to protest.

Once in the restroom, Sadie went into a stall where she could be alone. *Think. How are you going to handle this? What if Tammi is spreading the word about Gary?*

Her chest pounded, and she was suddenly having second thoughts about wearing the sweater dress as perspiration trickled down her back. Her mind was blank. Once again, out of habit, she started to pray, *Oh, God. Help me here.* How ridiculous! Like God was going to help her figure out another lie.

Sadie heard the bathroom door open. She recognized the shoes instantly: Tammi's black boots, Krystal's sneakers, and Mackenzie's flats. *Oh, crap!*

"We know you're in here, Sadie." Tammi announced.

"Um, I'm not feeling so great, you guys," Sadie said.

A set of sneakers stood in front of her stall. "*Oh, sure!*" Krystal was now crouching down, head low enough for her to glare directly at Sadie. "You aren't sick. Come out or I'll crawl in and drag you out."

Sadie braced herself against the wall and jabbed a

crutch toward Krystal's face. "You wouldn't."

The next thing she knew, Krystal was cramming her way under the door and suddenly was directly in her face. "Let's go," Krystal said, opening the stall door, where both Tammi and Mackenzie stood with wide eyes and open mouths.

Krystal tugged her arm and gave a little shove. "Head into the stupid pink powder room where we can talk."

"No." Sadie yanked her elbow away. "You can't just order me around." She hated that her voice came out all high-pitched and shaky.

Mackenzie frowned. "Um, I see her point, Krystal. You're being kinda pushy." Her lips now turned up into a weak smile. "Pun intended," she added as if to lighten Krystal's usual bully-like behavior.

Tammi tilted her head around Krystal and looked Sadie in the face. "Yeah, let's take it down a notch. We just want to talk to you. We're your friends."

"Oh, really? So, friends just bust into the bathroom stall. That's great. Plus, I hear the music. Church is starting."

Krystal stepped in closer again, arms folded across her chest. "Screw that! *This* is more important."

CHAPTER 9

KRYSTAL tightened her hands into fists and gritted her teeth, a piercing squeak resonating inside her mouth. She didn't want to see Sadie end up like her. But at least Bryce loved Krystal and was willing to do the right thing. *And* he was a good guy. Gary, although good-looking and all, was just a wanna-be rockstar who would soon be on the road touring, leaving a trail of broken hearts in his wake. Krystal was sure that Sadie was only another groupie to him and nothing more. Krystal was determined to convince her of this fact, even if she had to slap it into her!

"So, what's it gonna be?" Krystal asked Sadie, stepping in closer.

Sadie's lower lip quivered, but the look in her eyes was anything but fear. She was ticked off. Even though she was tiny, she was a force to be reckoned with. Sure, Krystal knew she could take Sadie, but not without a hair-pulling, nail-scratching fight. Sadie glared up at Krystal—her pupils were tiny dark dots, the opposite of her usual innocent baby blues with long fluttery lashes. If she wanted a fight, Krystal would give it to her. She *needed* some sense knocked into her!

Mackenzie's soft voice came from behind the standoff between Krystal and Sadie. She gently touched Krystal's shoulder, giving a slight tug as she edged her slim body between them.

"Hey, Sadie, we're just worried about you," Mackenzie said. "And Krystal's right. This is way more important than sitting in church as if nothing is wrong when we all know you've been seeing Gary and lying about it. Which, by the way, isn't like you. I mean, I think if it was one of us doing the same thing, you'd care enough to ask about it."

Tammi brushed Krystal's arm as she moved closer. "Yeah, let's go sit down. And, uh, take it down a notch. She glanced at Krystal then motioned to the nearby old-fashioned sitting room attached to the restroom.

With a clenched jaw, Sadie jerked her crutches close and started for the other room. Krystal followed along with the others. Sadie plopped down in one of the pink wingback chairs and folded her arms across her chest. Tammi and Mackenzie sat on a small loveseat across from Sadie. Rather than sit in the chair next to Sadie, Krystal sat on the fancy cherrywood coffee table directly in front of the two wingback chairs, shoving aside a fake flower centerpiece. She wanted to get up close and personal with Sadie. The room's frilly Victorian décor was in juxtaposition to the company it kept at the moment. Krystal breathed deeply and prayed a simple prayer in her head, *I need you to help me here, God. Please help me and all of us.*

Sadie's head swiveled from Tammi, to Mackenzie then to Krystal. "Well?" she said sarcastically. When no one spoke right away, she rolled her eyes, throwing herself into the back of the chair. "Tammi, I don't see how it's showing you care to body slam Gary." Sadie's voice was shrill.

Krystal turned to Tammi. "Seriously?" She couldn't hide the smirk emerging on her lips.

Tammi harrumphed. "Oh, don't even, Krystal. You would have decked the guy. But, yeah. I shouldn't have done that. I guess I just don't want you to make the same mistakes I have." Tammi scratched at her cheek. "Well, and like 'Kenzie said, it's not like you."

"Sadie, why don't you start by telling us the truth?" Mackenzie said. "We know you can make your own choices, but friends should be honest with each other."

Krystal glanced at her best friend. They still hadn't worked through what happened at the diner the other morning. Mackenzie was calm and wise in how she spoke. It took a lot to get her angry, but Krystal had upset her, and she chose to walk away rather than argue or lash out. It was a quality Krystal greatly admired and sort of reminded her of Lauren. Thinking of Lauren made Krystal think of adoption. She shoved that thought away for later. Now was the time to focus on little Sadie.

"It's like I told Tammi, you guys just don't understand. Gary is a great guy. He cares about me and accepts me for who I am. But it doesn't even matter because of my parents' archaic no dating rule. What choice do I have?" Sadie said.

Krystal was about to spout off when she heard Mackenzie's collected voice again. "*We* care about you for who you are too. You were the one who got us all to come to church and youth group. You've prayed for us and shared with us about your past," Mackenzie said. "Sadie, what I'm trying to say is, you trusted us enough to share your secrets, so please trust us now. We love you and don't want to see you hurt."

Sadie shook her head furiously. "Ugh! And what makes you think Gary is going to hurt me? You guys don't even know him." She wriggled in the chair. "You know what? You guys are judging him for what Dawn has done, and that's not fair! Have you even *really* talked to him?"

Again, Krystal was about to speak, but Mackenzie's voice broke through first. "Well, maybe we don't know him very well. But we know *you,* and you seem to be changing. And we shouldn't judge him as if he did the things that Dawn has," Mackenzie said, as Sadie nodded slowly. "But I think this is a Scripture. It's something my mom used to say—'Bad company corrupts good character.' I mean, I don't think he's completely innocent if he is okay with you lying and spending so much time with Dawn and the rest of the band."

"Yeah," Tammi said, leaning forward. "I mean, you end up either becoming like the people you spend the most time with or influencing them. I think Dawn is a major manipulator who has the entire band and many others under her evil spell. Sadie, look what she did to Krystal and to me."

"That's Dawn! Not Gary!"

"What makes him different?" Krystal finally got a word in. "He's sure willing to get you to risk sneaking out, and he doesn't care that you're a minor. Gosh, I hope you haven't had sex with him, have you? That's what he's after, Sadie!"

Sadie gasped, tossing one of her crutches at Krystal

when the bathroom door opened and Lauren entered, her eyes wide. "I wondered if I'd find you all in here. What's going on?"

Whew! Krystal was relieved to see Lauren. But wait, Sadie's sister, Ming, was behind her. This was about to get ugly, and once again it was her fault for flying off the handle. Mackenzie and Tammi were a lot better at this. Krystal just wanted to pick up Sadie and shake some sense into her. She couldn't believe that pipsqueak threw her crutch! Little brat didn't know how lucky she was that Lauren walked in.

Lauren's eyebrows rose as she tapped the toe of her boot. "Girls, why aren't you in church?"

"Because we thought this was more important," Tammi said.

Lauren took a seat in the chair next to Sadie and folded her hands in her lap. Ming followed and stood next to Lauren, her mouth a straight line, dark eyes on her sister as if she was the only one in the room.

"Okay, so tell me what's so important, then," Lauren said.

Krystal decided to keep her mouth shut. Better to let her friends handle this. Plus, she felt awkward talking to Lauren because of the whole adoption thing.

"Look, girls, I know you all have had a lot to deal with. Seriously, I know it's got to be hard," Lauren said.

Krystal could sense her gaze, but kept her eyes focused on her hands.

Tammi cleared her throat. "Um, I think it would be a good idea if Sadie spoke with you alone."

Ming nodded, and flipped a strand of shiny indigo

hair over her shoulder as she zeroed in on Krystal.

Krystal turned her chin up and away from Ming's glare. Was she ticked off? Well, maybe so, but Ming probably didn't know all the facts. Sweet little Jesus girl Sadie was being corrupted! Krystal looked at Tammi and Mackenzie and then at Sadie who seemed to shrink even smaller into the large pink chair, like Alice in Wonderland.

"Yeah," Krystal said, rising from the table, handing Sadie her crutch. "That's probably best."

Tammi stood. "Just be honest, okay, Sadie?"

Sadie's face was pale and pinched, her eyes no longer looking angry, but terrified. Krystal sort of felt sorry for her. *Sort of.*

Once Tammi, Mackenzie, and Ming had exited behind Krystal, they hesitated just outside of the restroom without speaking. The music had stopped, and Pastor Dave was preaching.

Ming glanced at each of them. "Uh, I get that you guys are her friends, but wow. You were all up in her business. And kinda harsh to leave her in there with Lauren."

"She's been lying to us, and we're worried about her. So, yeah, we're all up in her business," Krystal said with a shrug. She wasn't intimidated by Ming even though she was a few years older and probably cooler than she'd ever be. "What now? Should we just try to tiptoe in? Sit in the back, maybe?" Krystal asked.

"Yeah, in a minute," Mackenzie said. "But I was thinking maybe we could pray for Sadie. Ya know, she was always so good about praying for us."

Tammi shook her head. "Not sure what to say,

someone else do it."

Mackenzie looked like a deer in the headlights. And Ming scrunched her two eyebrows into one angry unibrow.

"Ugh!" Krystal said. "I'll do it. God, please help Sadie to be honest with Lauren. We also pray that you keep bad people like Gary and Dawn away from her. Thank you. Um, amen."

"I kinda feel like I threw her under the bus," Tammi said, glancing at Ming, whose eyebrows were now lifted high as if to communicate, 'Ya think?'

Makenzie shook her head and shrugged. "We all left her in there with Lauren."

Krystal scowled. "Pfft! She threw *herself* under the bus." But inside, she hoped Sadie would understand. She also hoped things would be okay between her and Mackenzie. She whispered a silent prayer for God to help her make up with her best friend and with Sadie.

CHAPTER 10

MACKENZIE's dad glanced at her, a genuine smile reaching his brimming dark eyes. "I'm glad you decided to come. I know you wanted to go out with your friends."

"It's fine. They said to text them when I'm done, and we'll meet up."

Dad opened the door, and they made the familiar trek to the visiting area. Mom stood and waved them to her table. Her father sped up his pace, arms reaching out for a hug. Mackenzie watched, a sharp zing twisting her heart, reminding her how tough this was on their marriage.

Mom looked over Dad's shoulder at Mackenzie and immediately rushed to hug her daughter. "You brought your portfolio. I'm so glad. Let's sit and take a look," she said, tugging at Mackenzie's satchel.

Her mother's shiny raven-colored hair fell over one shoulder as she tilted her head to view one of Mackenzie's favorite drawings—the one of the two of them at the beach. Mom's slender fingers glided along the sketch.

Oh, I hope this memory doesn't make her sad. Darn it!

Mom raised her head, and to Mackenzie's relief, a thin smile emerged. "This was a good day. You captured it so well in the expressions on our faces," she said. "It's perfect."

Mackenzie released a breath. "That means a lot

coming from you."

"Oh, honey. You've already surpassed my abilities. I'm so proud of you," Mom said, laying her hand on Mackenzie's.

Hearing her mother's words were like an early Christmas present. Maybe Mom was getting better.

Thank you, God.

Mackenzie picked up a thick French fry and used it to push the other fries on her plate. She could feel Tammi's glare coming from beside her. Bryce and Krystal sat across from them discussing what had happened with Sadie.

"How's your mom?" Tammi asked.

Bryce and Krystal stopped talking, and now Mackenzie could feel their eyes on her too. She continued to push fries around her plate. Why had she agreed to come? She just wanted to climb in bed and pull the covers over her head. She knew eventually Krystal would want to hash out what happened at the diner, but she didn't have the energy for it.

"She seemed better today," she said, still looking at her plate.

"That's cool," Tammi said with sincerity.

Mackenzie glanced at her. "Thanks. How's your dad?"

Tammi shrugged. "Don't know. Don't care."

"Yeah, understandable."

Krystal gave Bryce a shove. "Hey, get up so I can use

the restroom." She scooted out and made a dash toward the back of the restaurant.

Tammi started asking Bryce questions about adoption. Mackenzie could hear the pain in Bryce's voice when he explained he wanted to keep the baby, but Krystal didn't. She thought about the conversation at the diner and hoped Krystal wasn't as harsh with Bryce as she had been with her. Who was she kidding? She was probably worse. Mackenzie glanced at Krystal's empty plate as she listened to Bryce, when a gnawing sensation rose from her belly.

"Uh, I'll be right back," she said and headed to the restroom.

Mackenzie pushed open the door as a woman and little girl exited. She glanced around briefly. No one else appeared to be in there. She tip-toed past the sinks but didn't go near the stalls. Instead, she stood still and listened. Sure enough, there was someone in the handicapped stall at the end.

Krystal.

Looking over her shoulder, Mackenzie was thankful no one had entered after her. She padded closer until she was at the door of the stall next to Krystal's. And then she heard a soft gagging sound and another. Really? Why did she even come in here? Is this what their friendship was about? It dawned on her how their relationship began—well, actually collided—in a dirty school restroom. Mackenzie was depressed and in tears, hiding from the world, and Krystal, the popular track star, was hiding her problem of bulimia from the world. What a pair they were. Was there any hope? Mackenzie immediately recalled Pastor Dave's sermon from earlier. "Jesus loves us too much to allow us to stay the same," he'd said. "Christ is with you in your situation, helping and growing you … *if* you let him."

The toilet flushed and the lock on the door released. Mackenzie stepped in front of it, meeting Krystal's wide doe eyes.

"How could you?" Mackenzie heard her voice bounce off the walls like a loudspeaker at a concert. It sounded shrill and accusing, but she continued anyway. "You dare to accuse Sadie of sneaking around, and look what you're doing! And you're pregnant!" Mackenzie turned to walk away.

Krystal grabbed her arm. "I know." Her voice was barely a whisper.

Mackenzie turned to look at her friend, shocked at her humility. It was so unlike Krystal to let someone get away with talking to her the way Mackenzie had, much less admit she was wrong. Krystal released her arm and stood staring at the tile floor, looking small and helpless. Mackenzie sighed, thinking of the sermon again. God had brought them together—she was sure of it. But she had no idea what to do in this moment. The problems that she and her friends faced seemed insurmountable. They *were* a screwed-up bunch, as Tammi had said. But the fact their lives had become so entwined was evidence of God's love for all of them. And evidence they needed each other.

"Come here," Mackenzie said, wrapping her arms around Krystal's shoulders, who surprisingly allowed it for all of three seconds.

Krystal gently stepped back, freeing herself. "I'm so sorry."

"Are you talking about at the diner or what you were just doing?"

"Everything."

"I don't know what to say, Krystal. But it's hard to stay mad, because I know you're hurting. How can I help?"

"Just being my friend, even though I'm such a jerk, I guess."

Mackenzie shook her head and rolled her eyes. "Yeah, I guess I'm a glutton for punishment," she shrugged. "Glutton. Wrong word choice. It's just a weird thing Mom would say sometimes."

Krystal sucked in her lower lip, her brows connecting above her eyes. "Your mom. Jeez, I know you've got enough to deal with."

"Yep, I do. But ya know what?"

Krystal shrugged, her eyes focused on the floor again.

"We *all* have a lot to deal with. I was thinking how it's pretty crazy God brought all of us together—me and you, Sadie and Tammi. Well, and Bryce too, I guess. What I mean is, so we could help each other."

Krystal's chin was still lowered, as she nodded her head, glassy brown eyes looking up at Mackenzie like a little girl being scolded. "Well, that's for sure. Like Tammi said, we *are* a screwed-up bunch."

Mackenzie chuckled. "I know. I was thinking that same thing. But then I remembered Pastor Dave's sermon today."

"I thought about it too. Ya know, when I was in there making myself puke." Krystal laughed sardonically.

"Ironic, right? The thought of church used to make me so angry, I could gag. And now, I'm one of them—an actual Christian."

The bathroom door opened, and two elderly women walked in, chattering like crows. "Well, YOU are an old fuddy-duddy, Gail!" the shorter of the two women said, smacking the other with the back of her hand.

"No, I have common sense, Helga," Gail said. "A tattoo at your age. Ridiculous."

"Aw, you're wound tighter than a watch. Have some fun!"

Gail took her handbag and walloped Helga.

"What in the world are you doing, you fool?"

"Why, I'm takin' your advice, Helga, and havin' some fun," Gail said, dashing into a stall and slamming it shut.

Helga laughed deeply, finally noticing Mackenzie and Krystal. "Don't look so shocked, girls. We're just two crazy old ladies out for a good time."

Krystal smirked. "Is that gonna be us in fifty years?"

"I hope so," Mackenzie said. "Let's go, Helga!"

"All right, Gail," Krystal said, giving Mackenzie a shove.

CHAPTER 11

TAMMI was greeted with the familiar smell of Sunday pot roast when she opened the door. She breathed in deeply with a grin, realizing why they called it comfort food. Grandma sat in her blue La-Z-Boy recliner, knitting needles in hand. Grandpa was next to her in his matching recliner with the footrest up as he lay snoring softly, glasses on the bridge of his nose and newspaper sprawled across his lap.

Grandma set down her knitting. "Have a fun afternoon with your friends?"

Tammi nodded. "Is that another blanket for the homeless shelter?"

"Oh, this? It's a baby blanket for your friends, Krystal and Bryce." Her gray eyes sparkled. "I found the softest yarn. They call it chenille-style. Come feel this."

Tammi's gut recoiled, but she stepped closer and touched the yellow and green rectangle on Grandma's lap anyway, surprised at how luxurious the yarn felt against her fingers. "Wow, I want one of these. In purple, though." She winked, hoping Grandma didn't notice her reservation. Although Gram meant well, it was just strange to think of Krystal and Bryce as soon-to-be parents.

Maybe.

"It smells amazing in here, Gram. I hope you're

making biscuits too. I can help if you need me."

"I'll do that." Gram said.

"Just let me know when you're ready to start. I'll be in my room for a while," Tammi said, walking around Grandpa's extended legs and toward her bedroom.

"Okay, sweetie," Grandma called out a bit too loudly.

Grandpa snorted, newspaper rattling. Tammi smirked and continued walking to her room. Once inside, she slid off her jeans and sweater, switching into leggings and an oversized sweatshirt. Her mind wandered, thinking about officer Jason Hughes … *again*. Unfortunately, she'd only caught a quick glimpse of him talking with Grant as the two exited the church. But even that made her heart palpitate. Why did it matter to her? What did she think was going to happen? She was just a silly high school girl to him. But for some dumb reason, it did matter. She had replayed her encounter with him when he pulled her over at least fifty times. She even imagined kissing his gorgeous lips. Maybe once she graduated, he'd be interested?

You're being ridiculous. Stop!

She grabbed a book Lauren suggested she read, hoping to get her mind off Jason when she noticed an envelope on her bed with familiar handwriting.

TAMMI. Her dad always printed in all capital letters, slanting to the left. Tammi's skin grew clammy as she stood staring. *What does he want?*

Incest crept from beneath the dresser, thick tail swooshing between stubby lizard legs. Anger hopped upon Incest's back, digging clawed feet into the creature's sides.

Incest hissed—pernicious tendrils sprayed from its blue forked tongue as it drew close to Tammi's legs. Anger made a leap from Incest's back and clung to the end of Tammi's sweatshirt, shimmying upward until it reached her shoulders.

I hate you! The scaly brute said.

Tammi snatched the envelope and crumpled it in her fist. "I hate you," she said, throwing it with force into the nearby trashcan, causing it to wobble. She flopped onto her bed, curled on her side and drew her knees up, cradling them tightly within her arms. Incest pounced onto the bed. It circled around Tammi's head and laid down inches in front of her face, staring with bulging orange eyes. It reached out, twirling one of Tammi's dark curls through its claws, conjuring dreaded memories of a sticky summer night—her father's bare skin touching hers.

The room began to fill with unholy beings, clinging to the ceiling and slithering across the floor while chanting vulgar and hateful things as Tammi drifted off to sleep. The troll, Anger, strode to the wobbling trashcan and tipped it over. Her father's letter toppled out.

"Ta-a-m-m-i-i-i," Grandma's voice rang out from the other room.

The demons shrieked at the sound of the godly woman's voice. She and her husband always seemed to be praying, singing, or reading the Bible—all the while foiling their dastardly agendas. A knock on the door sent the entire gaggle sailing through the ceiling and oozing through the walls.

Tammi sat up as Grandma entered. "Oh, didn't mean

to wake you, sweetie," she said. "I'm gonna start those biscuits, if you want to help."

"Um, yeah. I guess I drifted off," Tammi said, pretending to wipe the sleep from her eyes.

Grandma's brows pinched. "Are you okay?" She said, eyeing the trash-strewn floor.

Tammi's gaze followed her grandma as she bent, picking up the crumpled letter. "You didn't open it."

"I don't want to."

Grandma sat down next to Tammi, the letter in her wrinkled hand. "He was afraid you wouldn't," she said. "I know he hurt you, but …"

"There's no *but*. I hate him. He's dying and I'm glad." Tammi stood.

Her grandma's face was ashen, and her eyes filled with tears. "Look, Gram, I'm really sorry if that hurts you. That's the last thing I wanna do. But you have no idea—" the rest of the words were caught like a bone in her throat.

"I don't know because you haven't told me everything. But I suppose I've heard enough," Grandma whispered, looking down at her wrinkled hands clasped in her lap. "It breaks my heart, Tammi, honey. You know, you don't need to be in his life in order to forgive him. If he hurt you the way I suspect he did, Grandpa and I don't expect you to see your father again. We only want healing for you. Forgiveness is part of healing. I hope and pray that you have been working through this with Lauren."

Tammi steepled her hands in front of her lips. "Thank you for saying that, Gram. Lauren knows. I'm sorry. I just don't think I can stand having to tell you and Grandpa everything. But you're right, you do know enough. He's a sicko. Enough said. Look, I need to get some air," Tammi said, grabbing her phone and keys from the nightstand. "I'll be back soon."

"You shouldn't drive when you're upset, sweetie."

"I'll be fine," Tammi said, shutting the door behind her. The last time she drove upset, she was pulled over by the sexy officer Jason Hughes.

DAWN'S bright red lips curled when she saw Tammi's car pass by as she pulled out of the drugstore parking lot. Following Tammi to a signal, Dawn sent a quick text while waiting for a green light.

DAWN: HEY! RIGHT BEHIND YOU. MEET ME AT THE GRIND? WE NEED TO TALK.

Tammi didn't respond. That figures. She'd been pretty angry, but Dawn knew she could win her over. At the next signal, Dawn texted again.

DAWN: IT'S ABOUT SADIE.

Still no response. Shoot! Dawn thought for sure something about Sadie would do the trick. She chewed her lip, calculating another plan when Tammi made a turn like she might be headed to the coffee shop. Dawn followed until they reached the Grind.

Tammi got out of her car and stood at Dawn's window with her arms folded across her chest. Warmth spread through Dawn's body. Her plan was working.

Dawn rolled down the window. "We should probably talk in my car." She motioned to the passenger's seat.

"It's kind of personal." She relished the glint in Tammi's gray eyes like a spider when an insect is caught in its web.

Tammi opened the door. The car filled with her scent. Tammi was even more beautiful when she was angry.

"I'm not in the mood for games, Dawn."

Dawn blinked her eyes slowly. "But games are such fun."

Tammi reached for the handle.

"Don't leave, Pet. I'm just joking," Dawn said, grabbing ahold of Tammi's sweatshirt.

"Out with it, then," she jerked away from Dawn's hand. "And I'm not your pet, you freak."

Dawn chuckled. "Feisty. It's so sexy."

Tammi shook her head, reaching for the handle again.

"Wait. You're going to want to hear what I have to say."

Tammi's eyes were steely. "Then *say* it!"

She might be a beauty, but she's pushing it with this nasty attitude. I'll make sure she suffers. But not yet. I need to win her trust first.

"Well, I'm afraid your little friend might be in over her head," Dawn paused, gauging Tammi's body language. Yes, the slumped shoulders indicated this news had penetrated deep. Good. She'd just wait a moment longer, allowing Tammi to percolate the information.

Satisfied, Dawn continued. "And I know how much you care about Sadie and want to protect her and all—her being so innocent and sweet. So, I thought you should know that Gary … well, let's just say, he sees lots of girls. If you know what I mean."

"Just great."

"Well, speak of the devil," Dawn said, motioning forward.

Gary strolled out of the coffee shop. A large-busted blonde had her arm looped in the crook of his. The two made their way to a black sports car where they paused to make out. Dawn knew Gary would be with the girl but had no idea he'd actually parade out the door with her. Perfect!

Tammi lurched like a leopard after prey.

Dawn locked the automatic doors and quickly pulled out her phone, snapping a picture. "Just send her this," she said.

"Let me out," Tammi growled through her teeth.

"If you attack him like some kind of animal, then *you're* the bad guy. Think about it," Dawn laid her hand on Tammi's shoulder. "Trust me. This way is better." Dawn could see the wheels turning in Tammi's mind. "I just sent you the picture."

Tammi glanced at the image now on her phone. Her hand fell limply in her lap, still cradling the cell. "I'm not going after him. Besides, he's already in his car with that sleaze."

"Okay, good. So, you agree. This way is much better." Dawn tapped the button to unlock the doors. "But I hope you'll remember this. I'm trying to make up for the bad stuff I've done." She rubbed Tammi's shoulder briefly then removed it so as not to anger her further. "I mean it, Tammi."

Tammi rolled her eyes and got out. The door shut with a thud. Dawn watched Tammi's tall, slim figure promenade in front of her car without so much as a look in Dawn's direction.

"You'll be sorry," Dawn whispered under her breath.

CHAPTER 12

SADIE dug at the hole in her leggings as her mom and Lauren talked about her like she wasn't even in the room. Sadie glanced at the clock on the mantle. Lauren had been at their home for half an hour. Thank God Dad had a meeting after church. The situation would be ten times worse if he were here. But it didn't matter anyway.

It was over.

Her so-called friends had managed to sabotage her relationship with the only guy she'd ever liked. And to top it off, she'd most likely be grounded for months.

"Sadie, did you hear me?" her mother asked.

"No."

"I said the worst part of this is the deception," Mom said. "I wish you would have just talked to me. It's not like I was never a teenager. I remember how it feels to have a crush."

Lauren stood. "I think I'll let you two talk alone, now," she said. "I'm here if you need me, Sadie."

Bleh. I doubt I'll be wanting to talk to you.

She nodded despite her feelings. It wasn't really Lauren's fault. Sadie frowned, a prick of guilt nagging at her. Whose fault was it? Her phone buzzed in her pocket as Mom got up to walk Lauren out.

Grrr! It was Tammi.

Sadie was about to put the phone back when she noticed it was a photo. She tapped to reveal a couple interlocked in each other's arms. Sadie tilted her head and drew the phone closer.

Gary!

She felt as if she were dropped from an airplane, plummeting to Earth. What was going on? Why did Tammi send this? Who's the girl? Sadie managed her way into the hall to call Tammi while her Mom and Lauren said their goodbyes. Tammi answered on the first ring.

"How did you get that picture?" Sadie knew she sounded frantic.

"Sheesh, no hello or anything," Tammi's voice was flat.

"Just tell me."

"The Grind. He just left with her. I wonder if he's taking her back to Dawn's apartment?"

Sadie heard the front door shut. "I've gotta go."

Stuffing the phone in her back pocket, Sadie hopped to the bathroom, bracing her hands on the wall. Once in the bathroom with the door closed, she opened Tammi's text again. Suddenly nauseous, Sadie leaned her head against the wall and squeezed her eyes shut. Hearing her mother's voice, she hobbled from the wall and flushed the toilet.

"Coming," she hollered, making her way back to the living room.

"Come sit by me, sweetie." Mom patted the couch next her.

This was a positive sign. But what did it matter if Gary was a pig? The image of him wrapped up like a pretzel with another girl burned in her mind.

Sadie sat, drawing in a deep breath. She was in so much trouble now—and for what? Her mom's blue eyes brimmed with tears, evidence of the pain Sadie had caused. "I'm … I'm so sorry about all the lies," she croaked. "I guess I'm grounded, right?"

Her mother creased her light brows. "I'll speak to your dad about that later. But you and I need to talk first. Are you really sorry or are you just sorry you got caught?"

"Apparently I'm not the only one who was caught." Sadie opened the picture of Gary and handed her mom the phone.

Sadie covered her mouth with her hands as tears began to slide down her face. Mom stared at the image for a moment then gave the phone a toss on the couch, pulling Sadie into a tight hug.

Mom rocked Sadie back and forth like a child. "Shhhh, shhhh," she murmured.

"I feel like such an idiot." Sadie's voice was muffled by Mom's shoulder. She pulled back to look at her. "The truth is, whenever I would feel bad for lying, I would get angry and blame you and Dad for your rules. I wasn't sorry until now. How could I be so blind? My friends tried to tell me, but I wouldn't listen. I can't believe he'd do this. I really thought he cared about me …"

Christmas music blared from the portable speaker, filling the Summerses' large kitchen with joyous sounds to match the delectable aroma of holiday baking. Sadie's mom, Pam, was known for her sweet treats. Pam operated a side business making cakes, candies, and goodies for friends and church members. Many of the recipes were secret, passed down from her great-grandmother.

Sadie licked icing from her fingers. "Inviting my friends over to make candies and cookies was a great idea, Mom. Thanks," she said, giving her a side hug. "I mean, it really helped me to break the ice with them after everything … you know … with the Gary situation."

Mom wiped her hands on her Christmas apron, smearing a smudge of green across Santa's white beard. "Well, with all that's happened over the past few months …" she let the unfinished sentence hang in the air before starting a new one. "It'll be fun. Plus, I needed the help. Only a few more days 'til Christmas. And this way, everyone will have some treats to take home too."

The timer chimed and Mom opened the oven door, a rush of warm air mingling with the aroma of cinnamon and spices. While her mom lifted the gingerbread cookies off the sheet and onto a rack to cool, Sadie arranged bowls of colored icing and festive sprinkles on the large granite bar in the middle of the gourmet kitchen. Sadie's little brothers, Jeff and Jake, raced in the kitchen sliding across the wood floor in their socks, each snagging a cookie on their way. Dad followed the boys, a wide grin engulfing his face as he did the same.

"Hey!" Jake said. "These don't have icing. And where's the chocolate chip ones?"

"That's why you need to wait until we're done. I thought you guys were going out with Dad," Sadie said, eyes pleading with her father.

"Don't worry, angel," Dad said, giving Sadie a peck on the top of her head. "We're leaving soon. But it smelled so good, we had to make a pit stop first."

"Thanks for letting my friends come even though I'm grounded," Sadie said softly in his ear.

Dad winked at Sadie as he grabbed hold of Mom's apron, pulling her into a playful smooch. "How about we bring home a pizza or Chinese, so you don't need to worry about dinner?"

"Chinese would be great," Mom said, kissing his cheek. "You and the boys have fun."

"Okay, let's hit the road!" Dad said. "Go get on your shoes and jackets."

The doorbell rang as the boys filed out of the kitchen. "I'll get it!" Jeff hollered. His feet pounded against the wooden floor as he ran to the door.

Moments later, Krystal, Tammi, and Mackenzie entered the kitchen.

"Oh, my gosh. It smells like heaven in here," Krystal said. "But I thought we were helping. You guys already made a ton of stuff."

"We are decorating gingerbread and sugar cookies right now. Later we'll make chocolate chip cookies and help Mom make fudge and other candy," Sadie said.

Sadie's mom handed each of the girls an apron and everyone got to work decorating. Tammi and Sadie piped icing faces and red and green clothes of the gingerbread men while Krystal and Mackenzie iced and sprinkled the sugar cookies.

"So," Krystal said, popping a bite of sugar cookie in her mouth. "Are we going to talk about the elephant in the room?"

Tammi stared at Sadie and raised a pierced brow. When Sadie didn't speak, Tammi said, "We all know what happened. And we all know you're sorry and we forgive you. We also know that Gary is a—" she hesitated, glancing in the direction of Sadie's mom, who was stirring cookie batter with her back to them. "Uh, well, we all know Gary's a jerk. But what we don't know is if you've told him about the picture yet?"

Sadie picked up a heart-shaped sugar cookie with red sprinkles and broke it in half, an apt symbol. "No," she said, tossing the broken cookie on the counter, holding back tears as she walked out of the kitchen.

CHAPTER 13

BRYCE sat on his bed and twirled a delicate silver ring between his fingers, rubbing the engraved letters inside the band—*I Promise*—a tiny heart next to the phrase. It wasn't fancy, but he hoped it expressed his love and intentions of marrying Krystal *someday*. Bryce wanted to buy an engagement ring, but his parents suggested a "promise" ring until after graduation next year—or at least until the baby was born.

Until the baby was born. That was another subject altogether.

Right now, he just wanted to find the perfect time to give the ring to Krystal. Maybe after the Christmas Eve service at church tonight. Perfect. But next he'd need to figure out a way to get her alone. Bryce placed the ring into the velvet box and whispered a prayer, laying back on his pillow, arms over his head with one hand still clamped around the box.

Would she wear it?

KRYSTAL fiddled with the bow attached to the plate of homemade goodies and waited for Lauren to answer the door.

"Merry Christmas!" Krystal said, handing a surprised

Lauren the plate as soon as the door opened. "Just a little something from my family."

"Aw, how sweet." Lauren winked. "*Literally*," she said, taking the gift. "Do you have time to come in for a minute?"

"Um, sure. But I know you probably have a lot to do, so I won't stay long."

"I'm doing some last-minute food prep for Christmas brunch tomorrow, and with the church service tonight, I better get it done now." She waved Krystal inside and headed for the kitchen. "Have a seat," she pointed to the breakfast nook. "I just need to pop this egg casserole in the fridge, and then I can sit and visit with you for a minute."

Krystal sat down. "Do you have family coming over for Christmas?"

"Oh, yeah," Lauren said, sitting across from Krystal. "My mom and dad, and my sister and her husband with their three kids are coming in the morning. I'm excited to see my sister's new baby, Abigale." Her smile faded. "How are you feeling? I mean, with the pregnancy?"

"Uh, all right."

Lauren nodded, her eyes on the placemat in front of her. She kept rubbing her hand across it. Was she wondering if Krystal had given thought to adoption? Of course she was. Krystal could see it all over her.

"I've been thinking about what you asked me. You know, about adoption."

"Have you spoken with Bryce or your parents?" Lauren's head snapped up, her eyes wide.

Krystal shook her head. "Not really. I haven't spoken

to my parents. I sort of mentioned it to Bryce, but he keeps saying he wants to raise *his* kid. It's like he thinks we can just be this happy little family or something. And he's been super sweet and everything, *but …*"

"Have you prayed about it?"

"That's the thing—" Krystal hesitated. Should she say anything? It would be horrible to get Lauren's hopes up when she hadn't had a serious conversation with Bryce or their parents yet. But the desperate look in this beautiful woman's eyes made her continue. Krystal knew Lauren would be a perfect mom. "I really think God wants you and Grant to raise this kid. I've thought about it a million times, but I—I've been scared to talk seriously to anyone other than Mackenzie. I was thinking I would do it after Christmas, ya know?"

Lauren's lips parted, but she didn't speak. She sat back in the chair and drew folded hands beneath her chin. Was she praying? Did she change her mind about adopting?

"Yes, I agree. You need to speak with Bryce and your parents, Krystal," she finally said.

"I'm sorry. I shouldn't have said anything yet," Krystal said, standing up. "I better go."

Lauren shook her head. "It's okay. I'm the one that asked about your pregnancy. The truth is, I was hoping you'd say something. *Anything.*" She was looking at the table again.

"So, you still want this baby?" Krystal asked, realizing her hand was on her belly.

Lauren's head raised slowly. Her brimming eyes glanced briefly on Krystal's stomach then up to her face.

"More than anything," her voice cracked. "But not if it isn't God's plan. Not if you and Bryce are supposed to raise your own child."

Krystal rubbed her neck. "I don't *want* to have a kid yet. I'm not ready. And as wonderful as Bryce is, neither is he. I want him to have a future, and I also don't want to force him into marrying me. I mean, I love Bryce. I do. But we're so young. I want to experience other things."

Lauren got up and stood in front of Krystal, placing a hand on her shoulder. "Let's pray about it now, okay?"

As Krystal listened to Lauren's selfless prayer asking for God's will, her mind flooded with fear and doubt. Despite the godly woman's prayer, a brazen and high-ranking demon called Death dared to encroach overhead. It had been waiting for a time to strike, hoping to rattle Krystal's tiny growing faith. The thing was a black shapeless shadow, hovering like a toxic mist. When Death didn't identify any of God's angels nearby, it slowly began to wrap around and around Krystal's abdomen. She squeezed her eyes tight, trying to concentrate on what Lauren was saying but her stomach began to cramp. Death opened its inky cavernous mouth revealing long jagged teeth, delighting in the torment. Krystal trembled with fear, screaming silently in her head for God.

A beam of white-hot light shot from Silas's eyes as he descended. A guttural moan escaped Death's mouth, releasing Krystal from its grip. The monster disintegrated into tiny black droplets then disappeared. Krystal sighed in relief, unaware of the spiritual battle that had occurred. Lauren concluded the prayer and wrapped Krystal in a hug.

"Thanks," Krystal said softly.

Lauren released her and smiled. "I'll keep praying—and so should you. God will give you the right time to speak with Bryce."

BRYCE removed the small black box from his jacket pocket. He rolled up a leg of his jeans and stuck it inside his sock just as Krystal entered the room. Did she see? She sat down in his dad's leather recliner, drawing her legs up. She was wearing the tight black leather leggings that made him crazy.

"What's up with you? You're acting all weird. And why didn't we go for dessert with your family?"

Bryce's heart pounded in his ears. He sat down on the floor in front of the chair where she was sitting and laid his head on her lap. He turned his head to the side so he could look up at Krystal's beautiful face. Her eyes sparkled like brandy, her long hair, nearly the same color, cascaded over her slender shoulders. God, he loved her so much.

He took in a staggered breath, hoping she didn't hear. "We didn't go for dessert because I wanted to give you something." He lifted his head from her lap and quickly slid his hand inside the sock. He set the box on her leg. But before he could speak, Krystal jerked her leg violently as if a spider had crawled on her.

And the box fell to the floor.

Along with his heart.

"Oh my gosh," Krystal eyed the box as if it were alive

and ready to attack.

Bryce grabbed the box and got up on his knees. He took the ring out and held it up toward her. "It's a promise ring."

Krystal drew a hand to her chest like she was having some kind of fit. "No … no," she whispered, shaking her head, eyes wide with pity.

Bryce dropped his arm to his side and sat on his butt hard, bruising his tailbone and his pride. He released all the air from his lungs, deflating like someone had kicked him in the groin. His mouth was watery like he might throw up too. This was his biggest fear come true.

Krystal fell to her knees in front of him and caressed his face with her hand. "I love you, Bryce."

His pulse quickened at her touch. "Then why—"

She covered his mouth gently with her hand. "I want you to listen to me, okay?"

He nodded, a wave of relief releasing a trickle of sweat down his back. Her hand still covered his mouth. She said she loved him … *that* was good. It was also good she was only inches from his face. He would have attempted a kiss but saw her eyes glistened like they were about to spill tears. He'd better listen now and kiss her after.

"I hope we can get married someday. I really do. But I don't want us to get married just because we *have* to."

Bryce tried to speak, but she pressed her hand harder on his lips, and raised her brows, letting him know she meant business.

"Let me finish, Bry. I've prayed a lot about this. I really think God wants us to let Grant and Lauren raise this kid. You know, adoption. And I want *you* to pray about it too."

Bryce gently removed Krystal's hand from his mouth and gaped at her.

I don't know if I can do this, God. If she loves me, how can she give up our baby?

CHAPTER 14

MACKENZIE and Harper cleaned up after the traditional Christmas breakfast of French toast casserole, bacon, and eggs. Only this year, Mom wasn't here to make it, but no one talked about that. Dad put on a Christmas playlist and began passing out the gifts. Despite Mom being in the hospital, the family managed to stay upbeat until Del spoke up.

"When can I give Mommy her present I made for her at school?" Del said, holding the gift wrapped in red paper with a white yarn bow.

"I can take your gift to her today, Son," Dad said. "I'm sure it will make her very happy."

Del leapt off the couch, flapping his arms like a bird and knocking down a bulb from the Christmas tree on his way down. The poor kid had accepted he wasn't old enough to see his mom at the hospital, and this was as good as it would get.

"Be careful there, Sport," Dad said, tousling Del's dark curly locks. "Go and get those pictures you drew for her too."

Del skipped away to his room and Dad turned his attention to the older kids. "I'm going to take Del to his friend Landin's house while we go and visit Mom."

Harper's eyes widened, and her mouth dropped open while Trey's face was unreadable.

"Um, does she know we are coming?" Mackenzie asked.

"Nope, it's a Christmas surprise," he said with a twinkle in his eyes. "I think it will be just what she needs." He nodded to Mackenzie then continued, "Let's get cleaned up."

As she cleaned the kitchen, Mackenzie tried to imagine what Mom's reaction would be—especially after what happened at the last visit. All Mom could think about was coming home. She'd even threatened to leave the hospital on her own. Mackenzie blinked, remembering the look on Mom's ghostly face when Mackenzie begged her to stay and get better. But maybe Dad was right. She sure hoped so.

The ride home from the mental hospital was silent until Dad turned on the radio. But not even Christmas music could lift the dark cloud that loomed. Mackenzie glanced in the backseat. Harper stared out the window despondently while Trey closed his eyes, shutting out the world. Mackenzie felt her phone buzz in her pocket. It was a text.

KRYSTAL: I HAVE A GIFT FOR YOU. ARE YOU HOME?

"Would it be okay if Krystal comes over? We have gifts for each other." Mackenzie asked her dad.

No response.

Dad stared out the windshield, hands at ten and two. Did he not hear her or was he angry that she asked to do something fun after Mom refused to see them at the hospital? Mackenzie turned down *Santa Baby* and asked again.

"Sure." Dad shrugged without looking at her.

Mackenzie texted back: **YEAH, PLZ COME OVER.**

KRYSTAL: MERRY CHRISTMAS, GAIL! LOL TAMMI AND SADIE WANT TO COME. IS THAT OK?

Mackenzie snickered remembering the two old ladies, Helga and Gail. She responded yes without bothering to ask her dad. What was the point?

As their van pulled in the driveway, Mackenzie spotted Krystal's car pulling up to the curb. Trey rose from his slumber just in time to see Krystal walking to the house. He sat up, wiping drool from his mouth and made a wild attempt at straightening his bedhead. His shoulder-length slick black hair looked good even when it was messy, unlike Mackenzie's unruly curls. Good grief. Did he really think Krystal would be interested in him? Come to think of it, Trey probably didn't know that Krystal was pregnant. At least she assumed by his ridiculous flirting he didn't know. If he continued making a fool of himself, should she tell him?

Trey opened his door and hopped out just as Krystal stepped into the open garage. "Hey, what's up, K? Merry Christmas," he said, going in for a hug.

Krystal scowled and a did a sidestep. "Nice try," she said, patting Trey's arm.

"Where's your Christmas spirit?" Trey said to Krystal's back as she walked toward Mackenzie.

"Humbug," she said over her shoulder, then reached to hug Mackenzie with a laugh.

"Oh, I see how it is," he said.

"You know she has a boyfriend," Harper said, rolling her eyes. "*Bryce Williams*," she said his name like Bryce was a celebrity or something. Well, he sort of was, at least at Arcana School of Fine Arts. Harper knew about the pregnancy and was probably trying to save her brother from embarrassment later.

Dad opened the door leading to the house and held it open for the kids to enter. The look in his eyes was a million miles away. Usually, he'd make a joke or join in the bantering. The kids filed into the living room while Dad headed down the hall.

"I'll be right back," Mackenzie said.

Trey waved his arm in a swatting motion. "Take your time. I'll just get your guest a snack."

Krystal snickered. "Relentless little sophomore."

"*Little?*"

Mackenzie shook her head as she left the room. Trey was probably puffing out his chest and strutting around Krystal like a peacock. Oh well. Krystal could handle herself just fine. Mackenzie's concern was on Dad. She approached his bedroom slowly and rapped her knuckles on his open door.

Dad poked his head around the corner of the walk-in closet. "'Kenzie? Why aren't you visiting with your friend?"

"I needed to see you first," she said, walking toward him. "I'm sorry, Dad. I know that was hard."

Dad's dark eyes glistened. "I feel like a terrible husband and father. I'm so sorry. Should've called first." He rubbed the back of his neck. "Poor Harper was so looking forward to seeing Mom for the first time. Did you see her face? She was devastated. I'm glad Del wasn't there," he said. "Oh, Landin's mom is bringing him home soon. Anyway, I should have realized after our last visit …"

Mackenzie stepped in closer and wrapped her arms around her father's waist, laying her head on his chest. "It's okay, Daddy. You were trying to do something nice. We all know that."

"Thanks, sweetie." He kissed the top of her head. "Go and visit with Krystal. I'll be fine."

As Mackenzie was leaving Dad's room, the doorbell rang. She heard Sadie and Tammi's voices as she approached the living room.

"Merry Christmas!" Sadie squealed, eyeing Mackenzie. "We come with good tidings and gifts!" Balancing her armpits on her crutches, she held up her wrists looped with gift bags stuffed full of red and green glittery tissue paper.

Tammi stepped around Sadie, shaking her head. Mackenzie couldn't help but smile. Sadie was right. They did bring good tidings. Lord knows her family needed all the *good* they could get.

Trey approached Sadie. "I'll take those for you."

"Aw, you are such a gentleman, Trey," Sadie chirped.

Trey turned as red as the tissue in the gift bags he now held while Krystal and Tammi both made gagging noises.

"Thank you, Sadie," Trey, said. "At least someone around here appreciates me." He gawked at Krystal and Tammi.

"That small bag with a snowman is for you, Trey,"

Sadie said.

Trey froze. "W-wait. Are you serious?"

"Of course. I brought a little something for everyone. I even texted Bryce, but he's with his family. Anyway, it's Christmas and I'm so grateful to have all of you in my life."

Krystal raised her brows. "You invited Bryce *here?*

Sadie nodded.

"Well, I didn't get you guys anything. I mean except for Kenzie," Krystal said. "What the heck, Sadie? But if you brought some of those amazing baked goods you and your mom made, that's perfectly fine."

Tammi scoffed. "Jeez, if she likes giving gifts, don't make her feel bad. That's just Sadie. You know that. Besides, I didn't get anything for anybody. So there."

"They're just little things from the dollar store, you guys," Sadie said. "Let's go sit down so you can open them."

"Okay," Mackenzie shrugged. "I didn't get any gifts for you guys either, but I think it's super sweet."

"So, Bryce isn't coming, though, right?" Krystal asked.

What was the deal with Krystal? Something probably happened with her and Bryce again. At least that'll distract me from my own life for a little while, 'Kenzie mused.

CHAPTER 15

TAMMI was glad Mackenzie's little brother coerced Trey and Harper to watch a Christmas movie in the den. She'd been contemplating whether to tell her friends about the letter from Dad. Maybe this was her opportunity. But what purpose would it serve? For some crazy reason, it nagged at her mind like an annoying child. She had always kept thoughts about her dad buried.

Yeah, and that's worked out just great. I'm a hot mess.

The only thing that seemed to help had been opening up to Lauren and her friends. Could it be *God* wanted her to talk? She'd considered speaking with Sadie on the way over but couldn't get a word in after she asked if Sadie had heard from Gary. It was obvious Sadie was crushed that Gary had not even so much as texted her on Christmas. That conniving Dawn probably showed Gary the photo of him and the tramp. Tammi could picture the glimmer in Dawn's eye and the shock on Gary's face. But did he own up to it or apologize? Of course not. What a loser!

But Sadie was putting on her "it's Christmas so we should be happy" attitude. Yet when Tammi used a foul word in reference to Gary—she hated when Tammi cursed—Sadie nodded her head without protest. Well, good. At least she was finally in touch with reality.

Tammi was still trying to think of a way to get back at that despicable wannabe-rock-star dirtbag.

"Um, hey, you guys," Tammi, said, pulling the crumpled paper from her pocket. Best to just start … somehow … "Uh, my dad gave me this."

Her friends stared, waiting for Tammi to speak, but she still couldn't manage to string two words together. Sadie scooted closer, reminding Tammi of the first night she ever went to youth group at Grant and Lauren's. Except at that time, Tammi thought Sadie was the most bothersome person on the planet, with her squeaky voice, preppy pink sweaters, and disgusting rainbows-and-butterflies disposition. Sadie had gushed over Tammi's arrival, acting like they were friends when they weren't. *Not yet.* But that was also the night when Tammi realized Sadie had the same kind of secret that she, too, had been hiding for years.

So much had happened since Tammi met Sadie, Krystal, and Mackenzie.

"What does the letter say?" Tammi jerked at the sound of Sadie's voice, drawing her back to the present. "Hey, do you want me to read it for you?" Sadie asked, gently laying a hand on her shoulder.

Tammi tossed the letter on the floor next to Sadie and stood up. "You can read it, but I can't listen. I'm going to go use the restroom."

She could feel her friends' eyes boring into her back as she walked out of the room. Then she heard Sadie's child-like voice begin reading:

My beautiful Tammi,

I know there is nothing I can say to fix the awful things I did to you. But I hope you can find it in your heart to forgive me. I'm not asking forgiveness for my own sake. I know I don't deserve it. But I also know how bitterness can rot the soul. I want you to be happy and free, Tammi.

Tammi covered her ears and hurried to the restroom. She shut the door, standing with her back against it. She wished she could shut off her unwanted emotions like shutting a door or turning a faucet. But life didn't work that way. She hugged herself tightly as if she could somehow squeeze out the hurt, the pain, the anger, the confusion. It was all too much. Why was he back in her life? Why couldn't he just die and take all these boiling feelings with him to hell? Why, God?

Silas appeared, shimmering and bright. The mighty angel held his massive arms over his head and began to pray, silver tears dripping from his flaming eyes.

Even after he dies, the feeling will remain. You must forgive him in order to be free from it.

NO! I will never forgive him for what he did. He doesn't deserve it!

I forgave you.

What was happening? Was God giving her these thoughts? Was this the Holy Spirit that Lauren told her about? It *had* to be. She'd never entertained thoughts of forgiving her father.

"Tammi?" came Sadie's voice from outside the door.

The handle wiggled and Tammi quickly stepped away. "Hey!"

Sadie's blue eyes peered at Tammi through a small opening. "I'm coming in."

"No, I'll be out in a minute."

Sadie shut the door. Tammi heard her crutches thudding against the floor as she left. Tammi felt like a jerk, but she needed time to somewhat compose herself. She grabbed some tissue and dabbed it beneath her eyes and then blew her nose. Glancing in the mirror, she messed with her hair then decided there was no point in prolonging the inevitable. She switched off the light and headed back, but her friends weren't in the living room. Clanging noises and voices were coming from the kitchen.

Krystal sat across from Sadie at the table, munching on cookies. Mackenzie was pouring milk into plastic cups.

"Sorry, you guys," Tammi said, sitting next to Sadie.

"It's cool," Krystal said, pushing the plate of cookies toward her. "Here, chocolate always helps."

Mackenzie passed out the drinks and sat next to Krystal. "So, what are you going to do? I mean about the letter?" Krystal asked.

Everyone leaned in.

"Gosh, Krystal," Sadie said. "That's super direct. Maybe she doesn't want to talk."

Krystal puckered her lips. "Uh, if she didn't want to talk, then why show us the letter, hmm, Sadie? And what's up with you and Gary? Have you talked to *that* idiot?"

"Seriously?" Sadie said. "What's up with you and Bryce?"

Tammi figured she'd better say something before a catfight broke out. Sadie could get pretty feisty, and Krystal was plain old mean.

"There's something else too," Tammi said, silencing her friends. "This was with the letter." She tossed another crumpled paper on the table. "It's from a bank. Fifty thousand dollars in a savings account with my name."

CHAPTER 16

SADIE scrolled through the pictures from Christmas on her phone. There was a cute one with Ming and her boyfriend, Josh. They were so adorable together. Sadie's chest constricted, making it hard to take a breath. No. She would not cry. But she had to know if Gary ever really cared about her. What about the song he wrote for her? Did he do that for all his girls?

She started to text him for what was probably the hundredth attempt, but once again, deleted it. Sighing, she gave her phone a toss on the couch and headed to the kitchen for a snack. She rummaged through the cupboards, but nothing looked tasty. She never thought it was possible, but she was sick of cookies and candy. She opened the fridge, staring blankly. As she was about to shut the door, her eyes landed on a bottle of wine from yesterday's Christmas feast. She recalled the wine Gary had given her at Dawn's apartment ... and what happened after. A surge of regret filled her.

Can you forgive me, Lord?

Ming entered the kitchen as Sadie shut the fridge door. "Hey," she said. "Any good leftovers?"

Sadie's heartbeat quickened as her sister came closer, as if somehow Ming could read her thoughts. "Oh, there's all kinds of leftovers," she said, playing off her silly fear.

"What did you have?"

"Um, I couldn't decide," she said.

Ming began to get out leftover containers and set them on the counter. She took out two plates as if Sadie was going to eat too. Sadie's stomach lurched when Ming removed the cover and the smell of turkey and dressing reached her nose.

"You know what?" Sadie said. "I'm not hungry after all."

"Okay, but come and sit with me. We only have a few more days before I leave."

Sadie poured herself a glass of water before sitting down. Ming stuck her plate in the microwave then grabbed a wine glass from the cabinet. Sadie tilted her head in disbelief before realizing Ming was pouring sparkling cider. Of course, it's only cider. The guilt was really getting to her.

"Hey, there's only a little more. Want the rest?" Ming asked.

Sadie shook her head, feeling the blood drain from her face.

"You okay? Is this about Gary?" Ming said, taking her plate and glass to the table.

"I guess," Sadie said. "He hasn't texted or called."

"Did you ever tell him you knew about the girl?"

"Nope. But I bet Dawn did. That girl is just evil."

Ming shrugged. "Well, I say good riddance." She took a bite of stuffing then continued. "You know, I have a friend that works at that new coffee shop on Broadmoore Street. Let's go check it out when I'm done. You need a new hangout."

Sadie nodded, feeling lighter. It probably was for the best.

Ming zipped her Toyota Prius into the last available parking spot at the Coffee Cabin. Well, a full parking lot was a good sign. Maybe this *could* be the new place. It was tiny but inviting. And it was a literal log cabin, complete with a chimney and smoke billowing from the top.

When they entered, a bell rang and a barista with a full fuzzy beard wearing a black and red lumberjack flannel shirt greeted them from behind the counter. "Welcome, ladies. Come on over for a sample of our house blend."

Ming and Sadie both took a small paper cup. The coffee was good even without her regular cream and sugar. "Yum," Sadie said.

"We roast and grind our own beans in the back." The barista pointed to a small glass room behind him. "I'm Eric, by the way—one of the owners."

"Whaat?" Ming said. "I mean, you look super young."

Eric's pink lips turned up from beneath his dark mustache. "Yeah, it's been our dream—my dad and me. As soon as I graduated with my business degree, we started making plans. Just opened last month. So far, business has been pretty steady."

"That's so cool!" Sadie said. "I'm gonna tell my friends about this place."

"That would be great. Please share about us on social media too," Eric said, handing them business cards. "So, how about a pour-over? Or did you want an iced coffee, espresso, a blended drink? We do it all."

The sisters ordered the Coffee Cabin's version of a caramel macchiato with an extra shot of espresso and hurried to the empty overstuffed chairs near a stone fireplace complete with a crackling fire. Sadie sipped her drink as she glanced around. The whole place was pinewood, including the ceiling, where white twinkle lights were strung. It was cozy and perfect.

"So," Ming said. "How's Krystal doing?"

"She seems to be okay."

"What are they gonna do? I mean, is she going to keep the baby?"

Sadie took another sip and shrugged. "The last conversation we had, Krystal said she didn't want to keep the baby, but Bryce does."

Ming was quiet for a moment as she toyed with her napkin, folding it several times. "Sadie, tell me about Gary," she finally said. "I was kind of hurt that you didn't talk to me. But I guess I understand why. But you led me to believe that you had talked to Mom when you didn't."

"I'm sorry, Ming. I lied to everyone because I knew you all wouldn't agree. It was dumb."

Sadie's mind flashed to the wine she'd drunk with Gary and how she didn't remember how far they'd gone. His hands had been on her bare skin, but his jeans were still on when she stopped him. Guilt began to bubble in her stomach. She belched and coffee came up her throat and into her nose. She quickly placed a napkin to her face.

"Aw, Sadie. I don't mean to make you feel bad. I just thought we were closer than that," Ming said, her eyes brimming over. "You didn't have sex with Gary, did you?"

"What? So, you just automatically think I would sleep with him because of my past?"

I'm not sure how far we went, but I don't think we had sex. No, his pants were still on. Stupid wine!

"I didn't say that. I was only asking. And you aren't the only one with a past."

Sadie chewed her lip. "Sorry, Ming." She gazed at the table. "I asked God if He could forgive me. And no, I didn't sleep with him. But I did stuff that I regret. We went to Dawn's apartment a couple of times. I feel so dumb. It's obvious he didn't really care."

The words had no sooner left Sadie's lips than Dawn and the rest of the band walked into the Coffee Cabin. Her pulse quickened and her hands began to shake.

"Oh, no," Sadie whispered.

Ming must have followed Sadie's glare. "They haven't seen us yet. Let's see if we can sneak out," Ming said.

While Dawn was busy flirting with Eric at the counter, and the rest of the group was entranced by the bean roasting room, Ming helped Sadie up. They stayed near the walls and made a dash to the door.

Just as they were making their exit, Dawn's voice rang out. "Hey, Gary, isn't that one of your groupie girls?"

Sadie willed herself not to turn around, but against her better judgment, she did. And there stood Gary, his face pinched and ashen. Sadie quickly turned away.

"Come on," Ming said, opening the door.

As the door closed behind them, Sadie could hear Gary calling her, but she kept moving until she reached the car. Ming quickly opened the back door for Sadie to toss in her crutches. Gary's voice came again from behind her, his footsteps drawing closer. She hurried to the front seat and shut the door, seeing Gary approaching from the corner of her eye, but she kept her face forward.

Ming started the engine and began backing up. Sadie looked out the window to see Gary in his black leather jacket and skinny jeans as he headed back to the coffee shop.

"Maybe I should have talked to him?" Sadie said. "I mean, I want to know why he hasn't even called or texted."

"You did the right thing." Ming glanced at her. "If he really cared, he would have called. Don't act desperate. He doesn't deserve you." She looked back at the road. "It's over. Let it stay that way."

Sadie glanced at Ming, watching her brush a strand of midnight blue hair from her pale face. Sadie turned her focus out the window. As the dreary gray sky and leafless trees whizzed by, she came to the realization that Ming was right. But for whatever reason, Sadie still wanted to hear what Gary had to say for himself. Maybe she'd call him later.

Her phone vibrated.

Or maybe she wouldn't need to …

She let Gary's call go to voicemail but planned to call back when she was alone.

CHAPTER 17

KRYSTAL's hands were folded tightly in her lap as Bryce's parents talked to her mom. Bryce's house was always so clean that it felt sterile. She glanced around, noticing the recent vacuum cleaner tracks in the perfect beige carpet. Not one stain. How was that possible?

This time, Krystal sat where she wouldn't have the portrait of Jesus glaring at her like the last meeting. Instead, Jesus was behind her, boring into the back of her head. *Great.* And as usual, the parental units talked as if Krystal and Bryce weren't in the room.

"Adoption is a good option," Bryce's dad said. "These kids aren't ready for this. We keep talking in circles, but I think it's something to seriously pray over."

"Peter, that's our grandchild you're talking about," Bryce's mom replied. "How do *you* feel, Gloria?" She turned to Krystal's mom.

Bryce shifted forward in his seat. "I've already told Krystal how *I* feel," he said. "And Mom, that's *my* son or daughter *we're* talking about," he said emphatically.

Krystal's blood boiled in her veins—one in her temple throbbed, ready to burst. All of them acted like this was *their* decision, yet she was the one carrying this stupid kid! She could have gone through with an abortion and never even told them. But she didn't. And truth be told, she *was* glad. Especially now that she had accepted Christ. It was bad enough she even attempted it. Krystal was still dealing with the shame and guilt of the whole experience at the clinic. But this conversation was making her want to scream!

It was still her body, right? Shouldn't she have the final say? She could hear Dawn's doomy voice tickling her brain, "It's your body, Krystal. Choose for yourself." Krystal shuddered, imagining what would have happened if she'd listened to that horrible witch who pretended to care. No, it wasn't just her decision. This was also Bryce's baby growing inside of her—as he continually reminded her and everyone. Suddenly her mind skipped to a Scripture from youth group: *"For you created my inmost being; you knit me together in my mother's womb."*

Krystal placed a hand on her stomach. This was *God's* baby. And she truly believed that God wanted Grant and Lauren to raise it.

"Listen to me," Krystal said, halting the conversation. "You guys haven't been listening to me. I *have* prayed about this … a lot. I think God wants Grant and Lauren to raise this baby. Did you know Lauren has had four miscarriages?"

Krystal's mom covered her mouth with trembling hands. Bryce's dad put his arm around his wife's shoulder, squeezing her close. The parents sat speechless, wide-eyed, and staring at Krystal.

"Have *you* guys prayed about it?" Krystal asked. "I mean, Mr. Williams just said you should, right?"

Bryce rose from his seat and knelt in front of Krystal's. "You know what? I admit, I've only prayed that God would help us and you wouldn't have an abortion. Even when you brought up adoption the first time, I just thought you were trying to find a way out. I didn't realize you've *really* prayed seriously about this." He squeezed her hand. "I'm sorry, K. I should have listened."

For the first time, Krystal felt real peace.

This was the right thing to do—for everyone—even if Bryce didn't realize it yet.

Mr. Williams rose, his eyes moist. "Krystal has a point. Why don't we *all* pray now?" He stood beside the chair Krystal was sitting in, both moms joining him.

While everyone's eyes were closed, shimmering lights like tiny specks of stardust rose into the air with each word. Silas stood behind the families, his enormous wings encircling the group as he too prayed in a heavenly language understood only by the Holy One and his angels.

BRYCE opened the Mustang's door for Krystal to get in. Finally, they could leave and have some time alone. He knew Krystal was probably done talking about baby stuff. But *he* wasn't. Probably best to wait a while before bringing it up again. He'd talk about something safe first to test the uncertain waters of Krystal's moods.

"Where do you want to eat?" he asked as he started the engine.

"I want pizza. But after we eat, can you drop me off at 'Kenzie's?"

"Pizza sounds good," he said, leaning over to kiss her cheek. "And sure, I'll take you to 'Kenzie's."

Even though I was hoping to spend time alone.

Krystal surprised Bryce and reached out to cup his face in her hands, placing her forehead against his. "Thank you for hearing me." Her breath was sweet and warm.

Well, I guess she does want to talk.

Bryce stared into her light brown eyes. He could see every golden fleck with her face this close. And she smelled amazing too. "I think you might be right," he whispered before he realized what he was saying.

He couldn't believe what just spilled out of his mouth. Bryce knew he had to be honest with Krystal, recalling the unexpected calm that settled over him while holding Krystal's hand during their parents' prayer earlier. Maybe adoption *was* what God wanted. Bryce pulled her into his arms as close as he could despite the stupid console between them. The warmth and curves of her body made him all too aware of how they got pregnant. But it wasn't just that he was incredibly attracted to her. He loved her. They were perfect together. No one knew him the way she did. And he still wanted her to wear the ring he'd bought.

He loosened from the embrace, pulling the black velvet box from his jacket pocket. His hand betrayed him, shaking as he held it out to her. Dang it!

He tried to keep his voice low and steady. "I still want you to wear this."

Her gorgeous eyes glistened. "Why?" she whispered.

"Because I love you."

Krystal blinked slowly, staring at the box.

Please say yes. I must be stupid to subject myself to her rejection again. Oh, God. Please let her say yes.

"Well …" She rolled her eyes. "Do I have to put it on myself?"

A smile burst through his lips as he opened the box, gently removing the ring and placing it on Krystal's slender finger.

"You're sure about this?" she asked, twisting her hand from side to side, looking at his ring on her lovely hand.

"I bought the ring because I love you and want to marry you *someday*. That hasn't changed."

"And how are you feeling about the idea of adoption now?" she asked. "I mean, you just said I might be right. You meant about Grant and Lauren, yeah?"

Bryce squeezed the bridge of his nose and breathed deeply. He was going to wait, but she opened up the subject. So, here goes nothing. "Well, I'm still not sure. I did feel kinda peaceful after the prayer. But it's scary, K. This is a human being and we're just giving it away to someone like it's a puppy or something."

"Not just *someone*. Grant and Lauren. They are going to be amazing parents."

He shifted in the seat. "Yeah, I know. But will we tell them when they're older that we're the *real* parents? Will we be in the kid's life at all? And would they even *want* us to be?"

Krystal shrugged, shaking her head. "I'm not clear on that part."

"Uh, well that's kind of a big deal."

"Tsk, I know that, Bry. I didn't say I have it all figured out."

Krystal plopped down on Mackenzie's bed. She'd come to feel at home in her friend's room with the soothing clouds painted on the baby-blue ceiling. Mackenzie sat down next to her and scooted back, drawing her skinny legs up as she leaned into the brass headboard. Krystal held out her hand, watching closely for Mackenzie's reaction.

'Kenzie's dark eyes widened beneath her long lashes as she grabbed Krystal's hand. "Are you getting married?"

"No. It's a promise ring."

"Huh?"

"Uh, it means he promises to marry me 'someday,' I guess. He gave it to me Christmas Eve, but I said that I wouldn't wear it. You should have seen his face, 'Kenzie. I felt like such a jerk."

"But you're wearing it now?"

Krystal explained everything—the ring, the talk with Lauren the other day, the meeting with their parents, the conversation with Bryce before pizza. Mackenzie listened attentively, nodding and saying "Uh-huh" every so often. 'Kenzie was the best listener. Everything about her said she cared. Her eyes never shifted. It was one of the things Krystal loved about their friendship. Suddenly, feeling sort of selfish for dominating the conversation, Krystal remembered that she hadn't asked about Mackenzie's mom.

"Okay, I'm done talking about me. Did you see your mom on Christmas? You texted that your dad was taking all you guys to see her."

For some reason, Krystal had a weird feeling that something was really troubling her friend. A creepy chill ran up her spine noticing Mackenzie had this faraway look in her eyes and her mouth twisted to the side of her face.

Not a good sign.

CHAPTER 18

MACKENZIE fingered the satin edge of the blanket on her bed as she considered Krystal's question. She wasn't looking, but she could feel Krystal's eyes on her, waiting for a response. Mackenzie was content listening to Krystal. She didn't want to talk about her own problems. Hearing everything her friends were going through helped her issues seem small. Feelings of shame crawled up her back and niggled at her conscience. What a terrible way to think. But it was true. On any given day, her friends had more drama going on than a soap opera.

Krystal, Tammi, and Sadie would not be the type of people Mackenzie would usually hang out with. Then again, she'd never had many friends since her family had moved a bajillion times. But what few friends Mackenzie had in the past were quiet and studious nerds like her. She would have never imagined becoming so close to Krystal. Sure, Krystal was a great student too. But the girl who started out as a bully had turned into the best friend she'd ever had. Maybe it was like what Lauren said. Maybe it was God's plan to draw them all together to help each other. Feeling more at ease, Mackenzie opened up to Krystal about how her mom refused to see the family on Christmas and about Harper's cutting. Then she found herself admitting how on many days it was the hardest thing to just get out of bed. Krystal listened without saying a word, allowing her to vent.

"The truth is," Mackenzie said. "I've got this nagging fear that she'll really go through with it. You know, killing herself. And if my mom is like that …" She couldn't say anymore. Why would Krystal want to be friends with a freak who could end up like her mom?

Unbeknownst to the girls, the room now swarmed with unholy beings who chanted despicable curses. Bats dangled from the ceiling while Suicide, Depression, and Pity encroached toward the bed, ready to administer more of their poison, up close and personal.

Krystal nodded. "Makes sense."

"Really?" This surprised Mackenzie.

"Yeah," Krystal said. "Why do you think I have body issues? And why do I push Bryce away? All you have to do is take a look at my parents."

Suicide's slinky black body wound through Mackenzie's dark hair. *S-s-s-ee, there's no hope for you. What's the point of living?*

Mackenzie gulped. *There's no hope for me.* Of course, she couldn't share her thoughts with Krystal. Or could she?

Suicide sensed its victim might consider revealing her thoughts. After all, it had become an expert on her mannerisms, quirks, and especially her weaknesses.

No one can know! Suicide hissed. *She'll want you to get help. Look what that did for your mother!*

Mackenzie frowned. No, she would keep those thoughts to herself. "Jeez, why can't we take on some of their good traits?

"Humans are stupid. Life sucks. We should all be

more like cats."

'Kenzie snarled at the thought of Krystal's creepy cat, Cheeto, and gave her arm a shove. "So cynical, *Helga!* And maybe I should bring Bristol over to meet your precious Cheeto!"

"Pfft. You keep that mangy slobbering mongrel at home. And you are just as cynical, *Gail*. It's just that I say it out loud."

Mackenzie's mind whirled. *She's right. But I can't tell her how often I think about dying. Wait, maybe she knows and that's why she's talking like this.*

"No way. I'm not as cynical as you." She lied to keep Krystal from knowing her secret. *Oh God, help me!*

"It's a good thing we have Sadie, though," Mackenzie said. "She seems to find the good in everything. I know it's God. Well, *and* her faith in God."

At the mention of God and faith, the horde of demons shook violently, some leaving and some dashing for cover. Would the angel of God appear and come to her rescue? Suicide dropped to the ground and slithered beneath the bed. There the slimy urchin would wait for another opportunity that would surely come.

Krystal nodded. "True. But ..." She rolled her eyes. "I actually consider myself a realist, thank you. And I always thought of Sadie as an—here's a word for you, Miss Straight A's—*anomaly*. That is, until lately. You know, with the Gary situation."

Mackenzie raised her brows. "Nice word choice, *Miss Competitive*. And yeah, I'm not sure if she's over him yet either." She pulled out her phone. "Tammi texted earlier about a new coffee shop that's really cool. I guess when

Ming and Sadie went to check it out, Dawn and the band came in."

"Oh no."

"Yep, and when Ming and Sadie tried to slip out while Dawn was at the counter, she must have seen them with her third eye in the back of her head or something. I swear, it's like she uses black magic." 'Kenzie shivered. "Anyway, Gary called out to Sadie and followed them outside. She ignored him, but Ming is worried that Sadie might fall for whatever lame excuse he was most likely going to dole out to her."

"Like I said, humans are stupid. Except for you." Krystal shook her head and stood. "Let's get a snack."

Mackenzie huffed. "Well, I'm preparing for the PSATs. And didn't you just have pizza with Bryce?"

Krystal glared at her. "I'm eating for two. Get me food." She turned, grumbling as she left the room, "*PSATs.*"

"I won't argue with a hungry pregnant woman."

"Mm-hmm, like I said, smart girl," Krystal said, turning to flip one of 'Kenzie's curls from her shoulder.

The girls passed Trey in the hall on the way to the kitchen. Like a dog, he turned and followed. At some point, Mackenzie needed to let that hormone-crazed brother of hers know that Krystal was pregnant. But then again, he would eventually figure it out. Yeah, just let him figure it out. He'd either hear the gossip or he'd notice Krystal's belly. The thought of Trey realizing he'd been flirting with a pregnant girl for months made her giggle to herself. He also seemed interested in Tammi, but the fact that she towered over him must have quelled his testosterone-led impulses, because he mostly just ogled Tammi without a word. It seemed Sadie was just too sweet and perfectly Christian for him to consider flirting with. Oh, if he only knew what she'd been up to lately. Might make him try chasing after Sadie instead of Krystal. Guys—bleh!

Trey treaded directly to the freezer, pulling out a gallon of ice cream. "Can I interest you in some ice cream, Krystal?"

"Bring it on," Krystal said, plopping down in a chair at the table. "What flavor? Not that it matters."

"Rocky Road," he said.

"Well, that's the story of my life," Krystal said, leaning back in the chair.

Trey got out two bowls and spoons then began scooping without bothering to ask if Mackenzie wanted some. Stupid boy. She reached over him and grabbed another bowl and set it next to the others. At least Trey scooped ice cream into all three bowls. He picked up his and Krystal's and headed to the table. He set Krystal's bowl down in front of her and took a seat, scooting his chair closer to hers. Mackenzie sat across from her friend. Trey glanced up, and Mackenzie gave him the stink eye. He ignored it, or possibly didn't even notice. He was hellbent on impressing Krystal.

Little footsteps pounded from the hall, making their way to the kitchen. "Hey! I want ice cream!" Del hollered.

Harper strolled in, giving Del's curly hair a tussle. "I do too, buddy. I'll get us some."

"If there's any left, bring it over," Krystal said. "I'm down for seconds."

Trey pushed his long dark bangs from his wide eyes. "I guess running track helps you burn off all those calories and keep that figure of yours."

"Oh my gosh. Shut up, Trey," Mackenzie said.

Harper set the carton of ice cream in the middle of the table and Krystal began to scoop what was left. "Well, I'm eating for two now, ya know."

Trey scowled. "Huh? Come again."

Uh-oh. Here we go.

"I thought with all the gossip at school that you knew," Krystal said.

The color drained from Trey's face. "Knew *what*?"

Krystal looked at Mackenzie, who was trying to subtly caution her not to say anything, nodding her head and shifting her eyes in Del's direction.

Of course, Krystal ignored Mackenzie. She shrugged her shoulders and said, "I'm pregnant," as if it was totally normal.

Trey dropped his spoon, letting it hit the floor with a clang. He bent to pick it up, knocking his head on the table as he rose. "Ouch." He rubbed his head as he stared at Krystal. "Is this a joke? Like are you messing with me because I—"

"You have a baby in your tummy, Krystal?" Del asked.

Mackenzie kicked Krystal's leg beneath the table. "You opened this can of worms."

Krystal set her spoon in the bowl and chewed her thumbnail. "Uh, yeah. Sometimes girls have babies?" She responded like she was asking a question.

Oh! My! Goodness! What the heck?

"How'd a baby get in there?"

Mackenzie kicked Krystal again, this time a lot harder. "Ouch!"

Trey stood up, raking his hand through his bangs. His face looked almost gray. "Come on, Del. You wanna go play a game? You can even bring your ice cream."

"Yeah!"

Relief washed over Mackenzie, but she knew Del would have questions later. She'd need to let Dad know about this.

"Way to go," Mackenzie said.

"I'm sorry. I really thought he knew. Should have thought about the kid being here, though. It's just that your brother is such a flirt. I better go," she said, setting her bowl in the sink and walking to the door without saying goodbye.

"Get back here." Mackenzie's voice came out harsher than she wanted.

Krystal turned around but didn't look at her. The proud track star slumped, looking at the floor.

Mackenzie sighed. "He would have eventually found out. Soon enough *everyone* will be able to see that you're pregnant. Besides, you don't have a car. I need to take you home."

Krystal's head jerked up. "Oh, yeah. You're right." Her brows scrunched together. "And you know what? I've been thinking about something. If everyone is eventually gonna know, then I might as well just go back to school when winter break is over. I hate independent study and being all alone at my house."

"Yeah, why not?"

"Really? You'll still hang out with me when I'm as big

as a barn?"

Mackenzie noticed her glassy eyes ready to spill. "Yeah, Helga. Remember? Friends even when we're old and gray," she said and gave her friend a hug.

"Thanks, Gail," Krystal whispered in her ear.

Will you still be friends with me if I end up in the loony bin like my mom?

CHAPTER 19

TAMMI stuffed the letter into her jacket pocket. She slid a fuzzy beanie down over her ears and headed to the car. A bitter breeze whipped back her long curls as if to prove winter had officially arrived. She climbed in and simultaneously started the engine while turning on the heater, which blew out icy air. She quickly turned it off. Best to let the poor car warm up. Kinda like herself in the morning before coffee. Revving the engine a few times, Tammi contemplated what she'd say during her appointment with Lauren, visualizing her kind but probing eyes. The woman had a gift. Lauren knew just the right things to ask. Well, she was a counselor after all.

But Tammi knew it was more than professional with Lauren. She actually cared deeply. Tammi thought of her more like the big sister she never had than a counselor. Lauren had even opened up some of her personal life with Tammi. Not only had Lauren experienced sexual abuse as a kid, but she had a Black mom and White dad. And just like Tammi, Lauren's Black side of the family had nothing to do with her. Lauren said it was hard for her growing up because she didn't feel like she fit in with the Black kids or the White kids—just like Tammi. Even though Lauren looked lighter than Tammi, it was comforting to finally have someone in her life who understood the complications that come from being biracial but being raised like she was White.

Gazing at herself in the rearview mirror, Tammi analyzed her raven-colored ringlets and full lips—dead giveaways she was part Black. Her gray eyes and light caramel skin proved she was also White. Lauren, on the other hand, had soft features and long silky hair. Tammi pulled a tube of lip gloss from her bag and applied it before backing out.

Tammi parked her car near the front of the church and hesitated before getting out. She'd rather meet with Lauren at her house as they had for previous appointments. But as more members of the church became clients of Lauren's, Pastor Dave allowed her to use one of the church offices.

Pushing past the fluttery feeling in her stomach, Tammi headed inside. A middle-aged secretary with a frizzy bob sat at a desk in the lobby. "May I help you?" she asked, looking over the top of her dark-framed glasses that were attached to a colorful chain looping downward like a necklace.

This was another reason Tammi didn't like meeting Lauren here. "I'm here to see Lauren."

"Oh, yes." The secretary glanced at her computer screen. "You must be Tammi. I'll let her know you've arrived. Please take a seat, sweetheart."

Tammi sat down and pulled out her phone. As she scrolled through Instagram, the door slammed open with a gust of cool air. Pastor Dave waltzed in and promptly hung his coat on a hook near the door.

"Brrr!" The pastor said to no one in particular. He took a few steps and smiled at the secretary, then his gaze landed on Tammi. "Well, hello." His tone was chipper, and a smile engulfed his face, making his eyes look like tiny crescents.

And another reason she didn't like meeting here.

"Hi, Pastor," Tammi said, then resumed scrolling through her phone.

Eyes still on the screen, Tammi caught a glimpse of a pair of black boots standing in front of her. Tammi lifted her head to find Lauren gazing down at her.

"Oh, I didn't hear you. You're like a ninja," Tammi mumbled.

Lauren grinned. "Yep, that's me. Come on," she waved over her shoulder. "My *new* office is back this way."

Tammi followed her down a narrow hall lined with evenly spaced pictures in whitewashed frames with Bible verses printed on pastel-colored matting. There was an antique white, floor-to-ceiling bookcase at the back wall lined with books and bric-a-brac. Lauren made a left down another hall and entered the first door on the right.

The moment Tammi entered, the knots in her stomach seemed to loosen. A few candles were burning, the scent of lavender and sage filling the small office. Three of the walls were painted a soft blue. Lauren's desk sat in front of a dark gray-blue wall with white shelves that held matching blue and white décor.

Taking a seat in the chair in front of Lauren's desk, Tammi took out the letter and bank statement and held them out toward Lauren. Might as well just jump right in. Lauren grasped the papers, squinting her eyes as she scrutinized them.

Tammi sat with her hands folded in her lap as Lauren's

eyes darted left to right across the letter from Tammi's dad. She finished reading and laid the papers on the desk.

Leaning forward, Tammi asked, "What am I supposed to do with this?"

"Well, first, let's talk about the way receiving this letter made you feel."

"Oh, *let's*. That sounds just grand." Tammi rolled her eyes. "I'm angry. Like *so* angry. When I read the first few lines, I felt like I was going to crack a tooth from gritting my teeth so hard. I didn't even finish. I threw it across the room. I didn't even realize there was an account with money at first."

"So, you've read the entire letter, right?"

Tammi nodded.

"We've talked about the emotion of anger and how it's usually secondary to your fear, sadness, and disappointment."

Tammi nodded again, a hard pebble forming into a rock in her throat. She brushed her long hair over her shoulder, glancing around the room. Anything to avoid tears … again. Oh, how she hated giving him that. He didn't deserve her tears. Nor the forgiveness he was seeking.

"Okay, let's just deal with the anger part," Lauren said. "Name three things about receiving the letter and bank information that make you angry."

The rock in Tammi's throat seemed to be growing. She choked it down as she snatched the letter.

"Right here." she pointed. "'*My beautiful daughter.*' I hate that." she continued, "And this: '*I don't have much time.*' Like, is that supposed to make me feel bad? And then this: '*But I hope you can find it in your heart to forgive me. I'm not asking forgiveness for my own sake. I know I don't deserve it. But I also know how bitterness can rot the soul. I want you to be happy and free, Tammi.*' Um, no! I can't forgive you! And yeah, you don't deserve it, you freak!"

CHAPTER 20

SADIE waved goodbye to the back of Ming's little Toyota as it rounded the corner. She watched the red brake lights disappear as her lower lip began to quiver. Sadie clenched her jaw tight only to turn and see Mom's glassy blue eyes as she leaned into Dad's shoulder. Winter break and New Year's Day had flown by, and now Ming wouldn't be back until spring.

"You still have me and the boys," Sadie said to her parents, pointing to Jeff and Jake who chased each other around the front yard.

"I have an idea," Dad said. "Let's go inside and play a game." He was obviously trying to lighten Sadie and her Mom's somber mood.

"Yay! Let's play Super Smash Brothers!" Jake said, running toward the house with Jeff on his heels.

Sadie didn't feel like playing a game. She was sad that Ming was gone, but even more sad about Gary. She checked her phone again and still nothing. Seeing him at the Coffee Cabin was driving her crazy. What did he want to say when he followed her and Ming out to the car? Although she'd typed a text at least a dozen times, she couldn't bring herself to hit send.

Her family made their way into the living room, Sadie lagging. By the time she sat down on the sofa, Jeff had already started the game. He tossed a controller to

Sadie, then turned back to face the TV. Sadie held the controller but didn't play. She kept thinking of reasons why Gary hadn't contacted her. *He probably thinks I hate him. That's it! He's ashamed and was going to apologize. But I didn't give him the chance.*

"Hey! Sadie's not even playing," Jake said, jolting her from her thoughts.

"I'm sorry, guys. I don't feel like it." Sadie stood and hopped over to her crutches. "I'm just going to go read," she said. "Or maybe call my friends."

"It's fine, honey," Mom gave a nod. "Maybe just you and the boys can play?" She lifted an eyebrow at Dad.

Uh-oh, was she going to want to spend some mother-daughter time? Sadie was hoping to finally call Gary. And knowing Mom, she was probably suspecting that.

Mom stood, a mischievous grin on her face. "Let's get some ice cream," she whispered as she passed by on her way to the kitchen.

Grrreat! Sadie followed reluctantly. Her mom knew Sadie couldn't resist ice cream.

When she got to the kitchen, Mom was already dishing up the best, Ben & Jerry's. There was store brand for the boys because "they didn't know the difference," her mom would say with a sly giggle while pushing the *girl's* ice cream toward the back of the freezer.

Well, this part wasn't so bad. But Sadie had an inkling that Ming may have told Mom about seeing Gary at the coffee shop.

Mom handed Sadie a bowl and sat down across from her. "Mmm," she murmured.

Sadie nodded, savoring the creamy flavor. "I bet Ming told you that we saw Gary, huh?" Might as well get it over with.

"She did."

"I have started a text to him a hundred times, but then I don't send it."

Mom set her spoon in the bowl. "Aw, honey." Her eyes filled with compassion. "Let him go," she said. "He isn't worth it."

Of course, she would say that. She didn't understand. But Sadie didn't want Mom to suspect that she was going to reach out to Gary. Sadie just had to know what Gary was going to say.

"Yeah, you're probably right."

"Do your friends know?" Mom asked. "I mean that you saw Gary and he tried to talk to you?"

"Umm, I texted Tammi." Sadie licked her spoon, trying to play it cool. "She basically said that he's a jerk and to forget about him."

Mom smirked. "Well, I happen to agree."

"Wow! Didn't expect that from you."

"What? Like a Christian woman can't call it like she sees it?

"Huh?"

Mom laughed. "What I mean is, he *is* a jerk! So, I absolutely agree with Tammi."

"Speaking of Tammi, I think I'll go give her a call if that's okay?"

"Sure, sweetie. I was just checking on you. But I guess you knew that since you brought up Gary yourself." She chuckled. "You're an intuitive girl."

Pfft! Mom was the intuitive one, as was Ming. The two of them were like hunting dogs chasing a rabbit. Yeah, Mom probably assumed that Sadie hadn't "let Gary go."

Sadie stood to leave but paused. "Thanks for caring." Maybe that would take Mom off the scent.

"Always," Mom said.

And Sadie knew her mom meant it.

Once she was finally alone in her room, Sadie sat in her fuzzy pink chair, phone in hand. She searched her contacts for Gary and was about to tap his number when a call came through.

Gary!

Sadie gasped, clutching the phone tightly.

Her mind whirled. *Should I answer? Duh, you were about to call him. But what if I don't? You have to!*

"Hello?"

"Hi, it's me."

"Mm-hm."

"I guess I've got some explaining to do."

Sadie let silence hang in the air.

"Uh, well. First of all, I'm sorry."

More silence.

"And … uh … are you gonna say something?"

"What are you sorry for exactly?" Sadie asked.

"I'm sorry that I hurt you."

"What makes you think that you hurt me?'

"Look, Sadie. I really messed up."

"How's that?"

"I think I made you think that we were—" he cleared his throat. "that we were an item or something."

Suddenly, there was no air and Sadie felt light-headed like she could faint.

"Are you still there? Do you understand what I'm saying?"

"So, when you say you messed up, what you really mean is that you like to mess around," Sadie snapped.

"Sadie, I liked you. A lot. But the whole thing with your parents, and stuff—"

He said liked. Past tense.

"Look, I don't want to be stuck with just one girl—I mean, I'm really not looking for a serious relationship, you know? Not right now anyways. You know, I'll be traveling with the band soon. And you're still in high school and everything. It just won't work. But I am sorry, and I hope we can still be friends. You're a sweet girl."

Sweet girl? Friends?

Again, Sadie found herself gasping for air like she was drowning. She could almost picture the salty waves of pain splashing over her face, tugging her downward. The realization set in like cold, hard cement: She wasn't special to Gary. All that "secret lover" crap. He'd used her! How could she fall for it?

But she had gotten through much worse than this. Everyone she loved was right. He wasn't worth it. And he would *not* break her!

"Sadie?"

"Thanks for finally getting the guts to call. I was beginning to think you were a cheater *and* a coward." Her voice was monotone. "But no, we will *not* be friends.

I have real friends that would never do something like this to me. And as far as accepting your apology—that will take a whole lotta Jesus. Right now, I'm feeling like you can shove that apology where the sun don't shine.

"Sadie, come on …"

"Don't call me again."

Sadie tapped the end call button, deleted and blocked his number, then tossed her phone on the floor triumphantly.

CHAPTER 21

KRYSTAL looked at herself sideways in the bathroom mirror and smoothed her hand over her belly pooch. She huffed and pulled off her shirt and gave it a toss. It landed on the floor near her cat, who stretched and squinted at her in response. Krystal grabbed her favorite school sweatshirt from track that hung on the back of the door and tugged it over her head. That looked better. Even though she was sure everyone at school knew about the pregnancy, there was no reason to flaunt it on her first day back. Was she crazy to return to school rather than do independent study in her safe little world at home?

"Well, I'm no weakling, right, Cheeto?" she said to her cat, whose yawn lacked the enthusiasm she'd hoped for. "I'm not going to hide away from everything and everyone for months. I'm eventually going to have to face them. Why not today?" She shrugged and waltzed out of the bathroom. Cheeto followed, striped tail in the air.

"Hi, sweetie. You sure about this?" Mom said, meeting her in the hallway.

Krystal squeezed her eyes tight and balled her hands into fists. "Yeah." She opened her eyes again and sidestepped her mom.

"I'm praying for you," Mom called out.

She knew Mom meant it. Krystal looked over her

shoulder as she took the first step down.

"Thanks, Mom."

Once in the kitchen, Krystal made it past her brothers' glaring eyes and poured herself a travel mug of coffee. She knew Kasey and Korey were embarrassed about her pregnancy, but the idea of her going back to school made it worse for them. She frowned. Her decisions were affecting more than just her. Well, there was nothing she could do about it now. She was having a baby and that was that.

Krystal added sugar and cream, grabbed a muffin and banana then walked out without saying a word. Thank God, Mackenzie would be there to pick her up soon. Of course, Bryce had offered to take her, but it seemed worse to pull up to the school with the seventeen-year-old father of her child. Krystal recalled the pain in Bryce's eyes when she turned down his offer for a ride. He could thank her later. She chewed her lip as she waited for Mackenzie.

Krystal perched on the arm of a chair near the window and began to pinch off bits of her chocolate muffin, popping them in her mouth absentmindedly. Before long, she'd eaten the whole thing. If it weren't for her brothers, she would have gone back for a second one. Where the heck was Mackenzie? As soon as the question entered her brain, Mackenzie's car pulled into the driveway.

Krystal grabbed her coffee and banana and hurried out the door. She plopped in the passenger seat of Mackenzie's rusted rattletrap VW, let out a deep sigh, and leaned against the headrest. "Am I doing the right thing?"

"Yes," Mackenzie said and put the car in reverse.

"Wait. Stop."

Mackenzie put her foot on the brake and stared at Krystal.

"I'm scared. I don't wanna do this."

Mackenzie took her foot off the brake and continued to back out of the driveway.

"Hey!"

"We've already been through all the pros and cons. You told me not to let you chicken out. So, we're going," she said. "Together. Helga." She glanced at Krystal with a smirk.

"Okay." That one word—*together*—gave Krystal her strength back. She was more grateful for her best friend than ever.

Mackenzie pulled into the school parking lot and coasted into her regular space. Bryce's car wasn't by the tree where he normally parked. Krystal scanned the lot but didn't see his car anywhere. Well, that was probably for the best.

"Let's go," Krystal said.

"Jeez, now you're in a hurry?"

"I want to get it over with. Plus, Bryce isn't here yet."

"Oooh," Mackenzie said. "Yeah, let's get going." She opened her door.

As Krystal joined Mackenzie on the walk from the parking lot to the campus, her lip began to tremble. Although it was freezing, a line of sweat trailed down the crevice between her shoulder blades. Soon, they were engulfed in the herd of students shuffling their way to class. Krystal was jostled from side to side, her arm slamming into Mackenzie's.

This day was going to suck.

BRYCE parked in his usual spot next to Mackenzie's car. He turned off the engine but hesitated. He squinted into a ray of sunlight that peeked through the dreary gray sky and noticed the silhouettes of Krystal and Mackenzie as they merged with the throng of students. He puffed out a slow breath. This day was going to suck. People would be whispering, snickering, and gossiping. Bryce ran a hand through his hair and imagined Krystal getting angry and punching someone. Why was she doing this? What he should have done was tell her it was a *great* idea— then she wouldn't have decided to come back to school just to spite him. He predicted baseball practice would be the worst. The team had already started messing with him *before* winter break, making sexual jokes and talking behind his back. Bryce figured that maybe there would be new gossip once they returned. Yeah, there was new gossip all right—Bryce's knocked-up girlfriend was back at school.

The putrid green demon, Shame, wormed out from beneath the seat. The rotten little fiend sensed Bryce's troubled emotions over the past few days and had waited for the perfect moment to strike.

You're pathetic. Your whole life is a mess and it's about to get worse, the thing whispered.

A larger, higher-ranking demon called Religion

appeared. *I will handle this,* Religion snarled.

Shame hissed and clung tightly to the leg of Bryce's jeans in defiance. Religion lowered its goat-like head, rushed forward, and speared clean through Shame, flipping the creature upward. Shame's blobbish body splattered against the window then disintegrated.

You are not a REAL Christian, Religion growled, edging closer to Bryce. *Everyone thinks you are a phony. And you ARE!*

"I'm such a phony." Bryce muttered to himself, wondering if he should just ditch school.

"No," he said, balling his fists. "If Krystal is going, so am I."

After all, it was *his* fault. He could've stopped that night when she came to his house and knocked on his bedroom window. Come to think of it, he was the one who pulled her into his bed. "Well, she didn't resist either."

Religion clawed up the seat and sat behind Bryce. The thing glared at the back of his head with blood-red eyes. *You knew that night it was wrong—against the commandments. But you are selfish and wanted sex.*

Bryce's phone vibrated in his pocket. He jerked and let out a curse. Religion leaned closer to Bryce's head, its gnarled horns brushing against his hair. *You're not a Christian. Going to church, doesn't make you one. Listen to your language. And your thoughts are evil. All you ever think about is sex.*

Bryce glanced at his phone. A text from Krystal: **WHERE THE HECK ARE YOU?**

He looked at the time. Somehow, he hadn't heard the bell.

BRYCE: ON MY WAY.

He stuffed his phone and keys into his pocket and

headed to class. As he walked the deserted halls, it was like his mind was stuck in a negative gear. He imagined Krystal with a big pregnant belly, waddling around campus. He remembered his dad's disappointed eyes when he found out about Krystal. He saw his mother's pale face streaked with tears.

Bryce stopped and ran a hand through his hair, taking a deep breath. His thoughts shifted to Grant and Lauren. *Is that what you want, God?* Peace washed over Bryce's tumultuous mind.

Could Krystal be right?

CHAPTER 22

MACKENZIE kicked off her shoes and left them near the front door. As she padded from the entry, Bristol bounded through the living room and greeted her with slobbery doggy kisses. She giggled and wrapped her arms around the German shepherd's furry neck. He was the perfect antidote to a difficult day.

As stressed as Mackenzie felt, she could only imagine how it had taken a toll on Krystal and Bryce. They'd walked into a proverbial hornet's nest. The pregnancy was big news at a small school—especially since they were two of the most popular students. Most people whispered and snickered behind their backs, but a few like Bailey and Ashley from the track team had the audacity to inundate Krystal with a bunch of questions. "Why didn't you use protection? Are you going to keep the baby? Are you scared?" As if they cared—yeah, right. All they cared about was putting others down so they could feel better about themselves. Mackenzie watched Krystal's face turn several shades of red as her hand crumpled into a fist before Mackenzie intervened.

"They aren't worth it," Mackenzie whispered in Krystal's ear. Luckily, Krystal listened as Mackenzie led her into the hall to calm her down. Although she admired her friend's confidence and gumption, Krystal could be a loose cannon. Mackenzie knew that from personal experience.

But now, all Mackenzie wanted to do was veg out in front of the TV before it was time to get dinner started. Thank God her Dad was picking up her siblings. She had the house to herself for a little while. It would be great if, somehow, she could escape even from herself. A nap could help. Her mind flashed to an image of her mother's body curled beneath the blankets with the drapes drawn.

That's exactly what Mom did—sleep to escape. And when that didn't work ... She shivered. *I'm so much like her. Except, I believe in God now. Is that enough?*

Mackenzie fought the urge to sleep. She grabbed the remote and stretched out on the couch, her feet hanging off the end. She surfed the channels and finally settled on a cooking show. As she watched a woman dicing vegetables, her eyes grew heavy.

Depression slowly descended to the hotel's basement. As the four-legged reptile trudged the narrow hallway that led to the conference room, the echoes of screams and groans became louder with each step. Depression shook, imagining the torment it might receive when the terrifying Duke Astaroth heard its report about Mackenzie's growing faith. Near the double doors, low-ranking imbeciles crouched in a corner, waiting their turn to meet with the dreaded Duke. Depression raised its chin in pride and walked away from the wide-eyed fools, refusing to let them see it tremble.

The double doors smacked open with such force the

entire building rumbled as if there'd been an earthquake. Out flew the goat demon, Religion, twisting through the air multiple times until it hit the wall just above and to the left of Incest and Depression. The thing landed in a motionless heap near Depression's clawed feet. If this happened to Religion, who was of higher rank, Depression didn't want to imagine what was in store for the rest of them.

Next out of the door skidded Bulimia, scraggly arms and legs flailing until it hit the wall a few feet away. Its yellow eyes rolled back into its deformed head.

"KILL THE CHILD AND KILL THE FAITH OF MANY!" The Duke's voice continued to shake the building. "ENTER THE REST."

Depression swallowed and stepped over Religion's body, leading the way inside. It sensed the others following. Heat pulsed through the room, flames licking the ceiling and walls. The Duke wasn't at the lectern this time. The great horned beast appeared like a hologram through a wall of flames that hovered in the center of the room. Depression stopped short as the demons following plowed into its tail and back legs. Depression didn't bother to respond. It gaped at the flaming monster, unable to speak.

Duke Astaroth's voice boomed. "Reinforcement clones will be arriving shortly. Your time has … *expired*."

Depression couldn't believe it. Clone replacements already? "No! Your grace, I have been a faithful servant. Let me suffer like a warrior. Do not send me away to the abyss with these ingrates!"

The Duke glared down at Depression. "Our time is

short. As it is written, only the strongest will remain until the great war that ends all battles. And you think YOU can endure?"

"I want a chance to."

In one swift motion, the beings behind Depression were caught up into the air. They screamed and hissed as they spun chaotically downward and disappeared into a black vortex of wind. A fiery claw reached down and grabbed Depression by the throat, flinging it across the room. Depression's head smashed into the cinder block wall. It slid down to the floor, unable to move.

There was a sharp ringing in Depression's ears, and its vision was blurry. The injured beast convulsed a few times as flames encroached nearby.

"You know the mission!" the Duke's voice boomed. "The mother is weak and yearns for death. Make sure she gets what she wants. The daughters have the same strongholds. Use them to your advantage. Now, get out of my sight! And take these two with you!" The demons of Fear and Suicide tumbled through the air, a tangled mess of feathers, wings, and scales. The tattered raven hit the floor with a splat, its body sprawled out flat like roadkill with Suicide awkwardly wrapped through one of its wings.

Obeying the Duke's command, Depression tugged the raven's feathers and gave it a shove through the door and into the hall. With its last bit of strength, Depression scrambled, legs going in all directions, willing itself out the door before the Duke changed its mind.

The trio would live to torment another day. And there was no room for failure.

Mackenzie woke at the sound of the door slamming. She sat up just as her family entered.

"What's for dinner?" Trey asked as he strode into the kitchen.

"Uh, I don't know. What are *you* making?" Mackenzie said. Sheesh! Why did he always think it was her job to cook?

"I want pizza!" Del shouted.

Mackenzie's eyes met Dad's. "Sounds good to me. Can we order one?"

"One? You better get two. I'm starved," Trey said, grabbing a box of crackers on his way out of the kitchen.

Dad smiled. "I tell ya what, Trey. Find a coupon that will get us two pizzas for under $20 and you can order it."

Harper pulled out her phone. "Oh, I'm on it. I'm quicker."

Mackenzie rose and headed to the kitchen to make a salad to go along with the pizza. Dad approached her while she was washing her hands. "Saw your mom today." His voice was nearly a whisper.

"What? She let you in?"

A pang zapped her chest as she remembered Christmas Day when Mom rejected seeing them. She must've been in a really dark place not to want to see her family. But then again, Mom was probably the one feeling rejected. All she wanted was to come home again. Mackenzie knew that wasn't a good idea and had begged her mother to stay and get the help she needed.

What if I end up like that?

Dad's dark eyes darted to her siblings in the other room. When he was satisfied they weren't listening, he answered. "Her doctor phoned and said she asked to see me. So I went."

"And?"

He shrugged. There was something in his eyes that made her uneasy. "I'm not sure what to say, really. I mean, it was good to see her face, but—" he looked off into nowhere. "She's just not herself. I spoke to the doctor about adjusting the medication again. But of course, that worries me after what happened before."

"Well, at least she wanted to see you. That's something positive." She tried to sound encouraging for Dad's sake.

"Yes. I just …" He shook his head. "No, you're right. I'll look at this as positive." He gave a weak smile. "And of course, we'll keep praying."

Mackenzie nodded. *Yes, keep praying.* She continued to dice a tomato, but it was all she could do to keep calm. There was an uneasiness that rose from deep inside. As she chopped, she thought about her sister and the cuts on her arm. She imagined them brimming with blood, sending small red rivers down her arms. A buzzing sensation bolted up Mackenzie's spine. Suicide slithered up her back while Depression and Fear loomed closer. They had been watching and waiting for the perfect moment to strike.

Fear descended, flailing its ratty wings and perched on the edge of the counter next to Mackenzie. *You'll go crazy too.* The thing squawked, bouncing up and down on spindly bird legs.

Mackenzie's hand began to shake, and she sliced

through the tip of her finger. The bright red blood contrasted with the white cutting board, making her woozy.

The knife dropped to the floor with a clang and the demonic trio cackled with delight at the sight of human blood. Mackenzie rushed to the sink and ran water on her hand, Dad following close behind.

"I'll be fine," she said. "It's only a tiny cut." But inside, she shivered with fear.

Satisfied, the pernicious beings zipped up and out of the house in a dark streak. Within moments they had joined the faceless demon, Death, whose inky body waved above the bed of Mackenzie's mother, Angela Stine.

This time, their mission could not fail.

CHAPTER 23

TAMMI fumbled to find the light switch on her nightstand. It was late, but sleep wouldn't come because although her body was fatigued, her mind wouldn't turn off. She shoved her arms into the sleeves of her robe and plopped down at her desk. Her gaze landed on the crumpled envelope from her dad and the blank sheet of stationary next to it. Tammi picked up a pen, her nails jabbing into her palms. Her hand began to shake uncontrollably. She scribbled and then gouged at the paper until it was ripped to shreds.

"I can't do this!" She flung the pen across her room as if it were a snake, unaware of the little demon reptile whose claws were wrapped tightly around it.

Incest sailed through air, landing with a whoosh in the corner. Its stubby legs scrambled until the thing was upright. It made a dash beneath the dresser, detecting an unseen heavenly presence. No way could the girl do that on her own. Incest curled into a tight ball as Silas became visible.

I'll be back again, the demon lizard hissed and slipped into the spirit realm away from the Holy One's warrior angel.

"What's wrong with me?" Tammi whispered, her face in her hands. "God, I need your help to forgive him. All I can feel is anger and hate. There is not one ounce of love for him. I don't care if I ever see him again. And worst of all, I *want* him to die. I'm glad he's sick. And that's evil … just like *him*! I don't want to be like him. Please help me, God."

Silas extended his arms in front of himself and just behind Tammi's head. Shimmering lights propelled from the angel's fingertips, encircling her like a halo. She laid her head down on the desk when Lauren's words flooded her mind, washing over the hateful thoughts like a cleansing rain.

Forgiveness doesn't mean you are excusing your dad's horrible behavior. What he did was wrong, and nothing changes that. But forgiveness frees you from the power he had over you … and continues to have because of your anger. You must make a decision not to allow him to have power over you. It's a process. It takes time to heal. The very fact that you are asking God for help is a step in the process. Give yourself the same grace that God has given you.

Silas flew above the sleeping town of Arcana just before dawn. The uppermost layer of the night sky shimmered with stars as the darkness began to surrender to the sun's increasing light. Earth was the perfect reflection of God's authority and control.

Eyeing the glow from a gathering of angels below, Silas descended through the pine trees, landing next to Theo, Jason, and Jonathan. The three stood erect, jaws tight as they faced Commander Philo. Within the trees and bushes blinked the tiny yellow and orange cattish eyes of fifty demon spies.

"It's come to my attention that the enemy has ordered thousands of replacement clones," Philo said. "Therefore, The Lord God has commissioned a dozen legions to be ready at His command."

Silas's blond brows furrowed. "Sir, are there new orders for us?" He glanced at his comrades.

Philo's eyes were like torches as he gazed over the company of angels gathered in the forest and then back to Silas. "Your orders remain the same. Stand firm, mighty soldier."

The illustrious veteran, Theo, took a step forward, fisted hand across his body armor. "I do not presume to question the Almighty, sir. But the attacks have been relentless."

Philo nodded. "I am aware of this. Nonetheless, the warrior legions will be released to fight at the Lord's command. In the meantime, stay close to the beloved souls that have been entrusted to you. I have called this meeting to strengthen you with prayer and the Almighty's blessing."

The four angels bowed their heads as Commander Philo began to pray in a heavenly language understood only by God and his angels. As Philo spoke, what looked like pearlescent blue flaming tongues of fire settled over each of the angels, causing the demon spies to shriek and disperse like roaches. Once Philo finished, the team of angels stood emblazoned in gold, silver, and bronze. With fortified power and strength, they let out a shout and shot upward becoming a part of the masterpiece of the early morning sky.

Tammi sat up and swiped the tears from her face. She wasn't ready to write the letter, but she knew God was helping her to slowly heal. She put her headphones in and scrolled through the songs on her phone until she landed on one Grant and Lauren had recorded. Tammi smiled when she heard Lauren's warm alto voice.

Tammi found herself singing the words to God like a prayer just as the first sign of daylight broke through her window. It was amazing, really. She never would have imagined herself singing Christian songs, going to church, and hanging around "believers." Yes, she really *was* different. It was the craziest thing ever. Tammi Gerard, the melancholy, tatted, and pierced emo girl was actually experiencing … could it be … joy?

Maybe she *was* crazy. She'd just moments ago entertained gleeful thoughts of her dad dying. Did she really want him dead? Tammi thought of his frail and pathetic-looking appearance. She'd always wanted him to suffer. And now he was. Is that what she wanted?

Feeling an urge to let out her tangled emotions, Tammi grabbed her guitar from the corner and began to hum until words flowed from her lips, warming her from the inside out. She stopped playing for a moment to hit record on her phone so she wouldn't forget the words and melody. As she continued, Tammi's heart ascended. Music had always been her refuge and escape, but this was different than the other times. Rather than escaping, she was drawing close to something. There was a connection to something holy and freeing that was guiding her. Inspiring her. She was writing a song to God.

Only you could come in and change my heart,
Could give me a brand-new start.
Only You forgive me of all my sins.
Say 'this day new life begins.'
Only you, ooooo,
Only you

CHAPTER 24

SADIE glanced around the quad outside of the cafeteria. Although it was a chilly day, students huddled under the metal covering. Her blue eyes scanned the picnic-style tables where she spotted Tammi by herself at the furthest one. Sadie meandered through the tables packed with students laughing, talking, and eating their lunches. As usual, Tammi seemed to be in her own world. She munched on some carrot sticks while gazing into the distance. Sadie set down her crutches and with a smirk, shoved a shoulder into her. Tammi scowled and rolled her eyes but didn't turn to face Sadie. Typical. Sadie leaned into Tammi a little harder this time as she plopped down next to her.

"Wha-a-a-t?" Tammi said, turning her head ever so slightly.

"I talked to Gary."

Tammi's head jerked in Sadie's direction. That got her attention! Tammi pulled one long leg from beneath the table and straddled the bench, now facing Sadie dead-on, her gray eyes wide. "You didn't call him, did you?"

"Nope."

"Oh no. You met with him?"

"Nope."

Tammi huffed. "Okay, what then?"

"I was thinking about calling him when he beat me to it."

"*And?*"

Sadie twisted a strand of hair between her fingers. How to say this without feeling like the fool she knew she'd been? *Oh, screw it!*

"You were right." Sadie looked away. Her lower lip began to tremble. Dang it! In an instant, shame had now turned into pain. She would not cry over that jerk! Sadie strengthened her resolve and faced Tammi again.

Tammi blinked then looked away. "I'm sorry."

"He—he said that he *liked* me a lot. Past tense. And that he doesn't want to be '*stuck*' with one girl." Sadie drew in a ragged breath. "Can you believe that?"

Tammi shrugged. "Um, unfortunately, yeah."

"Hmp! *And* he said—" Sadie lowered her voice to sound like a guy. "I'm so sorry. But I hope we can be friends." She laughed bitterly. "I told him that he was a coward and that we would *not* be friends because I already have REAL friends. And then I hung up."

"Good riddance!" Tammi stood. "Let's go. This calls for a celebration."

Sadie got up and followed Tammi. "Okay, but where are we going?"

"To get an ice cream in the cafeteria. They have Drumsticks today." Tammi said over her shoulder. "Where'd you think, Disneyland?"

Sadie hurried to catch up. Darn Tammi and her long legs! And darn the stupid crutches too! Sadie was glad her doctor's appointment was today. Hopefully the new prosthetic wouldn't need too much adjusting and she'd be able to wear it home. But even more exciting was that the new pointe ballet prosthetic may have arrived! She couldn't wait to get back to dancing. Of course, she'd been stretching and doing her barre exercises in the garage. But the new leg would mean getting back to actual dance class. Yes, dancing would help take her mind off of Gary.

Finally catching up to Tammi, the two entered the cafeteria. "Disneyland." Sadie huffed, shaking her head. "You sound like Krystal."

"What sounds like me?"

Sadie turned to see Krystal, Mackenzie, and Bryce. "Oh, hey, you guys!"

"Why are you talking about me?" Krystal asked, unwrapping an ice cream cone, and sinking her teeth in, bits of peanuts falling on her shirt.

"Ice cream!" Sadie said. "That's what we're here for."

"Oh, so ice cream means you talk about the pregnant girl?"

Tammi put her arm around Krystal's neck. "Yeah."

Sadie sucked in her lip. Not many people could get away with messing around with Krystal Peterson. Tammi was one of the few, and it was hilarious! But Sadie did feel a little bad since the past few days had been hard with Krystal returning to school. The gossip mill was in full force. Even a few kids from the youth group at church were joining in, and they were taken by surprise being called out by her. Well, good! She was proud of Krystal and Bryce for facing their peers, and she wasn't going to tolerate people talking bad about her friends. Everyone knew Krystal was pregnant. Why should she miss out on coming to school?

Krystal shook her waffle cone in Tammi's face. "Well, don't talk about me."

Tammi's teeth clamped on the cone in her face. Krystal snatched it away and drew her arm back, ready to fling the thing when Bryce stepped between the girls. "Whoa, whoa. You don't take a bite of a pregnant girl's ice cream cone."

"Yeah, I can see that," Tammi said, taking a step back. "It's like a lioness on a gazelle. Jeez, I'll go get you another one."

"You do that!" Krystal said, biting hard into what was left of her cone.

"Nah, I'll do it," Bryce said, heading back to the line.

Tammi rolled her eyes. "You've got that guy wrapped around your finger. Speaking of guys, I was getting an ice cream for our Munchkin here because she finally kicked Gary to the curb."

Mackenzie's eyebrows raised. "You saw him?"

"He called," Sadie said. "It was dumb. Said he doesn't want to be 'stuck' with one girl." She shrugged. "So, that's that. I'm done being sad over him. Plus, I have my appointment today. I'll be getting my new prosthetic and I can kick these stupid crutches to the curb too!"

"Good for you!" Krystal said. "He's a loser."

Mackenzie tilted her head, eyes narrowing. "Are you okay though, Sadie?"

A lump was hard in Sadie's throat. Under Mackenzie's caring gaze, tears threatened to fall. *No! Think of good things.* Then suddenly she remembered. *My pointe ballet prosthetic could be ready too!*

Sadie nodded. "I *will* be."

Sadie sat next to her mom in the waiting room, shifting in the seat and clicking her nails on her water bottle. She checked the time on her phone *again*. Jeff and Jake seemed content to play with oversized Legos in the little room adjacent to the waiting area, that is until Sadie's name was called. Now they were moaning and making a scene.

"Mom, I can go in alone so you guys can stay out here."

"Good idea." Mom nodded, a look of relief on her face. "Text if you need anything."

A nurse led Sadie down the familiar hall lined with ocean pictures. Sadie squealed the moment she caught sight of Tegan, the prosthetic specialist, who she now considered a friend.

"Tegan!"

"Hey, girl!" The prosthetist smiled, revealing pink gums below her wide lips. Tegan pulled Sadie into a gentle hug. "It's great to see you. Come on in." She waved her arm and entered an examination room.

Sadie followed. Knowing the drill, she sat down and got her pant leg situated to where her stump was exposed for Tegan.

After helping to attach the new prosthesis to the socket on Sadie's stump, Tegan rolled her chair back. She tucked a strand of amber bangs behind her ear, wrinkled her freckled nose, and gave Sadie a wink. "Okay, girlie. Time to test it out. Be sure and tell me if there is pinching or any pain whatsoever. We don't need to reopen that old wound."

Sadie tilted her head, eying the flesh-colored smooth covering below her knee. She preferred a more natural-looking leg to the titanium. She was grateful her parents had agreed to pay the extra money for what the insurance company considered 'cosmetic'.

There was a rap on the door and Sadie's mom and brothers entered just as Sadie stood and took a few tentative steps. "It's sooo good to be back!" Sadie said.

"Oh, yay! We're just in time," Sadie's mom gushed. "Aww, it's great to see you up and walking, honey."

"Uh-hmmm, you've gotta test it a lot more than that," Tegan said.

Sadie nodded her head. "I know, I know."

After a few small adjustments, Sadie was walking around the entire office and waiting room. What an amazing feeling of freedom! She couldn't wait to show her friends. As she rounded the corner on the way back to the examination room, she saw Tegan grinning from ear to ear, holding the new ballet prosthetic. "Ready to try it?" She dangled the pointed foot in front of Sadie.

"Are you kidding?"

Sadie sat down and removed the covering to reveal the metal beneath. Tegan showed her how to unscrew the lower leg and attach the pointed ballet foot. Once it was in place, Mom pulled a worn pair of pink satin pointe slippers from her bag and handed them to Sadie.

"Thanks, Mom. I didn't even think to bring those."

With the slippers on both feet, Sadie stood on her

pointed toes and walked gingerly about the room.

"Now remember," Tegan said. "There is new science being developed. I've even heard of bionic prosthetics for athletes and dancers. I'm not sure of the cost or how soon these will be available. But for now, you are back on pointe, Sadie! And you can still do some dancing with your other prosthetic too."

Raising her arms above her head like a ballerina, Sadie smiled. "I'm me again!"

CHAPTER 25

KRYSTAL's bare feet dangled from the examination table. She wiggled to situate the sheet over her legs, rattling the protective paper beneath. Mom sat across from her in a plastic chair, thumbing through a maternity magazine. Krystal didn't bother to tell Bryce or her friends she had a doctor's appointment. Of course, when Sadie mentioned having her own appointment, Krystal thought about telling them. The timing wasn't right, though. And Bryce would probably want to come along. No way! It was bad enough having Mom here. Then again, the thought of a vaginal ultrasound was terrifying. So, Krystal consented.

Her mom's eyes raised over the pages of the magazine. "You okay? You keep fidgeting."

"Uh, not really. But there's nothing I can do about it," Krystal said. "Why the heck is it so freaking cold in here? I mean, my feet are turning purple."

There was a light knock on the door and a short stocky woman in a white coat entered. The doctor looked to be in her forties and wore thick glasses with purple frames. Her hair was short with trendy highlights.

The woman reached out to shake Krystal's hand. "Hello, Krystal. I'm Doctor Barnes." Her grip was firm, making Krystal all the more nervous.

"And you must be Mom?"

Mom stood and shook the woman's hand. "Yes. I'm

Gloria. Nice to meet you."

The doctor rolled over a cart with a machine. "Since your periods have been irregular, I'll be doing a first trimester transvaginal ultrasound to determine the baby's due date and development …" The doctor's voice faded, and Krystal found herself nodding but not really hearing. Her mother came near and took hold of her hand as Krystal laid back on the examination table, placing her feet in stirrups. Krystal tucked in her lower lip and focused on the ceiling, where a mobile with gold and silver stars dangled. The heater must have finally kicked on, warm air from a ceiling vent gently blowing the stars back and forth on their iridescent strings. She pretended to leave the planet and float with the stars. That was probably why the thing was hung there.

Mom squeezed Krystal's hand tightly. "Did you hear the doctor, honey?"

"I'd say you are fifteen weeks along. This means you're in the second trimester. A typical pregnancy is approximately forty weeks," the doctor said. "Would you like to look, Krystal?"

Turning her head to the screen, Krystal sucked in a deep breath. She could see the baby's head and little arms and legs. It looked like an itty-bitty peanut human. Along with a whooshing noise came a rapid pattering sound—the heartbeat! She could see it too! And to think, she was going to have an abortion. The very thought now made her nauseous. How could God ever forgive her for listening to Dawn and going to that horrible clinic? But he had forgiven her.

Back at home, Krystal laid on her bed and held the black and white image of the baby growing inside her belly. She traced the tiny head with her finger. It seemed unreal. She placed the picture across her stomach and wondered whether the child was a boy or girl. What would their name be? He or she would probably be athletic and smart like Bryce. Would they have gorgeous green eyes and dimples like him too? She hoped so. Her lips turned upward into a grin when there was a knock at the bedroom door. She sat up to see her vision come to life as Bryce entered.

"Hey, your mom let me in," he said. "Sorry I didn't call first. Were you taking a nap?"

Krystal tucked the image beneath her leg and quickly drew her hand up to smooth down her bedhead. Why was she hiding this? Her heart rate increased at the scowl on his face. Did he know?

"What's up? he asked.

Krystal pulled out the image of the baby. "Come sit down." She patted the bed. "I have something to show you."

Bryce eyed her hand and sat next to her. She handed it to him. He tilted his head, brows knitting together. His eyes widened, his mouth rounding like the letter O. "What? Is this …" He looked into her eyes. "Is this the baby?"

She chewed the side of her lip and nodded.

An enormous smile engulfed Bryce's face. "Oh." He stood up, still holding the picture and pacing the room.

He turned to her again. "This is crazy! I can't believe it." A frown began to emerge. "Wait. When did you go? Why didn't you tell me?"

"Today. And I was embarrassed."

"Why would you be embarrassed?"

"Uh, because it's super personal. They put a camera … down there." She pointed between her legs. "Mom went with me. I'm sorry, Bry. I feel bad now."

Bryce sat down, placing his arm around her shoulder. "I guess I can sort of understand now that you explain it." His face was flush, and his eyes darted below her belly then back to the black and white image of the peanut human. "Do you know if it's a boy or a girl?"

Krystal shook her head. "Too early to tell." She glanced at the picture again. "I'm fifteen weeks, which means the baby will come by the last week in June … maybe earlier or later. She said it could be two whole weeks early or late. I sure hope it's early."

Suddenly, Bryce's soft lips crushed into hers. She kissed him back, a tingling sensation rising from her toes to the top of her head. He smelled like sweet soap and Old Spice. Bryce's hands rubbed up and down her body as she fell back onto the bed with him on top of her, kissing her neck and ears. She could hardly breathe. Krystal reached her hand inside Bryce's shirt, feeling his warm skin when, like an unexpected rain shower, he just stopped. He jerked up and ran his hands through his hair.

Bryce let out a heavy sigh. "I'm sorry. I got carried away." He turned his face the other direction. "That was dumb." He scooted to the top of the bed. "Sit up." His voice was gruff.

Krystal pushed herself up with shaky arms. "What the heck? Why should you be sorry? I'm wearing your ring—" She shoved her left hand in his face. "And we're having a baby. I think it's okay to make out."

Bryce flashed a sideways grin and shook his head. "Yeah, well, I wanted more than making out. And *that's* what got us *here*." He slid the picture across the bedspread.

Krystal rolled her eyes and huffed, tugging her fingers through the length of her hair to loosen a knot. "Get back over here."

One of Bryce's eyebrows arched as he slid near, his leg touching hers. "I love you, K. I promise." He lifted her hand that clutched the image of their baby and kissed her ring finger. "I can't get over this picture, though." His eyes darted at the sonogram. "Are you still sure about adoption?"

"Oh, my gosh. This doesn't change anything. We cannot raise this kid, Bry. Actually, maybe it does change things. I just want to get this over with. I want to run track again in my senior year. I want our lives back. I'm more sure now than ever. This kid deserves more than we can give him or her. Ya know?" she pleaded.

Bryce stood quietly and headed for the door, then stopped. "Which is it, Krystal?" He turned to face her now. "You want your life back or a better life for the baby? Because I wonder if it's more about what *you* want."

"Both, Bry. I can want both." Krystal got up and approached him. "And I already told you I truly believe that God wants us to let Grant and Lauren raise the baby. I thought we'd sort of agreed on that." She laid a hand on his muscled bicep, feeling him tense.

"Yeah, I did too. But now … I just need to think," he said as he turned and shut the door.

"And pray," Krystal said to the closed door, hoping he heard.

This is what you want, right God?

CHAPTER 26

MACKENZIE hurried toward the gym, eyes on her feet. All she wanted was to get out on the track. She glanced up just in time to avoid smacking into Brad Kozlowski from the baseball team.

"Well, hello," His deep voice and piercing blue eyes sent her heart into palpitations.

Did he know what he did to her? Was she blushing? Mackenzie forced a smile and scurried past him, then pushed open the door to the girl's gym. Although it had been three weeks since Krystal returned to school, things were still weird with the track team. Mackenzie was keenly aware of the whispers and stares. Avoiding contact with anyone on the way to her locker, she swiveled through the benches without looking up. She put in the numbered code and kicked off her boots and jeans then tugged on her running shorts. The locker room buzzed with chatter as the girl's track team prepared for practice. Pulling her hair into a high ponytail, Mackenzie headed out of the gym when she heard a voice from behind that sounded like Krystal. She spun around to see her best friend dressed for practice and talking with Bailey and Ashley. *What the heck? She didn't mention coming to practice.*

"Yeah, I can *still* run track!" Krystal said, her hands on her hips.

The sound of Coach's whistle silenced the room.

"Everyone outside to the bleachers for a meeting."

Mackenzie could guess what the meeting was about. She headed back toward Krystal as Baily and Ashley came in her direction. Bailey's blue eyes bulged like she'd seen something frightening. "Can she still be on the team?" she whispered. Mackenzie ignored her and kept walking until she reached Krystal.

"Um, hey, Helga. Why didn't you tell me you'd be here?"

"Don't get your panties in a wad, Gail. I didn't know I was until an hour ago. I met with Coach Lopez to ask her for a safe running plan while I'm pregnant. Long story short, she and Principal Rainey said I could still be on the team. I have other stuff to tell you. But obviously, not now." she said. "Let's go. I'll explain more later. Coach is gonna tell everybody right now they haven't gotten rid of me." Krystal nodded at the door. "This ought to be fun, right?"

How could a pregnant girl be on the track team? Krystal's belly pooch was hardly noticeable now, but Mackenzie tried to picture Krystal running beside her in a few months, looking like she'd swallowed a watermelon. She shook her head and walked alongside Krystal through the deserted locker room.

Mackenzie pushed open one of the double doors, bright sunlight making it hard for her to see. She shaded her eyes as they approached the benches where the rest of team came into view. Her heartrate jumped like a jackrabbit with each step. Everyone stared as they took a seat on the bottom corner bleacher. Mackenzie glanced at Krystal who seemed cool as a cucumber but she knew inside she was probably a wreck. Somehow self-confidence emanated from her—even now. Sure, she was headstrong and brave, but why put herself through this? Mackenzie knew the answer. Krystal was determined to stay in shape and not let this pregnancy disrupt her life. Oh, how Mackenzie wished she could be strong like her friend and not let her mom's illness affect *her* life. But it did. Mom's illness seeped into every cell of her being like a cancer. She was doomed.

Or more like … cursed.

Coach stood at the front of the bleachers facing the team with her hands on her hips, feet slightly spread. "Well, I'm pretty sure that most of you know that Krystal is pregnant. And if you didn't—well, Krystal is pregnant," Coach Lopez said matter-of-factly. "This team is not just a team. We are a family. And I want the gossip to end now. Krystal will remain on the team, albeit her running regimen will be different the rest of the season. The baby is due in June, so she intends to come back next year ready to compete."

Coach answered a few stupid questions like "Don't you think this is a bad example for our team?" And then everyone headed to the track in silence except for the sound of tennis shoes crunching the dirt. Mackenzie could feel the tension and couldn't wait to just start running. Only when running could she escape the sadness that clung to her, weighing her down. Of course, it would return. It always did. But for the next twenty minutes, it would be behind her rather than on top of her. She hoped for Krystal's sake things would get better, but knowing some of the girls, she had her doubts.

Mackenzie ordered two iced coffees and headed to the table at the Coffee Cabin where Krystal sat with Bryce and a few other friends from youth group. She almost hadn't come. What Mackenzie really wanted was to hang out with Krystal *alone* and hear about whatever else was going on. Not be all social. But instead, Bryce convinced them to come hang out at their new coffee spot.

Mackenzie forced a smile and sat in the empty seat next to Krystal. Glancing around, she noticed Tammi walk in carrying her guitar case. Would she perform here, now? Sadie strutted in behind *without* crutches, walking like there'd never been an accident. The two pulled up chairs and squeezed in around the already too-full table. Everyone around her laughed and talked, carrying on like everything was back to normal. Maybe it was. New hangout, same people.

So, why did it seem like everything was normal except for *her*? Despite all that had happened, her friends and everyone else were able to enjoy life. But it wasn't like that for Mackenzie. Sadness followed her *and* her family. It was like a black thundercloud lived over their house, ready to dump rain or stir up a tornado at any point.

The loathsome little demon, Pity, landed upon Mackenzie's right shoulder. The tattered-looking bird drew near her ear. *You're a loser. No one would like you if they knew how sad and pathetic you are.* The thing tapped its twisted beak into the side of her temple. *Loser!* Tap. *Loser!* Tap, tap. *Loser! Loser! Loser!* Tap, tap, tap.

Depression balanced its hefty lizard legs on her other

shoulder. Together the awful pair chided and cursed in stereo, holding Mackenzie prisoner in her mind of negative thoughts. Suicide wound around her waist, squeezing tightly. *You're just like your mother*, it hissed.

Mackenzie chewed on the loose skin around her thumb nail until she felt a trickle of blood running down her wrist. She pulled her hand beneath the table, wiping discreetly.

Sadie placed a hand on Mackenzie's shoulder. Pity let out a shrill cry then took flight, perching on a shelf across the room. "Are you okay?" she tilted her head, eyeing Mackenzie's hands beneath the table.

"Oh, it's fine. I just chewed a hangnail."

Sadie's light brows knitted together. "I used to do that. Sometimes I still do when I'm worried or upset. Is everything okay?"

Suicide squeezed tighter around her waist. *Don't tell her!*

"Everything's the same." Mackenzie shrugged. "But I'm fine."

"How's your mom?"

"The same." Mackenzie knew Sadie was trying to help. But she didn't want to discuss her mom—especially here with everyone around.

"That must be hard." The condoling look in Sadie's eyes made her feel defensive.

"Look, I don't want to talk about it!" Her voice came out louder than she expected. *Oh, crap!*

Everyone stopped their conversations and stared. Mackenzie slid her chair out, knocking into Krystal's. She stood and hurried outside where she laid her head against the building. The cold air blew her hair back bringing some relief. What in the world was wrong with her? Poor Sadie was only being a good friend. Behind her the door opened and footsteps approached. She didn't bother to turn around.

"Hey." It was Krystal.

Mackenzie stayed still and didn't answer, afraid of what might come out. Of course, Krystal came around and stood in front of Mackenzie. "Munchkin was being too pushy?"

Mackenzie nodded, avoiding eye contact.

"Yeah, but she means well."

"I'm not good." Mackenzie began to shiver.

"Oh, no. Is it your mom?"

"Kinda."

"What does that mean?"

A swarm of demons swooped overhead. *Don't tell! Don't tell!* They chanted. But little did they know, the mighty warrior angel, Silas, watched their feeble attack from the rooftop. He had been summoned by Sadie's prayers. Oh, how he wanted to draw his sword. But he had his orders and trusted the Almighty's timing in all things. Silas lowered his head obediently and began to pray, the timber of his deep voice filling the atmosphere with warmth.

Mackenzie squeezed her eyes shut trying to turn off the unwanted thoughts when a silent voice whispered from deep within her mind, "I love you. I'm here."

Oh, God. Please help me.

"Mackenzie, what's going on?"

"I ... I don't know how to explain it. And I really

don't want to."

"Well, I'm not leaving until you do." Krystal was staring at her and moved in close. Did she think she could bully her into talking?

"Hey," Krystal said, gently touching Mackenzie's arm. "I'm your friend. You've been here for me and I'm here for you too. That's how this works. You know, friends even when we're old and gray."

"I'm just sad all the time. I mean, I try to stay strong for my family. Harper is cutting, and this is so hard on my dad. It's like he's aged ten years." She paused, her lips trembling. How much should she say? Would Krystal still be her friend?

Swallowing down her fears, Mackenzie continued. "Some days, I want to just die. I mean it. Like I think I'd be better off dead than ending up like …"

Her voice was a strained whisper. "I think I'm going crazy like my mom."

CHAPTER 27

TAMMI situated herself on a stool near the front of the Coffee Cabin. Luckily, the co-owner Eric was elated to have her perform. "Whenever it works for you is great for us," he'd said. "I've heard you play at the Grind. Love your music. And it will be good for business. How much do you charge?"

Taken aback by the question, Tammi threw out the first dollar amount that came to mind, knowing she probably could have asked for more. But she didn't want to seem greedy, and there was the fact that she was an inexperienced high schooler. Plus, it was more than she'd ever made before—which was zero.

The only trouble was, being a new place, the Coffee Cabin didn't have a sound system or mics yet. But she actually didn't mind playing off mic in this cozy little place. It seemed right. An unplugged vibe partnered well with the roaring fire and rustic wood décor. And it put her more at ease. Tammi was a bit nervous now that she was getting paid. But the bigger concern was Dawn Rising. She hoped the band was too busy with their other better-paying gigs and wouldn't be interested in playing this tiny shop. She wouldn't put it past Dawn to play here just because Tammi was, although Tammi heard they'd be going on the road soon. They hadn't performed at the Grind lately, because they were getting ready for their big road trip spring break tour around the corner.

She felt a twinge of jealousy as she thought of Dawn Rising performing at some pretty major venues, including the House of Blues. There was no denying their talent and increasing fan base. The fact was they'd outgrown the small town of Arcana. When Tammi first heard them play, she'd dreamed of performing with them. Not only did she want to meet Dawn, she'd wanted to be *like* her … that was until she got to know her. It was too bad because Tammi and Dawn sounded great together. There had been a strong connection between them that somehow got twisted. Oh, well. What did it matter now? That dream was dead along with any type of friendship with Dawn.

Tammi had a feeling God had other plans for her music anyway. So, why was she bothered by their success? At least Tammi and her friends would be rid of Dawn and Gary. That was a good thing, right? Of course, it was. And yet Tammi felt empty and sad about not seeing the band around. She pictured Dawn's malevolent hazel glare and shivers poured down her spine, reminding her it *was* a good thing the band was leaving.

Closing her eyes, Tammi strummed a few bars and released the negativity of all things Dawn Rising. Without giving it a thought, the new song she'd just written seemed to roll off her tongue. As the words flowed out of her mouth, so did the jealousy, anger, and pain. Music had always been an escape, but this was something altogether different. This was soothing and healing, like chicken noodle soup when you're sick or a hug when you're lonesome—but better. Tammi sensed that this must be how God intended to use her music. For the first time in her life, she felt a sense of real purpose—and it was amazing!

Lauren closed the door to her office as Tammi took a seat. Although Tammi had grown to love Lauren like a big sister, she usually dreaded these counseling appointments—but not today. Today, Tammi could hardly wait to tell her about what happened when performing at the Coffee Cabin earlier.

Before Lauren had a chance to plant herself in the chair on the other side of the desk, Tammi pulled out her phone. "Listen," she said and played the recording of her new song.

Tammi slid the lyrics across the desk and watched Lauren's tawny eyes scroll from side to side as she read and listened.

When the recording ended, Lauren steepled her hands in front of her lips. "That was amazing!"

"God gave that song to me, Lauren. It's called Beautiful Scars. He's healing me, little by little. Just like you said." She couldn't stop smiling even if she wanted to. "And I sang it today at the Coffee Cabin. I think this is how God wants to use my music!"

Lauren rose and came around the desk. Tammi stood and met her in a big blubbery hug. After a few seconds, Lauren released her arms from around Tammi and looked her square in the eyes. "I'm so proud of you."

"Why?"

"Well, of course, God is the one to praise here. But Tammi, you had to be willing. You had to go to the hard places within yourself and invite God in to begin the healing. And you had to ask for help from me, your grandparents, and friends. You also had to trust God and surrender to him. It's hard, painstaking work. And it's not over. But now you are seeing that it's worth it." A tear rolled down her cheek. *"That's* why I'm proud of you."

Tammi's heart was so light, she could soar like she had wings. A huge weight she'd never realized she'd been trudging around was lifted. "Yeah, it *is* worth it." She chewed the side of her lip. "But I know there's more work to do. I mean, I don't want my dad dead anymore. But ..." She shrugged. "There's still ugliness in my heart. I want it gone, and I know I need God's help to get rid of it."

After leaving the appointment with Lauren, Tammi checked her phone, finding a text from Grandma: **Please pick up Grandpa's RX and some coffee creamer. Thx** ☺

Tammi stared at the words and sighed. Grandma didn't realize what she was asking. With her luck, Dawn would be working at the pharmacy.

God, I need you. She prayed and sang until she arrived at the drugstore entryway. As Tammi scanned the parking lot looking for Dawn's car, relief set in. She wasn't working today. Whew!

The electric doors whooshed open as Tammi strolled

in. An aisle filled with Valentine's Day displays caught her eye. Wow, it was almost February already. She paused, perusing a sea of red, pink, and white stuffed animals, trinkets, and candy. This wouldn't normally be her thing, but she was in the mood to shop. Maybe she could get a few little gifts for her friends and grandparents. She had her own money now. Tammi's lips turned up at the thought of how Sadie would appreciate even the smallest of gestures. She fingered a tiny pink bear holding a satin red heart that read "Best Friends" in white cursive stitching.

"Aww, how sweet." Dawn's unmistakable voice sent prickly goosebumps rising. "Best friends." Her voice dripped with sarcasm.

"I thought you were going on tour." Tammi turned to face her fear.

"We leave next week." Dawn's full ruby lips pouted. "Oooh. You're gonna miss me, huh, pet?" She reached up and brushed the back of her hand along Tammi's cheek. Her pupils were dark and reminded Tammi of a cat. "Not to worry. I'll always have feelings for *you*." she threatened through gritted teeth, giving Tammi's cheek a little slap with the back of her knuckles.

Tammi swatted at Dawn's hand just as she removed it, glaring down at her for a moment to let her know she wasn't afraid. Truth is, she actually was. Taking a step back, Tammi set the bear on the shelf and slowly walked away. She kept her pace, sure footsteps would follow, but there was no sense Dawn was behind her. Good. Maybe the threatening stare worked. Tammi grabbed some creamer from the refrigerated section and headed back to the pharmacy.

A long line snaked from the pharmacy area. Tammi fell in line with the string of people, hoping to avoid Dawn. Was she coming into work? Maybe she'd given notice because of the tour. Tammi tilted her head ever so slightly around the person in front of her to see if Dawn was behind the counter. There were two registers with pharmacy techs but no Dawn.

Someone closed in from behind her. There was a little nudge and then something sharp poked between her shoulder blades. "Looking for someone?" Dawn's voice was low, almost guttural.

Tammi spun around. "No. And what did you jam in my back?"

Dawn drew in close enough for Tammi to smell her minty breath. "Oh, just a knife." She said, dropping something on the floor at Tammi's feet as she pivoted on her high heel leather boots and walked away.

Dawn's long black coat fluttered like bat wings as she sauntered down the aisle and rounded the corner. Tammi turned back toward the pharmacy when her toe tapped something soft.

The little pink bear for Sadie looked up at her with outstretched arms, white threads dangling from them.

The "Best Friends" heart was gone.

CHAPTER 28

SADIE clicked her pink nails on the desk, eyeing the clock. Only one more period to go. Well, at least it was Spanish with Mr. Garcia. He was a fun teacher, and Tammi and Bryce were in the class. The bell finally shrilled as Sadie simultaneously snatched her backpack and jetted out the door.

Students lolled down the hall like a lazy river. Sadie weaved in between the slow movers to a pocket of open space. It was amazing to be rid of those dreaded crutches! As she turned the corner, there was another clog. She rubbed shoulders with someone who smelled like fabric softener and way too much Axe body spray when she spotted Bryce just ahead.

"Bry!" She jumped and waved, turning sideways to make it past two football players.

"Como estas, mi amiga paquita?" Bryce said.

"Muy bien! It's Friday *and* I have dance class today!" Sadie covered her mouth then quickly removed her hand. "Uh, I mean *bailar*." She smirked. "That's how you say dance in Español, right?"

"Sí, muy bien!" Mr. Garcia said as the two entered the classroom.

Tammi flopped her backpack down beside the desk next to Sadie, giving a nod. "Well, we've almost made it through the week. Can you believe it's already February?" She sat and rubbed the back of her neck.

Bryce leaned forward from the other side of Sadie. "Yeah, I know. It's been rough. I'm looking forward to the weekend." A thin smile accentuated his boyish dimples, reminding Sadie her good friend was about to be a father despite his young age.

Students continued to file in, sluggishly taking their seats. Everyone seemed ready for the weekend. Mr. Garcia passed out a pop quiz as students groaned. Sadie was glad she'd reviewed verb tenses last night. From the look on Bryce's face, he had not.

Sadie slipped into a dressing area of the dance studio. She sighed, looking around at the familiar Victorian style décor. Oh, how she'd missed this place. She plopped on a floral chaise lounge and rummaged through her dance bag. She removed everything which included her new pointe ballet prosthesis. Her heart fluttered with excitement. She quickly removed her school clothes and got dressed for dance.

Walking on her toes to the full-length oblong cherrywood mirror, Sadie admired what she saw: Black leotard, pink tights, *and* her pointe ballet prosthetic! She pulled her long tresses into a tight bun and waltzed out of the door. Mom was waiting on a bench outside of one of the classrooms of the dance studio.

"Oooh, look at you!" Mom's face beamed with pride. "You're going to dance 'En Pointe' again." She gave Sadie a quick side hug. "Come on, let's get you to practice."

Sadie peeked her head into the doorway of a classroom that was empty except for one girl. A long-limbed blond with a dark leotard stretched one leg on the wooden barre in front of the floor-to-ceiling mirror wall.

"Heather!" Sadie said. It was so great to be back with her favorite instructor.

The blonde spun around. "Wow, you look great," Heather said. "Are you ready to work?" She didn't wait for a response. "Girl, you better be. I'm gonna make you sweat!"

"Bring it on, sergeant." Sadie saluted.

Mom gave Sadie a peck on the cheek. "Next time, I'll practice with you two. So be ready." She shook her finger at Heather and Sadie. "But sorry, we already had the plans set with your brothers."

"No problem, Mom. I understand."

"I'll be back later," Mom said. "Did you say you'd made plans with your friends for tonight? I know it's Friday. I was thinking of ordering pizza."

Heather raised her brows. "Uh-hem. Ballerinas do *not* eat pizza."

"Oh, Sadie and I will have the one with cauliflower crust, kale, and tofu!" Mom winked as she took a few backward steps.

Sadie giggled. "Uh, I'm not sure about my friends. Tammi is supposed to text me later."

"Okay, we'll talk about it when I pick you up at 6:30." She pulled her phone from her pocket. "Oh, shoot! Gotta hurry. Bye." She rushed out, answering the call.

Heather informed Sadie they would need to work

their way into using her new pointe prosthetic and that they could practice with both. But Sadie only wanted to work with her pointe prosthetic to get used to it.

The instructor had Sadie begin with barre exercises and stretches. Then she moved into adagio and petite allegro. For the next hour, Sadie did center work advancing to chaîné and piqué turns. Her new prosthetic was wonderful, but it did not allow her foot to return to a flat position or demi pointe. She found herself a little frustrated at her limitations. But Tegan had assured Sadie that new technology was coming. She hoped it would be soon.

Heather wiped her forehead with a towel. "Well, that's enough for today."

Sadie beamed. "I feel like *me* again."

"I bet," Heather said. "Well, get some rest and go have fun. I'll see you Monday." Heather padded to the door then turned. "No pizza or junk food."

"But you said have fun!"

"Sadie, are you still interested in dancing professionally?" Heather's brows raised. "I mean, it's fine if you just want to get back into dance without that pressure."

"What? Of course, I'm still interested. You know my dream has been to get into Juilliard."

Heather stepped toward Sadie, placing the blue towel around her shoulders. "Let's talk for a minute before your mom comes, okay?"

Sadie's stomach did a summersault. "Sure. Be honest with me, Heather. I can take it."

"We talked about this before, but I'm not sure you

understand. This is going to be grueling work, Sadie. Live, breathe, and eat dance—*not* pizza and junk food. There are just things you must sacrifice. And we need to work on your modern dance for auditions. Then there's the issue of your height. At five foot two, you are considered short. However, your long neck and streamlined legs and arms help compensate." Heather dabbed the towel beneath her eyes and continued. "There are other great dance schools to consider. I graduated from Champman University. I'm not sure about Juilliard, Sadie."

"Yes, I remember the conversation. I told you I'm used to tough *and* sacrifice. I grew up in more foster homes than I want to remember."

Heather pulled in her lower lip. "Honey, I know you did. And I cannot imagine. But this is a different kind of hard. You told me to be honest. That's what I'm doing because I respect and care about you. I just don't want you to underestimate this challenge."

Heat rose from Sadie's belly to her neck and into her face. "And you shouldn't underestimate *God*. Listen, I know that God saved me from all the abuse, made sure that not only did I get adopted into a loving Christian family, but he gave me a mom who was a professional ballerina. And to top it off, he saved me from dying so that I can prove to the world that he is awesome." Sadie took a deep breath. "So, you see, Heather, I'm up for a challenge."

Applause broke out from the back of the room and bounced off the walls of the studio. Sadie turned to see her mother, father, and brothers.

"Well said and amen!" Dad said.

Mom approached. "We believe in you, sweetheart." She cupped Sadie's face with both hands. "And I will help you."

"And I'll eat your pizza!" Jeff said.

Everyone, including Heather, burst into laughter.

Silas stood at the back of the room, a wide grin on his bronzed face. "And I, too, will help, little one. God indeed has a purpose for you and each of his children. Glory be to God Almighty!"

CHAPTER 29

BRYCE laid on the bed beside Krystal, hoping she didn't hear his thudding heart. Her hip touched against his own when she scooted closer. They both knew it was probably not the best idea to be alone in her house together. They had an hour to kill before meeting their parents at Grant and Lauren's to discuss adoption. But as usual, their strong desire for one another won out and here they were in her room … on her bed. Bryce's insides flickered like a jar of fireflies at Krystal's touch. He rubbed his thumb across the top of her soft hand, drawing it to his lips, then turned on his side to face her. She drew closer and lightly kissed his lips, sending tingles up and down his spine. Oh, how he wished they were married now. He wanted her so badly that he physically hurt. Looking into Krystal's eyes after they kissed, he detected confliction and apprehension.

But instead of saying they should leave, she drew closer and laid her head on his shoulder. "I know it's the right thing to do, Bry." Her voice vibrated against his chest. "This is how I know it's what God wants." She pulled back and looked into his eyes. "After the sonogram, something changed. I'm not sure how to explain it. I—I felt love."

Bryce's heart pounded faster. "What?" The feelings of arousal were suddenly squelched. Did she want to keep the baby now after he was finally thinking adoption was probably for the best?

"Let me finish. I was confused by those new feelings for a few weeks. That's why I didn't bring up the subject of adoption anymore to you or *anyone*. I kept thinking 'how will I give up this baby?'" She paused and Bryce reached for her face. He rubbed along her jawline, waiting for her to speak again. What was happening?

Krystal propped up on her elbow and faced him with her head on her hand, then continued, "I stopped asking God about it. I was afraid that maybe I never really heard him. Maybe he wasn't even real. I got out my Bible and just started reading. I found this story about two women. Both lived in the same house and were pregnant and had babies. During the night, one of the babies died. The woman with the dead baby placed it next to the other woman who was asleep and took the live baby like it was hers." Bryce knew the story. He nodded for her to continue.

"The next morning, the lady who now had the dead baby realized it wasn't her son. Pretty crazy, huh?" Krystal said. "Anyway, the two women argued at home and finally went before the king. As they argued, the king said since they both claimed the baby was theirs that he would cut the child in half so both could have a part. But then the real mother spoke up in a panic and said, 'Please don't kill my son. I love him very much, but give him to her so he may live.'"

Bryce nodded, struggling to find words. But he *knew*. He'd known for weeks. Krystal was saying she believed God wanted Grant and Lauren to raise their child. But

186

did *he* believe this is what God wanted? Sure, it would be easier to go on with life as high school students. Would it really be easier in the long run? He wasn't sure. But adoption was now in motion.

KRYSTAL slipped off her pajamas and stood on the bathroom scale, squinting at the numbers. As suspected, she'd gained two pounds. How could she have gained two pounds in one week? The doctor said it was healthy for her to gain 25-30 pounds by the end of the pregnancy. Krystal figured she'd make sure not to gain more than 20 pounds. It was only the end of February and she had until June. At this rate, she'd be a whale! And it didn't help that Bryce had given her a huge box of chocolates for Valentine's Day. She bit the sides of her mouth remembering how she'd binged and purged late last night after eating the rest of the chocolate. It was wrong, but she couldn't help herself. And then what had she done this morning? Oh, only gorged herself on waffles, that's all! Even though Mom made a healthier almond flour recipe, it didn't mean it was okay to eat four of them plus turkey bacon and eggs!

Stepping off the scale, Krystal pulled her jeans over her legs but struggled to button them. She turned sideways and gazed at her profile in the mirror with her hands fanned across her belly.

Well, no wonder! She could just leave the pants unbuttoned and wear a bulky sweater ... *for now*. But it wouldn't be long before nothing fit.

Bulimia sat on the tiled countertop, its gangly legs swaying back and forth. *It will be two more pounds by the end of the week if you don't get rid of those waffles!* A sinister grin revealed pointed yellow teeth.

Krystal squeezed her eyes shut. I can't keep doing this!

You can't keep gaining weight! Bulimia said. *No one will know. Hurry!*

Krystal tucked her long hair down inside the back of her sweater and kneeled over the toilet. Bulimia jumped from the counter to her back. The thing tilted its deformed triangular head, peering over Krystal's shoulders with bulbous orange eyes. *Hurry up, you cow!*

But Krystal knew it wasn't right to jeopardize the baby's health the way she'd done the night before. "No!" she whispered. "What am I doing? Please help me stop doing this, God. This baby belongs to you and Grant and Lauren."

Krystal jolted up, which sent Bulimia sailing from her shoulder, skinny limbs thrashing to stay affixed. It landed on the tile then quickly skittered behind the toilet expecting God's angel to emerge. But nothing happened. The girl prayed in faith and was strengthened without the angel's presence? This wasn't good. The demon drew its legs up tightly. Duke Astaroth would not be happy about the development. It shuddered at the thought of the Duke's wrath. What to do?

Bulimia scanned the room. With no angel in sight, it edged out again, scampering up Krystal's leg and back to her shoulder. *You could just do it this one last time,* it said, massaging her scalp with its claws.

Krystal stepped back from the toilet, fighting the urge

to make herself throw up. This child did not belong to her. Krystal pictured Grant and Lauren's elated faces when their families met to tell them last weekend.

Now the goal was to make it through the next four months. But the binging and purging had to stop. Lauren had begun reading pregnancy books and asking Krystal about her diet, prenatal vitamins, and if it was safe for her to run track. She also asked Krystal if she'd been making herself throw up. Krystal lied, but she sensed Lauren didn't believe her. And Lauren would continue to press her about it. She couldn't bear to lie to her again. Maybe she should talk to Pastor Dave? No, she could handle this herself.

She was going to stop after this *one last time…*

CHAPTER 30

MACKENZIE tugged her green cardigan over her hips—if you could call them hips. She was a string bean just like her mother, and the green only seemed to emphasize that fact. Her sister, Harper, on the other hand, had a defined waist and hips. Krystal told Mackenzie not to complain about being thin, but she often wished she had some feminine curves. If it weren't for her long hair and some mascara, she'd look like a skinny junior high school boy!

Mackenzie eyed her sister through their shared bathroom mirror as they got ready for youth group. Grant and Lauren were having a St. Patrick's Day-themed Bible study since it landed on the actual day. Lauren's text said to wear green. Seemed kinda silly, but the couple always made things fun—and she could use some fun. At least that's what Krystal said when Mackenzie told her she didn't feel like going. "I bet Harper wants to go," Krystal added. And she was right—Harper seemed excited about it. So, Mackenzie agreed, and Krystal would be over soon to pick them up.

Krystal typically went with Bryce, so this was her way of making sure Mackenzie was truly going since she hadn't shown up at the Coffee Cabin to meet her friends two days ago. The thing was, it was getting more difficult to hide her depression. After her "breakdown" at the coffee shop last month, Krystal had been bugging her to talk to Lauren. Well, that wasn't going to happen. Besides, Lauren had her hands full with Harper and the cutting, Krystal's bulimia and pregnancy, and Tammi and Sadie with the abuse from their pasts. Mackenzie's issue paled in comparison, right?

Then why do I feel so crappy? Maybe I DO need help.

Mackenzie watched Harper affix a green bow to the messy bun at the top of her head.

Harper pointed to her hair. "Yes or no?"

She was really into this St. Patrick's Day Bible study party. And she looked adorable in her green shirt with little white polka dots. It was good to see her happy. Meeting with Lauren was probably helping … maybe it *could* help her too.

No. I can work through this on my own.

Maybe Mackenzie would feel better if she changed her outfit. "I think I'm going to put on a different pair of jeans," she said, turning to leave before remembering to answer her sister. "Oh." She faced Harper. "You look super cute. Yes, on the whole ensemble." She waved her arm from Harper's head to her feet in a sweeping motion and walked out.

Once in her room, Mackenzie slid into her favorite jeans, hoping to feel a little more enthusiastic about going. But she didn't.

Nothing seemed to help.

"Just pull it together," she whispered. "People will think you're a freak." She turned to find Krystal standing in her doorway.

Mackenzie gasped. "Hey! I didn't hear you ring the

bell."

"Guess not." Krystal's chin lowered. "You okay?"

"Yeah. Let's go."

"Gail, I heard what you said about people thinking you're a freak."

Mackenzie knew Krystal was trying to help, but she didn't want to risk blowing up on her friend, or worse—crying. Mackenzie threw her head back and sighed. She eyed the stupid clouds her mom had painted on her ceiling … back when she was acting somewhat normal. What happened? Did it start with feeling sad the way Mackenzie did? Mackenzie thought about how many times throughout the years she'd found her mother asleep with the blinds drawn, shutting out the world.

"Mackenzie, talk to me. I'm worried about you." She stepped forward, her belly protruding beneath her mint green sweatshirt, the rest of her body following.

Her friend didn't need any more stress than she was already dealing with. There was no way Mackenzie would concern Krystal with her ridiculous gloominess. "Oh my gosh." Mackenzie rolled her eyes. "There's no reason to worry. You know how I get nervous in large groups. I always have to give myself a pep talk."

Krystal raised a brow. "Uh, calling yourself a freak is *not* a pep talk." She walked past Mackenzie and sat on the bed. "If you won't see Lauren, then you better talk to me. I know something's wrong."

Mackenzie gritted her teeth. She'd rather not! "I don't want to talk. I told you I'd go to this stupid thing, now let's go." She walked out.

Krystal, Mackenzie, and Harper entered Grant and Lauren's tiny cottage-style home. As usual, a hint of something delicious hung in the air. The girls made their way to the enclosed patio where groups of teenagers stood around talking and eating.

"I'm getting some of those snacks," Krystal said, and turned back toward the kitchen. "You guys coming?"

Harper followed but Mackenzie wasn't hungry, so she looked for available seats to save. Sadie was sitting next to Bryce, waving her arm from side to side wildly like a little kid. Mackenzie edged past the other students and plopped in the seat next to Sadie. She tossed her jacket over the back of the chair next to her, saving it for Harper. Bryce's leather jacket hung on the back of the chair beside him for Krystal.

"Is Tammi coming?" Mackenzie asked.

Sadie and Bryce both grinned and nodded.

Did Bryce bring Sadie? Krystal probably told their friends how she was worried about dumb, miserable Mackenzie!

Out of nowhere, Brad from the baseball team plopped down in the chair next the one Mackenzie was saving, making her heart start racing like she'd run the 800-meter dash, He was wearing a fitted, plain white T-shirt and looking even more amazing than usual.

Bryce leaned around the girls to speak to Brad. "Dude, that seat is saved. Sorry." He must have been thinking of Tammi.

Brad scooted over one chair just as Tammi arrived. "Thanks," she said and sat next to him, leaving the one next to 'Kenzie open for Harper. "No problem, Tammi." Brad grinned from ear to ear and leaned in close. "I've been wanting to talk to you about your music," he said.

Tammi glanced at Mackenzie and rolled her eyes before turning in Brad's direction. Mackenzie felt conflicted. She'd seen plenty of guys crash and burn when attempting to be friendly with Tammi. Most of them deserved it too. But Brad was a nice guy. And cute. She'd been observing him since her first day at Arcana High, though he didn't seem to realize she existed. But, of course, he was interested in supermodel Tammi with her steely gray eyes. Mackenzie sighed internally, wishing she had just an ounce of Tammi's natural glamour. Maybe then Brad would notice her.

Krystal and Harper made their way to the table with plates of cookies and chips. Harper raised an eyebrow when she noticed Brad talking with Tammi. Mackenzie had made the mistake of telling Krystal and Harper about her crush on him before Harper started coming to youth group. Since then, Harper was playing cupid—or at least trying to get Mackenzie to talk to Brad.

Mackenzie stood. "I think I *will* get a snack." Anything to avoid Harper's embarrassing matchmaking.

Harper scowled at her, then turned toward Tammi and Brad. "Anybody want anything? 'Kenzie is going to grab some more snacks."

Little weasel! She felt herself blushing before anyone even responded.

Brad looked up at Mackenzie with gorgeous cornflower-blue eyes. "Could you bring me a Coke, 'Kenzie?"

He remembers my name? Duh. Harper just said it. Calm down. He wouldn't be interested in a weird, string bean brainiac. "Sure," Mackenzie said and quickly left the room.

On her way to the kitchen, Mackenzie heard Lauren calling her from the den. Mackenzie veered around a few students and made her way to the other room.

"Hey, how are you?" Lauren asked.

Mackenzie shrugged. "Okay, I guess."

Lauren tilted her head, chestnut-colored eyes probing. "I won't beat around the bush," she said. "I know things have been hard. I have time in my schedule tomorrow afternoon. How about you come over, and we can have coffee and talk?"

A burning sensation made its way into Mackenzie's face. Lauren's widening eyes indicated she could see the red splotches Mackenzie felt emerging on her chest and face. *Why am I so darn awkward?* "Uh, no thanks." Wait. Did she just say that?

Lauren placed a hand on Mackenzie's shoulder. "Oh, I'm sorry to make you uncomfortable."

The burning feeling bubbled inside like she was going to explode. "Look, I *don't* need counseling!" The words flew out loud and vicious before she had time to think.

Embarrassed, Mackenzie muttered "excuse me" and darted down the hall to the restroom and shut the door.

If I do need counseling, I really am just like Mom!

CHAPTER 31

TAMMI twisted a strand of wavy hair between her fingers while she listened to Brad drone on and on about music. Usually, she enjoyed music talk. This wasn't just about music—she could tell. Where were Lauren and Grant? Shouldn't study start by now? Sure, Brad was a nice guy and all, but she wasn't interested. Tammi also suspected that 'Kenzie might have a crush on Brad. No way would she jeopardize her friendship over a stupid guy. And besides, no matter how nice they seemed, all guys really wanted was to get into her pants. Tammi had learned that the hard way before she moved in with her grandparents. This Brad, with his charming blue eyes, would not be her next mistake. Plus, high school guys were immature. She pictured the rugged, yet gentle Officer Jason Hughes. He was tall and dark, with bulging biceps. A *real* man.

Stop it! She chastised herself. *He would never consider a girl in high school. He was a godly man who even took the time to pray with you rather than give you a ticket.*

"Sooo, I was wondering—" Brad leaned closer, yanking Tammi from the self-dialogue in her head. "Do you think we could, like, get coffee or something tomorrow?"

"What? No."

Brad's bottom lip fell open. He blinked rapidly a few

times before he attempted to speak. Tammi interrupted his stutter. "Uh, that didn't come out right." She toyed with her eyebrow piercing. "I—I'm not—"

Just then, Grant walked in with his guitar. "Okay, let's get started with some music."

Tammi chewed the inside of her mouth. She needed to say something to this poor guy who looked pasty and ready to throw up. She leaned in and whispered, "Sorry. I'm just not dating right now."

The sparkle was gone from Brad's blue eyes. "Okay." He shrugged and faced forward.

Tammi's stomach tightened. She backed her chair out slowly, rose and headed out of the room. When Tammi reached the den area, she saw the back of Lauren's head, where she sat alone on the sofa. Why wasn't she with Grant singing? Tammi took a few steps before Lauren turned, misty eyes meeting Tammi's.

Uh-oh. "Hey, everything okay?" Tammi wasn't sure if she should be there, but it was too late now.

Lauren's lips curved up slightly, but she didn't attempt to hide her sadness. "I just needed a minute to pray before Grant sends the girl's group out. We are dividing the study into boy and girl groups. Oh, and then we have a guest speaker. Why are you out here?"

Tammi felt bad for intruding and didn't want to tell her something as silly as she'd left because of Brad. A valid excuse popped into her head. "Uh, where's Mackenzie?"

"She's in the restroom." Lauren stood. "I'm going to grab a drink. Could you wait out here for Mackenzie?"

No problem with that! I'd much rather sit here for a while.

"Sure." Tammi sat on the sofa where Lauren had

been and drew her legs up. It occurred to her there must be a reason Lauren asked her to wait for 'Kenzie. Come to think of it, Mackenzie had never showed up at the Coffee Cabin the other day. A sour taste filled her mouth. Something was wrong, and Brad talking to Tammi probably made it worse—that is if Tammi's suspicion about 'Kenzie's feelings for Brad was right.

Mackenzie came around the corner. Her dark brows drew together in confusion at the sight of Tammi. "Hey," 'Kenzie said softly. "What are you doing here?"

"Getting away from Brad," Tammi said.

'Kenzie's eyes darted to the floor. "Oh."

"You were supposed to bring him a Coke."

"Psh, I don't think he'll miss it. He seemed enraptured with *you*."

Enraptured? Where does she come up with these words? "You like him, don't you? Is that why you left? Because I'm not interested in him like that." Tammi said. "Uh, but I think he'd be a great guy for you, though."

Mackenzie squeezed her eyes closed, head still down. Tammi was about to say something when Mackenzie opened them and glared up at her. "I kinda do like him, but he wouldn't be interested in a freaky geeky girl like me." She started to walk away, then turned her head over her shoulder. "Don't worry. I'm not mad at you or anything. You can't help that you're a guy magnet."

"Okay, but is there something else wrong?"

With a shrug, Mackenzie avoided answering. "Are you coming back in?"

"Yeah, after I use the restroom. Don't forget to bring Brad his Coke."

Mackenzie didn't respond to Tammi's attempt at a joke. With a blank expression, she turned and headed toward the patio without stopping by the kitchen first. Tammi frowned. Something seemed to be bothering her more than Brad. Mackenzie probably thought Tammi didn't even like guys after everything that happened with Dawn and, of course, because of her dad. And Tammi hadn't given Mackenzie a reason to think otherwise. Tammi's heart twisted, imagining how she used to be so "enraptured" with the alluring hazel-eyed beauty. She had never felt that way before. It was confusing. The entire mixed-up relationship with Dawn left her angry, sad, and a little afraid—especially after their last meeting at the drugstore before Dawn Rising had left for their tour. Even though she knew it was for the best, Tammi found herself thinking about Dawn and the band often.

Suddenly, Tammi's phone chimed—a text message from Dawn. A shiver trickled down her spine. What were the odds? The girl had evil powers or something. Tammi recalled Dawn's story about how she and her aunt had cursed her dad before he died. Her hand trembled as she tapped the screen. It was a voice text. Tammi tapped to listen. Dawn's voice was barely a whisper.

"Things aren't going that great here. I'm really scared," Dawn's voice trembled. "Look, I know I've been awful to you, but you might be the only person I can trust." There was a rustling noise and a long pause. "Um, gotta go."

That was strange. Probably another one of Dawn's sleazy tactics. She was a piece of work! The phone chimed again, but Tammi resolved not to look at it.

Yes, it was definitely for the best.

She rose from the sofa when the front door opened and there stood Jason Hughes. Tammi stared, frozen in place and mouth agape.

"Hi," he said, a smile in his deep voice. "The rest of the group on the patio?"

Was *he* the guest speaker Lauren was talking about? Jason looked amazing in jeans and a T-shirt, but in her mind, she always imagined him in his uniform that fit snugly over his muscular physique. Tammi's heart thudded hard and fast. She swallowed and tried to formulate words, but nothing came out. Instead she nodded and pointed to the patio like a mute idiot.

"What are you doing out here?" he asked.

Somehow Tammi found her voice. "Um, what are *you* doing here?"

"My sis—I mean Lauren," he corrected. "asked me to come and share my testimony. I'll be talking to the guys first, I guess. You aren't leaving, are you? I will be sharing more when both groups are together."

"No, I'm staying." He wanted her to stay! Testimony?

He must have sensed her question. "I'm going to share how God helped me get out of gangs and get sober."

Tammi was taken aback. "What?" Weren't they raised in a perfect Christian home? "Wait, how old are you?" As soon as the words came out, she wished she could take them back.

Jason laughed. "I'm a wise old twenty-two. Come on," he said. "Walk in with me." He tugged her sleeve, sending tremors down her arm.

CHAPTER 32

SADIE waited for Mr. Allen to look away, then popped a few forbidden gummy bears into her mouth as she finished her test. She folded her hands on the desk and waited. The class was quiet except for the occasional rustle of a turning page. Sadie decided not to chew the candy, but to suck on them so they would last. Her dance instructor, Heather, would throw a fit if she knew. Despite Sadie's little cheats in her diet, she was making strides with the new prosthetics. Heather and Mom worked her hard at Friday's practice. Sadie was sore all weekend but couldn't wait to get back to rehearsal today. All of her efforts would pay off *if* she made it to Juilliard. *If* she made it? Before the accident, the word "if" was not in her vocabulary. The bell shrilled, bringing Sadie back to the present.

Students began to file out of class. Sadie hurried past them, hoping to catch Tammi or one of her friends on their way to lunch. English class was furthest from the cafeteria which was a real bummer. Sadie took a shortcut through the arts building. The walls were lined from floor to ceiling with colorful murals painted by students. There was fresco, watercolor, graffiti and many other styles that somehow all worked together to tell a story. Mackenzie's contribution was a depiction of Sadie dancing. Her long hair swirled about her as she leapt through the air, wispy limbs floating gracefully. Mackenzie gave her feathery wings like a fairy. Sadie paused and marveled at her friend's talent—not just the art, but the feeling it invoked. Dancing truly did make Sadie feel like she had wings. At least it used to. She was glad to be back to dancing, but it was not as freeing with the prosthetics. Surely, it would get better. She just needed more practice. Another thing that helped her feel free was finally being open with God about her experiences with Gary. It felt good to be honest in her prayers again. How silly to think she could hide anything from God—he knew everything—and he still loved her. Sadie ran her fingers over the bumpy texture of the mural, grinned, then headed out of the building, picking up her pace again.

Sadie arrived at the open double doors of the cafeteria and stepped inside to the loud chatter and laughter that bounced off the walls and vaulted ceiling. It was pizza day, and a line twisted like the letter S to the back of the room where she stood. She moved a few feet forward and took her place at the end, bobbing her head as she looked for her friends.

"Oh, jeez," Tammi said from behind her.

Sadie spun around. "I know! This will take forever, and I'm starved."

Tammi rummaged through her satchel and pulled out a chocolate chip granola bar. "I'll split it with you." Her full lips turned up.

Sadie watched her friend's long slender fingers tear into the wrapper. Everything about Tammi was sleek and elegant. Her stylish features used to clash with her e-girl rock-star image. But Sadie noticed a gradual transformation since they'd first met last fall. Tammi used to rarely smile and wore mostly black clothes and dark eyeliner. Today, her smile reached her gray eyes and she wore a light blue sweatshirt that made her grayish eyes pop even more. The fact that Tammi looked happy made Sadie bubble with joy because she knew why—God. Of course, Tammi's "happy" was controlled and subdued. But she seemed to be in an extra good mood. Sadie wondered if it had anything to do with what Lauren had talked to the girls about last night at study. Hmmm … or maybe it was Lauren's brother, the policeman, who gave his testimony last night. The two somehow knew each other, which Sadie found *very* interesting.

"So, how do you know Lauren's brother, the cop?"

The glimmer in Tammi's eyes dulled and her pupils grew large. "Uh—" She played with the foil wrapper. "Well, he pulled me over a few months ago."

"What? You never told me you got a ticket!"

Tammi explained how she'd encountered Dawn and how upset she was the day Jason pulled her over. As she continued her story, Sadie noticed the awkward tone in her voice. Tammi's eyes darted this way and that, avoiding Sadie's.

"Oh my goodness. You have a crush on him!"

At that moment, Krystal and Mackenzie got in line. "Who? Who?" Krystal asked.

Tammi glared. "You sound like an owl." She turned to Sadie. "And *you* have a big mouth."

Sadie sucked in her cheeks. It *must* be true if Tammi was getting this bent out of shape. But Lauren's brother was too old for Tammi—just like Gary had been too old for her. A sharp jab stilled her heart for a moment. *Gary*. She missed him. But not exactly. She missed who she had *thought* he was. She missed the idea of someone truly finding her special. Would she ever find real love? What decent guy would want her if they knew her past? She didn't have time for guys if she was going to get into Juilliard. Heather's words echoed in her mind: "Live, breathe, and eat dance."

"You like him! I can tell," Sadie said. "Tammi and *Officer Jason*—" Sadie made air quotes with her fingers—"met when he pulled her over a few months ago."

Krystal smirked and shook her head. "Well, who could blame her? He is one fine specimen of a man. Like, did you guys see how ripped he is?" She giggled, totally ignoring the part about how Tammi got pulled over. Guess that didn't matter.

Mackenzie harrumphed. "Uh, did you guys even listen to his testimony or were you too busy checking him out?"

"Yeah!" Sadie said. "And what about the talk Lauren had with us before we listened to Officer Jason?"

"I listened," Krystal said. "His bad boy past made him even sexier."

Sadie frowned. She wanted to know what everyone thought about the lesson, but all her friends seemed interested in was Lauren's cute brother. Ugh!

Tammi cocked one of her eyebrows. "What the heck? Good thing Bryce didn't hear you. I guess all the pregnancy hormones are raging." she said. "And yeah, obviously he's hot …" She paused and everyone leaned in. "And cool … and nice."

"*And* ... you like him," Krystal said.

"The truth is, I've been thinking about him since the day we met. But I know it's stupid for a lot of reasons. First of all, I'm a seriously messed up person. You guys know that." She turned to Sadie. "And I'm not sure how I feel about Lauren's lesson. Anyway," she said, now glancing between the girls. "Even though he's only twenty-two, that's too old for me. *You* should know about that, Sadie." Tammi's forehead wrinkled. "But when I see him, I get the jitters and break out in a sweat. When he showed up last night, I was so awkward. He came in when I was alone in the living room."

Mackenzie squinted. "Ah, that's why you were there when I came out of the bathroom, and that's why you aren't interested in Brad."

Krystal looked at Mackenzie. "Huh? I thought *you* were interested in Brad?" Mackenzie eyes were wide and unblinking.

A heaviness settled over Sadie as her friends discussed guys. She understood all too well what Tammi was saying about being "messed up" and falling for a guy that was too old. Of course, Gary didn't want her. And no one would *ever* want her. She glanced down at her prosthetic leg.

I'm just too broken—inside and out.

She tugged Tammi's sleeve. "Hold my place in line. I'll be back."

Sadie made her way to the restroom and stood in front of the mirror. The demon called Abuse hovered overhead, watching with amber-colored eyes that appeared too large for its misshapen head. One eye bulged outward and the other upward like a chameleon. Its mouth opened and revealed jagged teeth, ready to attack.

Abuse drew close and distorted its voice to sound like Sadie's foster care mother, Isabel. *You skanky mutt! No one will ever want you!*

Sadie trembled at the horrific memory. But then, like an unexpected cooling breeze on a warm day, Sadie remembered youth group last night. Lauren spoke with the girls about what she called "self-talk." She gave examples of how she used to think bad thoughts about herself, especially when she looked in the mirror.

"Some of the bad thoughts were because of the sexual abuse from my uncle. I called myself dirty, fat, stupid, and a lot of nasty things. It was even harder being biracial. I didn't feel I fit in anywhere," Lauren said. "But then I learned what God says about me." She paused, picked up a stack of papers and began to pass them out. At the top of the handout was a picture of a medieval princess wearing a crown and body armor. The beautiful girl looked strong and held a sword in her hand. The paper was entitled "Who I Am in Christ." Below the warrior princess girl was a list of Scriptures.

"Because God is the King of Kings and I am his daughter, that makes me a princess—a *beautiful* princess. And that means so are each of you!" Lauren said with a glimmer in her eyes. "Over the next week until our next group meeting, I want you to read this list of Scriptures about who you are in Christ. Find a few that stand out to you and write them on an index card and tape them to your mirror at home. Then read them aloud to yourself when you look in the mirror," Lauren had said. "We'll talk more about this over the next several weeks."

When Sadie got home from study last night and removed her prosthetic leg, she looked at herself in the mirror and read one of the Scriptures aloud as Lauren said. But all she could see was a mutt trying to pretend she was a pedigree. As she zeroed in on her stump where her leg used to be, it only emphasized her brokenness. When she turned to hobble away, her eyes flicked to something shiny on the top of the mirror. It was the tiara she'd worn at last summer's performance—when she had both of her legs.

Was God telling her something?

Sadie glared at her reflection in the school restroom mirror as she done at home last night. *Help me, God. I can't see myself as a princess. I feel filthy and broken. And I still feel bad about what I did with Gary.*

Silas arrived and stood near Sadie with a smile on his usually stoic face. For the Holy Spirit of God had enabled the angel to see Sadie as the Lord Almighty saw her—dressed in a dazzling pure white gown with a crown of jewels on her head, long blond hair flowing beneath.

Sadie squeezed her eyes shut for a moment, picturing herself as a princess, when suddenly words in her own handwriting on a notecard flashed in her mind:

"This means that anyone who belongs to Christ has become a new person. The old life is gone; a new life has begun!" 2 Corinthians 5:17.

A new person? Can this really be true? Yes! I'm going to believe it's true.

The door opened and in walked Tammi, Mackenzie, and Krystal.

"Hey, why'd you get out of line?" Sadie asked.

"Duh, we could read you like a book. We know when something's wrong," Tammi said. "Plus, the line for gross cafeteria pizza is too long."

Sadie rushed over and hugged Tammi, then backed up and glanced between her friends, touched by how much they cared even if they looked confused at the moment.

"Well, nothing is wrong anymore because I've made a decision," Sadie said. "I'm going to believe those Scriptures Lauren told us about last night. Ya know, the page with the princess?"

She paused and stared at her friends. They were all sort of scowling at her but nodded in agreement anyway.

The warrior angel began to pray. His words were silver beams of light shooting up and out of the ceiling, while glittery sparks fell back down, gliding over the girls like snowflakes.

Sadie continued, "I was just staring at myself in the mirror thinking how messed up I am. But that's not true. That's who I *was*. The stuff that happened with Gary too—that's who I was. So, I'm going to believe what God says about who I am *now*. Just like I believed God would get me out of those awful foster homes. And he *did* get me out. Just like I prayed for you to sing again, Tammi. And just like I prayed for all of you to become Christians. And you guys *did* become Christians. I believe what the Bible says. I'm not the same person I used to be."

Sadie stopped talking when she noticed Tammi, Krystal, and Mackenzie's faces were streaked with tears. None of the girls realized that Silas was behind Sadie, his wings spread wide and muscular arms raised toward heaven as he sang. His booming voice reverberating into the heavenly realms where a host of angels joined in beautiful harmony. The demonic creatures who also had access to the heavenly realm shrieked in pain, shooting from the sky in sooty trails like comets as they fell to the earth.

"I'm a new person—God's princess! And so are all of you!"

CHAPTER 33

BRYCE rolled down the windows and started the drive up the winding road to his favorite spot to think. The pavement ended and he continued slowly along the bumpy dirt road another twenty yards until he reached the crest that overlooked Arcana. The car rolled to a stop, and he killed the engine. He got out and walked to the front of the car, leaning his backside against the hood. A warm spring breeze pushed back his hair. Something about coming to this place usually helped him sort through things and get some perspective. He needed that now more than ever.

Seeing the latest sonogram image of the baby left Bryce feeling depressed. Although Krystal had given him the option of coming to the ultrasound appointment, Bryce had declined. Grant and Lauren were there to see their baby on the screen, and that was how it should be, right? He knew it was best for them to raise the child, so what was going on with him? Krystal said it made her all the more confident of their adoption decision when Grant and Lauren cried as they watched the little arms and legs moving. When the technician asked if they wanted to know the sex, everyone said yes. It was a boy.

A boy.

Bryce sighed. Was it too late to say he wanted to raise his own son? They'd already signed paperwork and everything. How could he think of doing such a thing to Grant and Lauren? They were probably choosing names already. But the thought of giving up his son made him physically ill. He couldn't even eat dinner last night after Krystal left. Her trembling hug and watery brown eyes told him she might be struggling too. That, or she sensed he was. Plus, she'd called early this morning. Today was a Saturday and unlike her to be up before noon. Bryce had been in bed but awake. He didn't pick up. Instead, he'd texted and said he would call later. Now, here he was all alone and mixed up as ever. Maybe a walk in the woods would help.

Bryce locked the car and started into a slow jog up the dirt path toward the trees. His calf muscles protested at the incline and increasing speed. Soon his jog turned into a sprint. Sweat dripped in his eyes, every muscle in his body pulsated, and his lungs screamed, but he kept going until the path ended at the opening to the forest. Bryce halted and bent forward, heaving staggered breaths.

The April morning had warmed up after the rain from the night before, but it was cool and refreshing under the canopy of trees. Bryce raised his face upward. Light filtered down the leaves in broken patterns, refracting like changing colors coming through a stained-glass window of a cathedral. In many ways, the forest was holy like a church.

Oh, God. I need you. I'm really confused. Please show me what to do. The thought of giving up my son is killing me.

Commander Philo, Silas, and one hundred angelic warriors gathered within a clearing of the forest not far from where Bryce was now on his knees in prayer. The entire company of God's beloved servants halted their meeting to bow and pray with him, imparting peace that would guard the young man's heart and mind through the power of the Lord Jesus.

When Bryce rose to leave, their meeting commenced once again.

"As you can see, the Almighty has called for reinforcements," the commander said. "The enemy clones have doubled in number and been released. Duke Astaroth is coordinating a massive attack—perhaps more than one."

Silas's eyes were steely and his mouth a hard line. He stepped forward. "Sir, there were numerous evil spirits at Angela Stine's room in the mental care hospital— too many to count. But worse, I sensed Duke Astaroth's presence. Although I did not see the beast—I believe it was cloaked."

Philo nodded. "The Duke is indeed powerful. But prayer from God's saints weakens his ability to remain cloaked. We must help them to remember to pray in humility as the young Bryce did today. We must also impress upon them the Scriptures to strengthen their faith. Sadie's belief and influence has infuriated the evil ones," the commander said. "Theo, urge Pastor Dave and his wife, Grant and Lauren, the grandparents, and other obedient saints to fast and pray for the four girls and Bryce." He turned to Silas. "The Lord has ordered Jason and Jonathan to aid with your mission, Silas. You are to watch and pray. God is strengthening their faith in the power of prayer. Do not raise a sword until I give the Almighty's order."

Silas's mouth pulled into a grim line. The angel bowed his head in obedience. "Honor and glory to the Holy One," he said, then raised his face. "I pray his orders come swift and furious, sir."

"Indeed, they will. For it is a fearful thing to fall into the hands of the living God," said Commander Philo as he turned to face the company of angelic beings behind the others. His eyes blazed like white fire. "As for the rest of you, be in prayer constantly, alert and ready for new orders."

The commander's deep voice was more sober than usual. "A storm is brewing."

KRYSTAL listened to the tinkling rain outside her window. Gray clouds had rolled in last night, bringing heavy showers and hail, keeping her awake. Her thoughts mimicked the thunder that rumbled outside. Throwing off the comforter, Krystal padded across the room. She paused when something bright caught her attention from the corner of her eye. A tiny burst of sunlight had pushed through the blinds and illuminated the white index card with a Scripture she'd taped to her mirror. Krystal paused and read the Scripture, remembering what Sadie and Lauren had said about being a princess.

Bulimia slugged from beneath the baseboard, clamored up the mirror, and sat above the index card, swinging its stringy legs. *A fat, pregnant, unmarried teenage princess. What a joke!* it said and laughed like a hyena.

Krystal frowned at her reflection, scrutinizing her crazy hair and pasty skin. Her eyes scanned down to her enormous middle. She turned sideways. Her belly protruded, and so did her butt! Her eyes scanned lower. Her legs and feet looked puffy and swollen.

Fat cow! Elephant legs! Bulimia hissed.

Krystal looked up at the Scripture and read it again, this time out loud. "For we are God's masterpiece. He created us anew in Christ Jesus." She looked herself in the face and deliberately smiled. Seeing her own dimples and twinkling light-brown eyes, she thought, for the first time ever, she looked beautiful. "I know I'm not the same. God really *has* been changing me."

Bulimia was shot backward and slammed into the wall. The thing slid to the floor and shook its knobby head as its victim strode out of the room. Krystal used the restroom then padded downstairs.

She sat on the couch next to her mom. "Can we talk?"

Mom closed her Bible and faced Krystal. "Sure."

Krystal frowned. She knew she was interrupting Mom's Saturday morning prayers but figured now was the best time for a talk. She sat beside her mom on the couch, bringing a satin throw pillow to her chest to squeeze. "I think Bryce is having second thoughts about adoption after I showed him the sonogram picture from yesterday's appointment."

Mom nodded, her eyes wide and glassy. *Was she having*

second thoughts too?

"And how about you, honey?" Mom asked.

Krystal laid her head back against the couch and shut her eyes. Mom's fingers ran gently through her hair. Krystal rolled her head to one side and leaned into her mother, breathing in her familiar warm scent. Mom pulled her into a hug. She remained in her mother's embrace, feeling like a little girl again, safe with mommy. But she wasn't a little girl. She was a mother herself with a child growing in her belly. A little boy. And that fact suddenly confounded her.

Krystal loosened from her mother. "I—I'm confused now." She wanted to say more but was at a loss.

Mom shrugged gently. "To be honest, so am I."

"Oh, great. You *too*?" Krystal said. "We signed paperwork and Grant and Lauren are over the moon excited. You saw them. And they will be the best parents …" She steepled her hands in front of her mouth. "Bryce and I are in high school. We are still kids. This child deserves parents like *them* not us, right?"

"Krystal, there's something I have come to realize. You and Bryce are young, but you are *not* kids. You may be immature in some ways still, but you are growing and learning." Mom took hold of Krystal's hands. "What I am saying is, as much as I'd like to, this is not my decision to make. It's not Mr. and Mrs. Williams's either. We can guide you and pray with you. But you and Bryce must decide what you believe God is directing you to do. And whatever you decide, I will be here to help you. I'm sure his parents will be too. Keep in mind, you are going to need our help, at least the first few years. That is, if you decide to raise this baby."

The air left Krystal's lungs. She freed her hands from Mom's and placed them across her belly where the baby was now moving. "He's kicking!"

Mom put a hand on Krystal's bloated stomach and smiled. "You and Bryce need to talk … and pray."

"What about Grant and Lauren? And what about Bryce's parents? I don't know if Mr. Williams will be happy about this. He seemed relieved when we chose adoption."

"We *all* need to pray," Mom said, cupping Krystal's cheek. "You look tired."

Krystal frowned. "I hardly slept last night. I wanted to call Bryce but didn't want to wake him. I waited until seven, hoping he'd be up. He didn't answer but texted and said he'd call later." She pulled her phone from the pocket of her sweatpants and glanced at it. "He still hasn't called. I'm a little worried."

Just then the doorbell rang. Mom looked out the window to the front porch, smiled, then rose from the sofa. "It's Bryce. I'll let you get it," she said and left the room.

Krystal opened the door. Bryce entered and pulled her into his arms.

Oh, God. What are we going to do? What do YOU want us to do?

CHAPTER 34

MACKENZIE stared across the table at her mother's graying straggly hair. She'd aged so much over the past months. Then again, it was the end of April and Mackenzie hadn't seen her mother since just before Christmas. This wasn't Mackenzie's choice. Mom didn't want to see anyone after Dad's attempted Christmas Day surprise visit with the family. Back in February, she'd agreed to see Dad again. He'd been coming to the hospital every other day since.

Although the guilt ate at her, Mackenzie was relieved not to see her mother. It made her more aware of how much she was like her. She'd stopped asking Dad how Mom was. So had her siblings. The hollow look in Dad's eyes told them more than they wanted to know. But out of the blue, Dad asked Mackenzie to come with him today. He said Mom had requested to see her. That was strange because other than a tense hug when they arrived, Mom hadn't even glanced in Mackenzie's direction. She barely looked at Dad. Why had she asked her to come?

Duke Astaroth descended inside the mental care hospital. A noxious fog obscured the enormity of the creature. Glowing orange eyes bulged from within the cloud, roving back and forth. The visiting room was replete with hundreds of nefarious beings awaiting orders from the Duke. Depression, Fear, and Suicide grimaced in delight. With Astaroth's powerful presence, they were sure they could finally accomplish the mission.

With a thunderous crack, Silas and Theo appeared in the hospital, blazing swords drawn. Depression, Fear and Suicide zipped beneath the table where Mackenzie sat with her family.

Astaroth's voice boomed. "You have no control here, angels of God! This hospital belongs to Lucifer."

"God Almighty reigns over ALL of heaven and earth," Silas said.

The Duke opened its enormous mouth full of jagged teeth. Flames shot forth as the beast spoke, "The Prince of this World is Lucifer! And I, Duke Astaroth, rule this city and this hospital."

"You have no authority other than what has been allowed by the Great I Am," Silas said. "We are God's angels and have been given sovereignty to fight for the ones who belong to him. Depart now or join the others in the abyss!"

Silas thrust his sword into the fiery cloud. A resounding yowl resembling that of a prehistoric creature rattled the building. Duke Astaroth shot upward and then vanished, but its guttural squall echoed from above. "I will be back for the ones that belong to ME!"

Silas and Theo slashed at the remaining demons until the room was clear of their filth … for now. They knew the Duke was after Mackenzie's mother, Angela, and would return again. Unlike her daughter, Angela did not believe in the Lord God, which gave the demons temporary dominion over her. The unholy beings tormented Angela as they had done to Mackenzie's great-grandmother, great-great-grandmother, and for many generations past. The Duke was furious when the lineage of bondage to depression had been broken the day Mackenzie accepted Christ. Now the demonic mission was to convince Mackenzie that the blood of Jesus could not keep her from the same fate as her mentally ill mother. But the prayers of her friends and church family had been interfering with their progress.

Mackenzie watched as Dad tried to engage Mom. He reached over and stole one of her fries and popped it in his mouth. This was something he'd done for years, and always brought a grin to Mom's face. But not today. Her dark eyes didn't flinch. She hadn't touched the fries or the chocolate shake Dad brought for her.

"Mom, why did you ask for me to come today?"

Dad's head jerked in Mackenzie's direction. Mom continued to stare at her uneaten fries. Mackenzie opened her bag and set her art book on the table. She slid it across to Mom, but Mom didn't react. The visiting room was noisy with multiple conversations and yet somehow her mother's silence was deafening.

Mackenzie scooted out her chair with force, causing it to screech across the linoleum floor. "If you aren't going to talk to me, I'm going to leave." She stood and stared down at her mother.

When Angela still didn't respond, Mackenzie looked to her father. "I'll meet you in the car."

Mackenzie stuffed her art book into the bag, wrinkling the other papers inside. In her attempt to straighten the now tattered papers, one dropped to the floor. Mackenzie snatched it up and spun around to leave. But as she grabbed the handle of the visiting room door, she felt a hand on her shoulder. She turned to face her mother's glistening eyes. "I love you, 'Kenzie."

"Oh, Mom. I love you too."

Suddenly, Mackenzie became aware of the paper she was clutching. It was the one Lauren called "Who I Am in Christ." Out of compulsion, she handed it to her mother. Angela Stine's dark eyes scanned the page briefly. She looked up, meeting Mackenzie's worried gaze, and pulled her daughter into an embrace.

Mom's warm breath was in Mackenzie's ear. "You won't end up like me," she said and turned to walk away.

"Mom, wait."

Angela turned and faced her, a weak smile stretched across her trembling, cracked lips. Mackenzie didn't know what to say. The two of them stood for a moment with only a few feet between them, and yet it was as if there was an invisible chasm. Mackenzie's throat was tight, and her breathing came in short gasps. When she didn't speak, her mother turned and began walking. Mackenzie watched her mother's slow gait until she reached the table where she sat down next to Dad.

Mackenzie sipped her coffee and waited for Krystal to arrive. At first when Krystal texted asking her to meet, she almost told her no. Seeing her mother had left her feeling even more empty. And her mother's words haunted her. It was as if she could see straight through Mackenzie and knew her worst fear was to become just like her mother. So, Mackenzie decided it would be good to see her friend. Maybe she'd even bring it up to Krystal, or knowing K, she'd probably ask.

The door opened and Krystal stepped in, her beach ball of a belly preceding the rest of her. She eyed Mackenzie and walked in a waddling motion to the table. She was all tummy. If you saw Krystal from behind, you'd never know she was pregnant.

Krystal tugged on the chair and slowly descended into it. "Ugh! Everything is a major effort. I'm *this* huge but still have like seven more weeks. And I'm getting stretch marks."

"Are they sure you aren't having twins? Ha ha! Just kidding." She hoped Krystal wouldn't mind her sarcasm, after all, Mackenzie had picked it up from her quick-witted best friend.

Krystal's eyes were dark and stern. She pushed a black and white sonogram image across the little round table. "Only one," she said. "It's a boy."

Mackenzie sucked in a breath, then gazed at the image and back up to her friend. "Wow, a boy."

"Thanks for meeting me. I know Tammi and Sadie wanted us to come later, but I really needed to talk to you alone."

"Yeah, I need to talk to you too," Mackenzie said. "But

we can talk about that later." Mackenzie glanced back at the picture of Krystal and Bryce's baby—or should she say Grant and Lauren's? "Hey, is he sucking his thumb?"

Krystal nodded and a tear slid down her cheek. "We're having second thoughts, Kenzie. I can't explain it, but I … I *love* this baby."

Mackenzie stared at her friend in disbelief. "You guys signed papers. They'll be heartbroken."

"I know," Krystal whispered to the table.

What could Mackenzie say? How could she help?

"You and Bryce have to tell them."

CHAPTER 35

TAMMI set her guitar case and music stand against the wood-paneled wall near the front of the room at the Coffee Cabin. She glanced around at the open tables. The place was usually busier on a Saturday evening. Maybe it was the rain. Tammi recalled the night of the accident when rain poured down in sideways silver sheets on the dark road home before her car collided with Sadie's. A shiver wiggled down her spine. But ironically, it was the accident that brought her to Sadie, her best friends, and to God. Tammi knew that despite the horror of the accident, God had saved her that night—in every sense of the word. She whispered a heartfelt thank you and took a few steps over to a nearby table to wait.

Sadie strolled in and waved her hand profusely in typical Sadie fashion as she made her way to the counter to order. Tammi smirked. As soon as Sadie got her ballet prosthetic, she'd bounced back from being rejected by that dirtbag, Gary. One more good reason that Dawn Rising was gone. Even still, the band's success irked Tammi. And she still had conflicting feelings about Dawn, who continued to keep in touch by an occasional text as if they were friends. Tammi had ignored the last few and hadn't heard back since. Dawn had resorted to asking Tammi to "pray" for her. Yeah, right. Tammi knew Dawn didn't want prayer. It was just another one of her games. Still, her texts seemed desperate. Maybe she was in over her head? Tammi shrugged.

Sadie set her coffee drink on the table. She squatted next to Tammi and held her arms open wide for a hug. Tammi stiffened and snarled, but leaned over in her chair slightly, allowing Sadie to wrap her up.

"When will you get used to the fact that I'm a hugger?" Sadie giggled and squeezed tighter, then released.

"When will you get used to the fact that I'm *not*?"

Sadie blew a raspberry at Tammi, little droplets of spit spraying.

Tammi gave her a shove. "Gross!"

Sadie covered her mouth and giggled as she plopped into a chair and took a sip of her extra-large, chocolatey iced-coffee drink. "Do you have time to sit and talk for a little while before you start playing?"

"Yeah. There's no set time or anything." She eyed the enormous blob of whipped cream in Sadie's drink. "I thought you were on a strict ballerina's diet. And how's that going, by the way?"

"I've been practicing two hours every single day after school for almost three months. I can afford a cheat now and then." She placed her index finger over her lips. "Shhh, don't tell my mom or Heather, though."

"Pfft, no worries there."

Sadie's eyes widened and she bounced in her seat like she was riding a horse. "Oh, oh, oh! I'm going to be performing in a show in May. You have to come!"

"Sure. Just give me the date and time and I'll be there. You should invite everyone else, too." Tammi said, opening the calendar on her phone.

Sadie told her the date and rambled on about her practices and what the show was going to be about. She flitted from talking about ballet, to schoolwork, and to what God was showing her in her Bible reading time. Tammi listened and marveled at her friend's ever-resilient faith and outlook on life and people—even those who'd abused or neglected her. Tammi wondered if she could ever have even a fraction of the forgiveness for her dad that Sadie demonstrated.

"Whew! Enough about me," Sadie said. She took a deep much-needed breath and blinked her baby blues at Tammi. "How are things going with your dad?"

"Way to get right to the point," Tammi said. "How do you do it? I mean, how have you been able to forgive people like your foster mom and the men who she let abuse you?"

Sadie's lower lip twisted, and her eyes turned to watery pools. "Oh, Tammi." She set her small hand on Tammi's. "It helped that my mom taught me things before she died. One day after my dad beat her up, I told her that I hated him. You know what she said? It was okay to hate. But to only hate the sin, not the sinner."

Tammi squeezed her hands into fists. "I want to forgive him. I'm really trying."

"All I know is I needed God's help to forgive," Sadie said. "And it isn't a one-time thing either. I had to forgive my foster mom over and over while I lived with her. It got easier when I finally moved out, but even then, it was a process. Sometimes, I still get those hateful feelings and I have to ask God to help me hate the sin and not her. But also—and this is super important—I'm not the same person I was, and neither are *you*, Tammi. Look at this."

Sadie scrolled and tapped the screen on her phone with her pink nails. Satisfied, she slid the phone toward Tammi to take a look.

"This means that anyone who belongs to Christ has become a new person. The old life is gone; a new life has begun!" 2 Corinthians 5:17.

Tammi scanned the first line when she rested on the word "*new*." A fluttery sensation filled her, and worked its way into her tight gut, releasing the knots. As if a light clicked on in a dark room, she began to understand.

God made her new. Forgiveness was a process.

"Thanks, Sadie. That really helps."

A large grin engulfed Sadie's face. "Talking with Lauren and another counselor helped too. I never thought it would help to talk about it with anyone. It seemed better to let it all stay buried, ya know? The abuse was like a monster that I needed to keep locked up. Like if I let it loose, somehow it would take over me. Lauren told me that was a lie from the devil. And she was right. You *are* still meeting with her?"

Tammi couldn't believe how similar her own feelings were to Sadie's, especially the monster part. "Yeah, I'm still meeting with Lauren. It's been good. I think the poor woman has her hands full with all of our problems!"

Sadie shrugged. "We've been here for each other too. I'm so glad to have you, Krystal, and Mackenzie."

"So am I." Tammi stood. "I'm gonna get started," she said, grabbing her guitar strap and putting the instrument over her shoulder.

"Oh, yeah!" Sadie hollered. "Don't forget, we are

princesses."

Tammi pulled open the sides of her mouth with her fingers, stuck out her tongue, and crossed her eyes. "Yeah, like Princess Fiona, that ogress from Shrek!"

"Not funny! I mean it."

Tammi rolled her eyes. Truth be told, she'd had enough of the mushy-gushy emotional stuff. And the whole princess idea was, well, ridiculous.

Tammi blinked her eyes rapidly as Grandma spoke. She heard what Grandma said but was trying to make sense of it.

"The doctors say your father's cancer is in remission." Grandma's words faded to the background as Tammi's heartbeat thundered in her ears.

Remission? Does this mean he isn't going to die? Tammi's mind swirled with a tornado of wicked thoughts. Suddenly, she was ten years old again, and her dad was rubbing his calloused fingers down her bare legs in the middle of the night.

Incest crept from behind the sofa and edged up to the cushion behind Tammi's head. The scaly little brute rubbed one of her curls between its talons. *He deserves to die for what he did to you!* It hissed.

Tammi covered her face with her hands. "No, no, no!"

"Oh, honey." Grandma squeezed Tammi's hand. "I know he hurt you. But maybe God is keeping him alive a little longer so your father can receive Jesus and forgiveness for his sins."

"Forgiveness? He deserves death!" Tammi shot up from the couch and pounded out of the room, a slew of demons flying after her in a dark, rancorous cloud.

When Tammi got into her room, she grabbed her phone, stuffed it in her bag and rushed out the front door as Grandma called to her. Tammi slammed the door without responding. The sound caused her to shudder, but she kept moving until she reached her car. The sun had set behind the hills, and it was beginning to get dark. She'd just put the car in reverse when her phone rang, the car announcing, "call from Lauren." Grandma was worried and probably called Lauren.

Tammi pulled out of the driveway and rounded the corner, ignoring the call. When she made it onto the dark open highway, she put her foot on the gas, the speedometer hitting seventy. A siren screamed from behind and red lights flashed through her rearview mirror. Tammi cursed and slowly pulled the car over. Her insides quaked as she waited. She rolled down the window to speak with the officer that approached.

Her stomach did a flip flop.

Of course, it had to be Officer Jason Hughes.

Tammi's gut clenched as he approached the window. "I'm sorry," she said pathetically.

Jason crossed his arms, biceps bulging. She expected a lecture but instead, there wasn't a hint of accusation in his gentle eyes, and his deep voice was soft. "Okay, what's wrong?"

"Let's just say my life hasn't improved since the last time you pulled me over. Just write me the ticket I deserve and get it over with."

"That will come later." His tone remained calm. "But seriously, I care about you. Talk to me, Tammi."

Hearing him say her name was her undoing. "Look, I know you mean well. I'm shaking like a leaf here. You're a hot guy in a uniform who's too old for me. And I hate men. And I hate that I'm feeling this way."

What the heck, Tammi?! How did my thoughts escape my mouth?

Jason's dark brows raised. "Not all guys are terrible, ya know. Well, all the ones your age probably *are* jerks." He shrugged. "It's obvious you've been hurt. My advice is to wait until after high school before even bothering with guys. Heck, after college."

Tammi nodded. Let him think this was all about some dumb high school breakup. Jason didn't need to know the depth of her hatred toward men. That is, except for Grant and her grandpa. They were the only good ones.

"As I said before, don't drive when you're upset." He began scribbling out her ticket. "Maybe talk to my sister?" He said, handing her a yellow slip of paper.

Tammi took hold of the ticket. "Gee, thanks." She quickly stuffed it in her purse. "No, seriously. Thanks for caring."

"I'll be praying for you, Tammi. It's gonna be okay." The radio on his hip made a squawking noise. "Gotta go. Drive safely." He took a step back and smiled, pointing at her briefly. "And see you in church."

Maybe there *were* good men out there. And maybe *someday* she'd be ready for a healthy relationship with one.

DAWN closed the door to the hotel room and stood with her back against it. She heaved a breath and squeezed her eyes shut as fear sliced through her. The tour was getting out of hand, and she needed to find a way out. More like Dawn Rising's manager, her uncle, was out of control.

The parties with crazed fans, drugs, and alcohol were thrilling at first. But now she was feeling used. Uncle Luther didn't really care about her or anyone in the band. All he cared about was money and sex. When she refused to be bartered for sex with his greaseball friends, he slapped her across the face in front of everyone at the party tonight. She knew it was time to leave. But how? She had no one to turn to. No one truly cared about her. Even her cousin, Gary, was too wasted most of the time to notice things were spiraling.

Dawn paced the room, racking her brain, when she thought of Tammi and her church friends.

CHAPTER 36

SADIE stepped inside the second and third grade classroom at church and smiled as she breathed in the familiar smell of glue and paints. The walls were a welcoming bright yellow with a red border. Posters of cute baby animals with Scriptures beneath hung alongside a large whiteboard at the front of the class. Sadie had been preparing a lesson all week and was excited to see her Sunday school students. Something about those little innocent faces brought so much joy into her life. She could tell the kids loved her almost as much as she loved them. Sometimes, she would see a student at a store during the week. Whether boy or girl, they would light up and usually run to her for a hug.

There was a new girl named Mallory who concerned Sadie. She had big brown eyes, dark hair and was extremely shy. And she didn't like to be touched. When Sadie found out Mallory had been recently adopted, her stomach churned, and bile rose into her throat. Now, Sadie prayed every day for Mallory, asking God to watch over the child. As Sadie got the supplies for the craft ready and began setting things out on the table, she prayed by name for each of her students.

She'd just finished the preparations when her little brothers slammed open the door with hurricane force and ran inside as if the storm was chasing them.

Jake set a plastic grocery bag on the table. "I have the snacks!"

Jeff stuck his face inside the bag. "Chocolate chip cookies? Hey, how come your class gets the good snacks?"

Sadie chuckled. "You'll have to ask your teacher about that. Or maybe ask Pastor Dave. Now go on out until it's time for class, you two."

Jeff punched his younger brother Jake in the arm, and the two raced out of the room as suddenly as they'd arrived. Their feet made loud splat, splat, splat sounds on the tile floor in the hallway, growing faintly into the distance. Soon the classroom was silent again, and Sadie continued her preparations. Maybe she should consider teaching elementary students as a career. It was the most rewarding experience to know she was making a positive impact on children the way her favorite teacher, Mrs. Adams, had on her life.

Sadie recalled Mrs. Adams's kind brown eyes, patience, and encouraging words. She even drove Sadie home a few times when she'd missed the bus. The first time was an accident. The next three times were on purpose so Sadie could spend time with her favorite teacher. Living in several foster homes during third grade left her feeling lonely and unwanted. It seemed like the only person who really cared what happened to Sadie was Mrs. Adams. But then Sadie changed schools and her next teacher was old and cross.

Why do some people become teachers if they don't even like children? And why am I considering teaching when I'm going to be a dancer?

The thought lingered for a moment. A teacher.

Hmmm …

Bryce honked from the driveway, and Sadie hurried toward the front door. "Mom, Bryce and Krystal are here. See ya after Bible study."

Sadie walked toward the car when Bryce got out to move the seat forward so she could climb in the back of his Mustang while Krystal remained in the passenger seat up front.

"Thanks for picking me up, guys," Sadie said. "Oh, before I forget, I want you guys to come to my dance recital that's coming up soon."

Krystal looked over her shoulder. "So, the new leg thingy really works? Sorry, I always forget what it's called."

Sadie shrugged. "Yeah, I can dance, but there are a lot of things I can't do like before. Hopefully, the technology with prosthetics improves so that it moves more like a real leg. But the main thing is, I can do what I love again." She frowned and glanced down at her prosthetic. Would she ever be able to dance like she used to? How was she going to get into a school like Julliard?

"Yeah, that's true. I know I can't wait to run like I used to before I became a pregnant whale," Krystal said. "Hey, do you think maybe Tammi or Mackenzie can take you home? Bryce and I are staying afterward to talk with Grant and Lauren."

Sadie pushed the worried feelings aside and leaned forward toward Krystal. "I'll text Tammi now and see. I was going to ask her to just bring me, but you guys live closer."

Bryce grinned at her through the rearview mirror. "No biggie, Munchkin. And I think it's cool that you're dancing again. We'll be at your recital."

As the friends arrived at Bible study, Sadie wondered why Bryce and Krystal were staying afterward. Probably stuff about adoption. Sadie watched Krystal tread the walkway lined with yellow and red rosebushes. She looked great. Her shiny light-brown hair cascaded down her back, and her flawless complexion was peaches and cream. But Sadie wondered if Krystal still battled with bulimia. She should probably check in with her about that. Sadie whispered a prayer thinking how it was almost May, and the baby wasn't due until late June. How much bigger would Krystal's belly get? Yeah, Krystal was probably really struggling with the weight gain. Still, Sadie had a hard time understanding how Krystal ever saw herself as fat. She had a tall and slim but muscular build. Bryce and Krystal made the perfect athletic couple.

Before the three entered the house, Sadie tapped Krystal's shoulder. "Hey, can we talk out here alone really quick?"

Krystal scrunched her brows together, forming a V. "Uh, okay." She glanced at Bryce. "Girl talk. See ya in there." She stepped back out. "What's up?"

Suddenly, Sadie was regretting her split-second decision to ask Krystal about her bulimia. She swallowed hard and forced a smile. "Well, first of all, you look so good. I mean it. Like your hair is so shiny and long."

Krystal's eyes narrowed. "Oh my gosh. Cut the crap.

My stomach looks like I swallowed a beach ball and my feet are watermelons! What's this about?"

Sadie's lower lip dropped. She should have known better. As she was about to speak, both Tammi and Mackenzie were on their way up the walk. Maybe this wasn't such a good idea. Then again, maybe it would be good to ask Krystal with some support. Yeah!

Tammi and Mackenzie approached. "What are you guys doing out here?" Tammi asked.

"You aren't still making yourself throw up, are you?" There! She did it.

Krystal placed her hand on her temple as if she had a migraine. "Seriously?"

"I don't think it's a bad question given you're prego and ready to pop soon," Tammi said.

Krystal looked at Mackenzie with a beseeching look. "'Kenzie, *you* know."

Mackenzie nodded. "She was struggling at the beginning. So, I keep tabs on her. We talk every week about how she's doing."

"What she means is," Krystal said. "'Kenzie caught me throwing up and beat the crap out of me." Krystal elbowed Mackenzie. "Well, not really. But she yelled at me and made me talk to Lauren. It's only happened a few times, though. I'm good. For reals."

"So, why are you staying afterward tonight to talk with Grant and Lauren?" Sadie asked. "I need a ride home from one of you, by the way." Sadie glanced at Tammi then back to Krystal.

As Krystal was about to answer, two guys from church started up the walk toward them. Krystal motioned with her head to move their conversation off to the side of the house. The three friends followed. Something was up. Sadie could tell by the way Bryce and Krystal were so quiet in the car on the way over.

"Bryce and I want to keep the baby."

CHAPTER 37

KRYSTAL scooted closer to Bryce on the sofa. He took hold of her hand and squeezed a little too tightly. She gave him a scowl, and he loosened his grip. A line of sweat trickled down the side of his face. Krystal chewed her lip. Her nerves were on edge, too, popping inside of her like one of those bug zappers on a hot June night. Grant and Lauren sat on the sofa across from them, looking like excited children on Christmas morning. How in the world were they going to tell them?

"Sooo, we have some news to tell you," Grant said, smiling as he spoke. "We wanted you both to be the first to know. We were going to ask you guys to stay after study, but you beat us to it."

Krystal's heart palpitated. Could this get any worse? What? Had they chosen a name for her baby already? Bryce's grip tightened again. Krystal shook her hand inside of his and he loosened.

Lauren's face beamed. She turned to Grant. "Let's say it together."

"We're pregnant!" The couple hollered in unison.

"Oh, look at their faces, Grant." They smiled at each other. "We've known for a while, but because of my, uh, *history*—we waited.

"Waited and prayed," Grant said.

"The baby is due in early August. The heartbeat is

strong, and all tests indicate a perfectly normal pregnancy and baby," Lauren said.

Krystal stared at Lauren's belly. Come to think of it, she *had* been wearing looser clothing. But she didn't look pregnant. Krystal placed a hand on her bloated belly. She had about eight more weeks and there was no doubt of her being pregnant. In fact, people had started asking if she was due soon. And what did this mean anyway? If they were finally having their own baby. Her heartbeat thudded harder. Bryce shifted next to her and Krystal gave him a glance. His green eyes were wide, and he looked a little pale. She raised her eyebrows. They'd agreed that he would initiate the conversation.

Before Bryce had a chance to open his mouth, Grant began to speak again. "There's more, guys." He stroked his goatee then continued. "It might sound a bit strange. The Lord gave me a dream about the two of you—"

Lauren cut in, "And about us."

Grant nodded. "Yes, honey. I'm getting to that." Lauren smirked as her shoulders sank back into the loveseat. "Anyway," Grant continued. "In the dream, we were at the park with you two … and our boys. We both had sons. I'm guessing the boys were about three years old, and they were playing in the sand as the four of us watched. And then your little guy, who had bright green eyes and dark curly hair, ran to Bryce holding something. He said, 'Look, Daddy!' And then I woke up."

Lauren leaned forward and elbowed Grant. "Tell them *when* you had the dream, honey."

"I had the dream in September."

Krystal's head was spinning. She didn't find out she

was pregnant until December. Krystal turned to Bryce. He was frowning as if puzzled. He let go of her hand and leaned forward, lacing his fingers together, hands between his knees.

"What does this mean, Grant?" Bryce asked.

"Well, when we found out that Krystal was pregnant, I remembered the dream and told Lauren about it. We prayed and hoped. We wondered if it meant we were supposed to adopt."

"But you said the little boy in the dream called Bryce Daddy," Krystal said.

Grant took a sip of his water bottle and nodded. "Yeah, I wasn't sure what to make of that. What did you guys want to talk to us about?"

Bryce's chest rose and then fell. "I—I don't know what to say about the dream except that it makes sense. Guys, Krystal and I have prayed so hard about our baby boy." His voice wavered and he paused a moment. "I've rehearsed over and over how to say this, but there's no easy way. We, Krystal and I, we want to raise our son."

Krystal held her breath and watched Grant and Lauren's faces. The room was so quiet. It didn't seem like anyone was breathing. Suddenly, the baby kicked within her. Then again, and again. She put her hands across her stomach. Maybe the kid was going to be a soccer player. He'd never kicked this much.

Lauren stood and moved over beside Krystal. "Oooh, he's kicking. I can see it!" She placed her hand on Krystal's belly. A tear slid down her olive-toned cheek. She looked into Krystal's eyes with so much love that Krystal, too, began to cry.

"I'm sorry, Lauren. I just can't do it. I love this baby."

"Oh, Krystal." Lauren cupped Krystal's face. Her brandy-colored eyes were brimming and full of compassion. "You don't need to be sorry. This is yours and Bryce's child. God knew. He knew, and he gave us our own baby. But even if I weren't pregnant, we would not want to adopt your son knowing you wanted him. It's amazing to see what God has done!"

BRYCE opened the car door for Krystal and helped her into the seat. His car sat kind of low, and she was having more difficulty getting in and out of his Mustang. Man, her stomach was really big. Seeing her like this was weird. But it was also so awesome to know his son was growing inside there. He sat in the driver's seat and glanced over at her in the moonlight. Her beautiful face glowed.

"Hey," he said. "Can you believe how well that went?"

"I'm speechless," Krystal said. "This has to be God."

He could see the whites of her eyes in the dim light. It was so good to hear her acknowledge it was God. It was an answer to his prayers.

Krystal continued "And our parents took it pretty well too. Well, our moms seemed happy. I couldn't tell about your dad. He's hard to read."

"Yeah, that's the way it is with him." Bryce didn't want to linger on that. "I have an idea. Let's go get ice cream!" Bryce knew she'd love that. Wait, was that a good idea? He still worried about her struggle with bulimia.

He didn't want to spoil the mood, but Bryce decided this might be the best time to ask how she was doing.

"Ice cream is always a good idea."

Bryce put his hand on hers. "I've gotta ask you something. It's important, and I want you to be honest."

"I already told you I want ice cream."

Bryce chuckled nervously. "Yes, ice cream is important. But seriously, K. You aren't going to eat it and then go throw up, are you?"

Krystal turned her face away.

Uh-oh.

Bryce lifted his hand from hers and took a strand of hair, twirling it between his fingers. "I love you, K. And I love our baby. I'm just making sure …"

She faced him again, the moonlight revealing a sheen in her eyes. "I did it off and on in the beginning. But I haven't for over two months. Lauren is checking up on me, and I've asked God to help me too. I won't hurt our baby, Bry."

Relief washed over him. He was thankful for Lauren and that Krystal was committed to being healthy. He was also grateful that she didn't blow a gasket and punch him or something. "Okay, good."

"Well, are ya gonna start the car, or what?" Krystal said.

Bryce shook his head and laughed. She was back to her sarcastic self—just the way he liked her. He turned the key and the engine came to life. He revved it a few times. That sound never got old. His dad had helped him install an amplified exhaust tip. They used to work on the 'Stang all the time *until* … Bryce didn't want to think about the disappointment he brought to his family. And now that he and Krystal had decided to keep the baby, Dad seemed more distant. The moms, however, were overjoyed. No matter what, Bryce knew it was going to work out. And everything that happened tonight with Grant and Lauren proved that God was going to help them.

KRYSTAL twisted the long-handled spoon inside the frosty silver cup containing her chocolate malt as she peered across the table at her gorgeous boyfriend. Is that what he was now—her boyfriend? She was wearing his promise ring, and they were going to be parents. Would they end up married after high school? She tried to picture a life with Bryce. Krystal thought about Grant's dream. Their son was going to be adorable! Bryce's gaze drifted across the room. Krystal turned to see what had caught his attention. Heat surged into her face when she saw he was looking at the cute blonde waitress with big boobs! And she was headed to their table.

"Can I get you anything else?" Blondie asked, batting her lashes at Bryce.

Krystal looked at the name badge that hung just above her left breast—Tori. Bleh!

"Uh, yeah. Can I get some water?" Bryce beamed.

"No prob," Tori said. She leaned across the table in front of Bryce and picked up his empty plate. "I'll just take this out of your way."

Krystal was disgusted. "Excuse me, Tori. You didn't

ask if *I* needed anything else."

Tori raised a perfectly manicured brow but didn't ask. When Krystal glared at her without ordering anything, she turned on her heel and walked away.

"Wow, that was rude," Bryce said.

"I know. What a witch. She was all flirty with you."

"What? I meant *you* were rude. She was just doing her job."

"Her job is to reach across you and put her boobs in your face?"

Bryce's chest rose as he released a heavy breath and rubbed his jaw, his lips twisting sideways. "It's getting late. We should go." He grabbed the check and headed to the register to pay.

Krystal took another sip of her malt but had trouble swallowing. What was once creamy and tasty was now thick and sour. She swigged it down anyway. No point wasting it. She followed Bryce out of the diner, resisting the urge to talk about what happened. Bryce's avoidance of conflict usually drove her crazy, but in this instance, Krystal knew it was wise to keep quiet. Plus, she felt a little nauseated. Things had gone so well with their parents and Grant and Lauren, but she'd let her jealousy ruin the night. Once in the car, Bryce put on some music. They didn't say a word the entire ride home. Bryce walked Krystal to the door and kissed her cheek, then turned to leave.

"Sorry, Bry. I guess I'm feeling a little insecure about this—" Krystal pointed at her belly.

BRYCE looked over his shoulder. "I know. I love you, K," he said, stepping off the porch. He sluffed down the driveway to the car. Krystal's porch light turned off, and Bryce backed out of the driveway. Why the heck had he looked at that waitress? He loved Krystal, but he couldn't help but notice the sexy waitress was flirting with him. It felt good. What was wrong with him? Things had gone so well tonight, and he'd blown it.

Guilt and Shame surfaced near Bryce's feet.

And you call yourself a Christian! The little ghouls said in unison as they climbed into his lap.

Bryce pounded the steering wheel. "What a *great* Christian!"

Next time, don't be as obvious. It's not a sin to just look!

All I did was look, though. If Krystal hadn't noticed, it wouldn't even matter. But Bryce knew better. He was only making excuses. He'd talked to Grant about his issue with pornography and the shame it always brought. Things had been better … until tonight.

Shame clawed up Bryce's arm and onto his shoulder, yellow eyes boring into his neck. *Phony!*

He was such an easy target. His battle with lustful thoughts made him forget about the power the Holy One provided. The weak-minded boy made their job so easy that they almost didn't need to do a thing. He was his own worst enemy. Nonetheless, the three despicable demons chanted curses and harassed him the rest of the drive home just for kicks.

The Duke would be pleased.

Bryce pulled into the driveway and cut the engine. He laid his forehead on the steering wheel and began to pray.

He recalled the last conversation with Grant about the thoughts that plagued him—he wasn't a good enough Christian. Grant called it spiritual warfare.

Recognizing what might be happening, Bryce raised his head, "Get behind me, Satan! I'm not a slave to sin anymore. I *know* who I am. Nothing can ever separate me from God. Victory is mine through Christ!"

Lust, Guilt, and Shame shrieked, dropped to the floormat, and oozed out the crack of the door. Their old tactics were losing effectiveness. The Christian was growing stronger in faith.

The Duke would be furious.

KRYSTAL closed the door and trudged upstairs, feeling heavy-hearted and just plain old heavy from the extra weight she carried. Why had she done that? But Bryce *was* checking out that waitress. Of course he was. She was thin and beautiful. And poor Bryce had a pregnant girlfriend ready to pop. Soon his freedom would be gone. She glanced at the promise ring on her left finger and cringed.

Mom came out of her room as Krystal made it to the top of the stairs. "Hi, how did it go?"

"It went great, Mom. Can we talk in a little bit? I need to pee and change into my pajamas. I'm so tired."

"Sure, sweetie."

Krystal went into the bathroom and shut the door. Bulimia and Anger joined her, one sitting on either side of the counter. Out of habit, Krystal stepped onto the scale. She gasped at the ever-rising numbers.

Fat cow! Bulimia chided.

Krystal stepped off the scale and covered her face with her hands. Anger hopped on her shoulder. It turned one of its deformed heads close to her left ear. *He's a pig!* The other head drew close to her right ear. *He'll eventually leave you for someone prettier and skinnier. Or he'll cheat on you!*

Bulimia edged closer, laying a yellow-clawed hand on Krystal's stomach. *You didn't need that chocolate malt, cow. Hurry up and get rid of it!*

Krystal got on her knees and bent forward in front of the toilet. As she started to stick her index finger down her throat, she stopped and sat back on her bottom.

"No! I'm not going to do it," she whispered.

In a flash, Bulimia and Anger skittered inside of the shower and cowered in fear. A smoldering dark cloud descended above Krystal. The room was engulfed as the head of the dragon-man, Duke Astaroth, appeared within the cloud. The beast extended its scaly arms toward Krystal, growling and speaking curses. As Astaroth chanted, its orange eyeballs rolled backward into the sockets, revealing only the whites.

Suddenly Krystal was clammy and dizzy. Her mouth became watery and before she knew it, she was bent over the toilet vomiting to the point of dry heaves. When the spontaneous convulsions finally subsided, Krystal scooted on the tile floor and sat with her back against the wall.

She wiped her mouth with shaking hands.

"Oh, God. Something must be wrong. Help me."

CHAPTER 38

MACKENZIE sluffed off her backpack and eased into her usual seat in trigonometry class just as the bell rang. She removed her denim jacket and dabbed the sweat from her forehead. The weather had warmed up, reminding her there were only three more weeks of school before summer break. She had a lot of studying to do if she was going to keep her straight-A record. When she unzipped her backpack, the pouch with pens and pencils spilled beneath her feet. Heat rushed to her face and her heart pattered. She quickly crouched down to pick up the mess. *What a klutz!*

As she tossed her supplies into the plastic zipper bag, she noticed a pair of battered Vans approaching and glanced up nervously, nearly conking heads with Brad Kozlowski as he bent down in front of her. His bright blue eyes stared into hers momentarily, then dropped. His hand brushed across her knuckles when he placed one of Mackenzie's pens into the pouch. A shock wave darted up her hand. He grinned and handed her a green colored pencil. She took it, and promptly looked down, hoping he didn't notice how splotchy and red she knew her face must be. She gathered the rest and sat back in her seat. Brad did the same.

Mr. Spellman droned on about ratios, cotangents, and triangles, but Mackenzie could hardly concentrate after her encounter with Brad. Oh, no! She never thanked the guy. He probably thought she was an idiot. She could say something after class—that is if she could muster the courage. Something about him made her insides feel like Jell-O.

Class came to a close, and Mackenzie grabbed her jacket and backpack while she kept an eye on the back of Brad's blond head in front of her. He stood and turned in her direction, eyes looking into hers again. Oh, gosh! Her heart did a backflip.

"Hey," she said. "Thanks for helping me earlier." Her voice came out like a whisper. How lame.

Brad winked. "No problem."

Mackenzie forced a shaky smile and spun around to head for the door. She entered the hall bustling with activity. Several conversations were going on at once as students stopped to chat or talked as they walked. Mackenzie joined the throng on their way to the cafeteria.

Rather than meet up with Sadie and Tammi, Mackenzie went out to her car, where she could unwind after the embarrassing encounter with Brad. He probably thought she was nuts for goodness' sake! She could also find out why Krystal wasn't at school.

Once inside her old VW, she muscled down the window by the hand crank. At least the rain had stopped. But now it was warm and sticky, so the breeze would help. Mackenzie pulled out her phone. Sure enough, there was a text from Krystal.

KRYSTAL: THE BAD NEWS-GOT REALLY SICK LAST NIGHT. GOING TO THE DR. THE GOOD NEWS-THINGS WENT GREAT LAST NIGHT WITH GRANT AND LAUREN. TEXT YA LATER.

MACKENZIE: ARE YOU BACK YET? WHAT HAPPENED? CALL ME. I'M IN MY CAR FOR LUNCH.

Mackenzie leaned her forehead against the steering wheel as she waited. She hoped Krystal was okay. And what about the baby? A heaviness seemed to lay on her shoulders like a weighted blanket. Why couldn't she shake this looming depression? She thought about Grant and Lauren and was curious how they took the news. Mackenzie had grown to love the young couple and didn't want to see them hurt. But Krystal's text said it went great. That was hopeful—and surprising.

Maybe I should tell Lauren about how bad this depression is.

Mackenzie eyed the phone cradled in her palm. She started a text to Lauren. After a few sentences, she backspaced. It was too long and sounded way more dramatic than she wanted. She started again, this time asking if Lauren could meet for coffee. Her index finger hovered above the send button.

Depression sprang up from the floorboard and clawed its way into Mackenzie's lap. The little brute knew a meeting with the God-fearing woman would be fatal to its mission.

She knows your mom is in the looney hospital. She'll advise for you to go there too!

Mackenzie tapped the delete button and was about to put it away, when a text came from Sadie: WHERE ARE YOU AND KRYSTAL?

MACKENZIE: K IS SICK. I'M IN MY CAR.
SADIE: TAM AND I ARE COMING OUT.

A sense of relief and peace filled Mackenzie. Even though she wasn't sure she had the energy to be sociable, she was glad her friends were interrupting her ever-looming vortex of depression. She gazed out the open window with anticipation. From a distance, she saw the tiny figures of her friends slowly grow larger. Tammi's tall slender frame towered over Sadie's, whose long blond locks flowed gracefully in the breeze. Mackenzie pulled out her sketchbook and began drawing. That was another thing that helped. And going to Bible study, hearing the music and learning about God helped too.

Tammi stuck her head in the passenger window. "Where's K?" She opened the door and slid into the seat, giving her long waves a toss. Sadie climbed into the backseat.

"Her text said she wasn't feeling well and went to the doctor. Haven't heard anything back, so I just came out here."

Tammi leaned over and looked at her sketchbook. "Can I see your drawings?"

Mackenzie handed her the book. Tammi flipped through a few of the pages and paused on one of Mackenzie's more intricate charcoal sketches of herself with her Mom. Tammi's head popped up. Her piercing eyes stared into Mackenzie's. "You really have a gift."

Sadie leaned forward. "It's amazing, 'Kenzie. But both of you have this far-away look. Why?"

Tammi nodded, staring at the picture. "That's what makes it so amazingly real. I could write an entire song or poem from those melancholy dark eyes." She looked back up at Mackenzie again. "You're feeling sad a lot, huh?"

Mackenzie's breath staggered and heat surged up her neck and into her face. She felt exposed beneath Tammi's stare. She knew her friends cared but was afraid to share just how difficult it was to live in her own skin. Would they think she was like her mother? Who was she kidding? She *was* like her mother.

Sadie leaned forward from the back seat and placed her hand on Mackenzie's shoulders. "It's about your mom, huh?"

Tammi tilted her head slightly. "No, I think she's afraid she *is* her mother." The words hung in the air for a moment before she spoke again. "But you're not. 'Kenzie, look at me."

Mackenzie stared at the dirty floormat. A tear trickled down her cheek. She swiped it away and slowly raised her head.

"You have your mom's gorgeous dark eyes, her flawless pale skin, and you are a talented artist like her. But you will *not* end up in the hospital like her," Tammi said with determination.

Mackenzie thought about the last words her mother had spoken to her: "You won't end up like me." How did Tammi know? Mackenzie hadn't told anyone, not even Krystal. In fact, her mother's words left her confused. Why would her mother say that?

"How can you be so sure?" Mackenzie whispered.

"You are stronger because you have God now."

Sadie's hand squeezed Mackenzie's shoulders. "And

you have us."

Mackenzie met their eyes, thinking how comforting it was to not feel alone for once. "Thank you," she whispered as her phone buzzed. "It's Krystal. I'll put her on speaker."

Mackenzie answered. "Hey, you're on speaker. Tammi and Sadie are here. What's going on?"

Krystal's voice rang out, "Well, I got really sick last night and still didn't feel good this morning. My mom was worried about something called preeclampsia. My urine test turned out okay, but I guess my blood pressure was kinda high and my feet are really swollen." She paused and the phone made a scratchy sound like she was moving around. "Soooo, I have to be on bed rest for a few days and then go back to the doctor again. But the baby's heartbeat was strong. That part is good. But it looks like I'll finish the school year on independent study, which sucks."

"I'm glad you and the baby are okay," Mackenzie said. "But what about the talk with Grant and Lauren?"

"You guys should come over after school so I can tell you about it. It's so cool! I gotta go. My mom's hollering at me."

Mackenzie ended the call and looked at her friends. "Do you want to go over there later?"

"Of course," Sadie said excitedly. "So, does this mean they're keeping the baby?"

Tammi shrugged. "We'll have to wait to find out the details. Hold your horses, Missy." She looked at Mackenzie again. "Have you told Lauren you've been feeling depressed?"

"Not really. I kinda don't want to."

Tammi glanced back at Sadie then to Mackenzie again. She was relentless. "Uh, if Sadie and I can talk to her about sexual abuse and abortion, you can talk to her too. I mean, you don't need to make an official appointment. Like, you could just stay after study or have coffee with her. We could go with you if you want. I know I'm being pushy, but it's 'cause I care, and I know how bad depression can be."

"Yeah, you are being pushy. But I get it," Mackenzie said. "I'll text her and ask if she could meet with us. Uh, maybe we can have her come to Krystal's house one of these days after school and we could all talk?"

"That's a great idea!" Sadie said.

"Yep," Tammi agreed.

The bell rang. Mackenzie and her friends gathered their stuff and left the car. As the three walked back toward the campus, a ray of sunlight burst through the dreary dark clouds. Mackenzie's face muscles loosened under its warmth, allowing a gentle smile to unfurl as she raised her chin. She breathed in the scent of the rain on the asphalt and for the first time in a while, she felt hopeful.

CHAPTER 39

TAMMI took her journal from the desk drawer. When she opened it, a yellow slip of paper floated to the floor. The speeding ticket from Jason Hughes. As she bent to pick it up, her phone buzzed with an incoming call from Dawn. That was strange. Dawn never called. She always texted. Tammi frowned and chewed the side of her mouth while the phone continued to buzz.

Not sure why, Tammi decided to answer, "Hello?"

Dawn's voice was sultry as ever which grated on Tammi's nerves. "Hello, yourself."

She heard Dawn breathing, but neither said anything for a few awkward moments.

"Sooo." Dawn broke the silence. "The band is back in town for a few days. I'd like to see you. Meet me at the Grind?"

"Why would I do that?"

"I have important things to talk to you about."

Tammi sighed. "Look, Dawn—"

Dawn interrupted, "I really need to see you."

"Yeah, see, that's the thing. *I* don't need to see *you*."

"That's harsh, don't you think?"

"No, I don't. The truth is, I'm a Christian now. I've changed."

"Well, funny you should say that, because that's what I want to talk about."

Tammi huffed. "Oh, I bet. You want me to *pray*? I thought you were into casting spells."

"I'm serious. Aren't Christians supposed to help others?"

Dawn was a piece of work! She'd even use Tammi's newfound faith in her manipulation tactics. Well, it wasn't going to work! But what if she really is serious? Pft! Not a chance. She's into witchcraft and curses and some weird voodoo stuff. Images of the Valentine's Day bear and Dawn's creepy apartment flashed in her mind.

"I'm busy. I gotta go," Tammi said and ended the call.

For some reason, she felt bad for Dawn. That was new too. In the past, she wavered between being obsessed and repulsed.

Pray for her.

Where did that thought come from? Could it be what Grant and Lauren referred to as the Holy Spirit? It had to be. Tammi would never think of praying for Dawn on her own.

Summoned by the Spirit, Silas appeared in Tammi's room and stood close behind her, a wide grin on his usually stoic face. The mighty angel laid a hand on her back and a glow covered her like a golden spotlight. It was Silas's joy to aid God's children in discerning the voice of the Holy Spirit. Tammi didn't know it yet, but the Almighty had given her the gift of discernment. She was in the infancy stage of her faith. This made her a threat as well as vulnerable to the kingdom of darkness. All Christians were a threat, but the new ones were like babes, seeing the spiritual journey with brand new and hopeful eyes. The demons would try to weaken her with disappointments, trials, doubts, and temptations. Silas had orders to stay close and to pray over her.

Tammi folded her hands on the desk. "God, Dawn needs you. Help her to find Jesus the way you helped me. And show me what to do about her. Amen."

When Tammi opened her eyes, she noticed the ticket beneath her feet and picked it up. She still hadn't told her grandparents. She knew that wasn't going to be a fun conversation, but avoiding the issue was only making it worse. There was a fine that had to be paid right away. Well, at least she had earned enough money playing at the Coffee Cabin to pay. Hopefully, that would help alleviate some of their disappointment.

As Tammi looked for a place on her desk to set the ticket, she focused on a single sheet of paper with the words: "Dear Dad," at the top. The rest of the page was blank. Each time she tried to write something, her mind was tormented and her heart was hard. If she began to pour out words on a page, would her resolve break and crumble? Would she completely fall apart? Tammi had started the letter when she thought her dad was dying. But now, not only was his cancer in remission, but her grandparents had also gotten him a job at the homeless shelter downtown. "We pulled some strings," Grandpa had said.

Her grandparents volunteered at the shelter every Tuesday. Tammi had gone with them a few times to help in the past, but she wouldn't dare step foot in there now and risk looking into those ice-cold wolf eyes. In fact, she couldn't wrap her mind around the idea of ever seeing her father again. Tammi covered her face with her hands.

Silas's jaw twitched and stiffened. He knew too well the pain this dear child had endured. He sensed her inner turmoil and it broke his heart. The mighty angel dropped to his knees and spread his arms toward heaven. Silver tears streaked his rugged face as he prayed to God Almighty. When he finished, Silas rose and spoke words of encouragement over Tammi.

"Oh, God. Help me," Tammi whispered.

"Yes, dear one. Cry out to your heavenly Father. He has been with you all the time that your earthly father was too broken to be who you needed," Silas said.

Tammi stared at the blank page when she remembered something both Lauren and Sadie told her. Forgiveness was a process. It was something only God could help her do. Yes! Suddenly her mind was clear, and her heart was ready. Tammi grabbed the pen and began to write. Tears and words flowed. And to her surprise, it did not break her —it gave her strength.

> Dear Dad,
>
> The things you did to me were disgusting and evil. You stole my innocence. I was just a little girl, grieving the loss of her mother. I needed a daddy. Instead of keeping me safe, you raped me—over and over. You made me have an abortion. I had nightmares for years. I still feel sick when I think of you. But I want you to know a few things.
>
> I'm a Christian now. I am finding strength and hope through Jesus. I still cannot say that I forgive you. But I'm working on it—for my own sake. I won't let the hatred I've had toward

you keep me prisoner anymore. You don't get to have that power over me. I don't ever want to see you again.

I give you to Jesus. I give my hate to Jesus.

Tammi

Tammi sighed. She breathed in deeply as relief filled her. It was like she'd stepped out of an ancient, black, pit-like cell and into the glorious light of a new day. She took out two envelopes from the desk drawer. In one, she placed the letter to her father. She folded the ticket, stuffed one hundred and fifty dollars in the middle of it, and placed it in the second envelope. She left her room with the envelopes in hand. Once in the kitchen, Tammi wrote a note to her grandparents and left it near the envelopes on the counter where they would be sure to see them. She grabbed her bag and headed out the door.

Once in her car, Tammi took out her phone and texted Dawn to meet her at the Grind. If Dawn truly wanted to talk about Christianity, Tammi had lots to share.

CHAPTER 40

May

SADIE pulled her hair into a tight bun and wrapped it with a pink ribbon—the finishing touch to her ballet ensemble. She stepped back from the mirror and twirled. Her spin still had a mechanical look. No matter how hard she trained, her stiff prosthetic didn't bend and rotate like her real leg. And it never would. A beautiful dark-haired dancer named Claire stepped in the room wearing her rose gold satin pointe shoes and a shimmering tiara. She was the star of the performance and rightly so. She had everything a school like Juilliard would be looking for. Claire was the picture of grace with her long arms and legs. She was also the perfect height and weight for a ballerina. Even before the accident, Sadie's shortness was a problem. But now that didn't really matter anymore.

Claire waved Sadie over. "I think you're amazing, Sadie. You are so brave," she said. "You have a lot of people out there cheering you on. I peeked in the auditorium. It's a packed house. Your group is right up front."

Sadie forced her best smile. "Thanks, Claire."

"I'm feeling kinda nervous. Are you?"

The room grew noisy as a group of other dancers came in and went straight to the mirror. Sadie and Claire stepped out of the way. The other girls giggled and talked as they messed with their hair and make-up.

"Yes, I'm nervous. I've never danced in public with this prosthetic. I'm worried that even though I'm one of the dancers in the back, I'll be a distraction."

Claire tilted her head. "Sadie, you must really love dancing."

Sadie nodded. It was true. She'd been enchanted with dance since she was a little girl.

"That's all you need to think about." Claire smiled. "Well, that's what my mom tells me. It helps too."

"I think that's great advice." Suddenly her prosthetic felt a lot lighter.

The dancers took their final bows. Out came the ushers bearing armfuls of flowers. The applause, whistles, and cheers echoed throughout the theater. Despite the bright stage lights, Sadie could make out her fan club in the front row. Her family and friends were on their feet. Sadie felt giddy, like she could soar across the room. She wasn't the best dancer—not even close. But she'd held it together and enjoyed every moment of the performance.

As the dancers flitted off the stage, the applause continued to ring out. Sadie made her way to the dressing area and changed into her regular clothes. She tugged her hair free from the bun. The weight of her thick long hair pulled tightly to the top of her head usually gave her a headache. But not tonight. This night had been amazing, thanks to what Claire said to her—and it was about to get even better. Sadie ran her fingers through her blonde waves and hurried to meet her family and friends. Everyone was going out for dessert, then Sadie and her friends were going to Lauren's house for an end-of-the-school-year sleepover. It had been Mackenzie's idea, which surprised Sadie. She was proud of her friend for opening up to Lauren about her depression, and it seemed as though it was already helping. Lauren, the awesome person she was, invited the girls to her home for their year-end get-together.

Sadie exited down the stairs and ran into the waiting arms of her mother.

"Oh, I'm so proud of you! You were wonderful up there."

While Sadie hugged her mom, she noticed someone she wasn't expecting—Ming! The two squealed, jumped up and down then, and hugged each other. Dad and Mom wrapped their arms around both girls. Dad said, "I love my girls."

Sadie stepped out of the embrace from her family and into another from Lauren, as Tammi, Makenzie, and Krystal waited their turn, all of them beaming at her. For the first time in her life, she truly felt like she belonged. She wasn't an adopted mutt. She was a daughter, a sister, and a friend.

Lauren led the four girls into the kitchen. "I know we just had dessert, but ..." Lauren waved her hands over the counter like Vanna White from *Wheel of Fortune.* "May I present—the sleepover feast!"

"Holy crap!" Krystal said. "This is a pregnant girl's dream come true." Her eyes roved the counter and stopped. "Wait a minute. Why is there a tray of vegetables?"

Lauren laughed. "We must have balance. Plus, we are both eating for two now." She rubbed her baby bump.

It was still unbelievable that Lauren and Grant were having a baby. And Krystal and Bryce would raise their own child. Totally a God thing.

Everyone loaded paper plates with goodies, went into the living room, and plopped on their own pallet of blankets and pillows strewn across the floor. Music played as the girls nibbled, talking and laughing about fun memories from the school year. It was hard to believe their junior year was almost over.

When Krystal's plate was empty, she rolled on her side to get up. Her big belly made her frivolous attempt hilarious. They all howled as she flailed about overdramatically, feet kicking like she was trying to swim sideways across the carpet. Krystal eventually maneuvered close to Tammi and snagged a brownie from her plate. Tammi started pelting Krystal with carrot sticks and grapes saying, "The baby needs sustenance!" Lauren joined in, tossing a powdered donut that hit Krystal between the eyes. Soon treats were being flung from all directions.

Sadie aimed a pretzel stick at Tammi before scooting out of the line of fire to watch. For all the difficulties this school year had brought, it also led to blessings Sadie would never have imagined in the dark days after the accident. She was smiling contently when a cheese puff hit her cheek, yanking her from her thoughts.

"You think that prosthetic leg and sweet voice of yours means we won't attack?" Krystal said, with a mischievous grin. "I don't think so. We all know how strong you really are, Munchkin!"

Soon Sadie was assaulted with pretzels, licorice, and powdered donuts. She grabbed a white napkin and waved it in the air. "I surrender!"

Lauren stopped the music as the play fight and giggling subsided. "Okay, you guys. Time to clean up. Plus, I have gifts for all of you to open."

After the room was clean, the girls sat on their makeshift beds as Lauren passed out gift bags with brightly colored tissue paper. Sadie's was hot pink, Krystal's gold, Tammi's dark purple, and Mackenzie's turquoise. Sadie loved how Lauren knew each of them so well.

Sadie was the first to pull out her gift. "Awww," she said as her friends echoed her sentiment. It was a stunning framed black and white photo of all four girls with Lauren in the middle. Grant was a skilled photographer and he'd taken it in front of his and Lauren's darling home before one of their Bible studies. Somehow, he'd captured the uniqueness of each girl. The tallest, Tammi and Krystal, were like bookends. Tammi was on the left with one arm raised in the air, the other wrapped around Sadie's neck. Krystal was on the opposite side, leaning her head on Mackenzie's shoulder. They all sported wide grins. Sadie fingered the slick black frame, noticing there was an inscription embossed in silver calligraphy at the top:

God's Warrior Princesses—Beauties from Ashes—Isaiah 61:1-3

The rattling of paper had stopped, and the room was quiet as each girl gazed at the gift. Sadie sensed her friends were as touched as she was.

Mackenzie cleared her throat, and everyone looked in her direction. "This is the best gift, Lauren." Her voice crackled and her eyes remain focused on the frame in her lap. "I … I just don't feel like a princess or a warrior, though."

Lauren sat next to Mackenzie. "How you feel doesn't change the truth. And the truth is, you *are* God's princess. The day you gave your life to him, you were adopted into the royal family. It says so in the Bible. Remember the handout I gave to you called "Who I Am in Christ?" There are several Scriptures on the sheet that prove it."

Mackenzie looked up. Her lips trembled and a tear trickled down her pale face. "I gave it to my mom." Her eyes darted to her lap again.

Krystal spoke up. "That's pretty cool. You never told me that. What did she do?"

"It was the last time I saw her. I told you how she wouldn't talk to me, so I got up to leave, and she followed," Mackenzie said. "Well, I gave it to her. She just stared at it for a while, and then she hugged me and told me I wouldn't end up like her. That was it. Then she just walked away." Mackenzie's eyes were focused on her lap again. "But that's the thing." She glanced up briefly. "I'm scared I *will* end up like her. It's like I'm haunted with those thoughts daily."

Lauren edged closer to Mackenzie. "That is exactly what the devil wants you to believe. But it's a lie." Her eyes scanned each girl's face. "It's called spiritual warfare.

We talked about it at Bible study."

Krystal frowned. "Uh, yeah. I remember that lesson— it creeped me out. I mean, it seems kinda 'out there.'" Krystal made air quotes with her fingers. "And how the heck are we supposed to defend ourselves against the devil, huh?

"I know it sounds like I'm talking about a horror movie or something. But I think each of you have experienced *real* evil for yourselves and know that it does exist. But, so do God and his angels, and they protect us. We are going to be studying this subject at youth group over the summer," Lauren said.

"Well, let's get started now, General Lauren," Sadie said. After her near-death experience during the accident, and the healing she'd experienced since her horrific time in foster care, she had no doubts about the existence of angels and demons.

Lauren gave a nod. Her sparkling eyes grew serious. "Remember the book of Ephesians tells us we are not fighting against flesh-and-blood enemies but against evil rulers and authorities of the unseen world, against mighty powers in this dark world, and against evil spirits in the heavenly places. The evil spirits don't want you to embrace who you really are. They also look for ways to trip you up and tempt you. They watch for your weaknesses and harass you. They also know your strengths, and they tempt you to become prideful and think you don't need God—or that maybe there isn't a God after all. Basically, the devil and demons stop at nothing to keep you from your God-given destiny."

The air conditioner kicked on, causing Sadie to jerk.

Tammi was toying nervously with her eyebrow ring while Krystal and Mackenzie both picked at their nail polish. Everyone seemed to have scooted in closer, wide eyes directed at Lauren as she continued. "You are not just sweet little princesses. You are warrior princesses. Did you notice it says that on the frame? I want you to always remember who and *whose* you are. God has given every Christian a purpose, destiny, and heavenly weapons, because as long as we are on this planet, we are at war. And God wants me to help you know about him and to train you for battle," Lauren said. "But for now, I want you guys to do a few things to prepare for our summer study, okay?"

Everyone nodded. Sadie got out her phone to type Lauren's assignment.

Lauren asked the girls to write out Ephesians chapter six verses ten through eighteen. She also told them to write a list of their strengths and weakness.

"Homework? Ugh! We're going on summer break," Krystal said.

"You are the one who asked for this," Tammi said, giving Krystal a small shove. "We kind of all did."

Krystal puckered her lips and shrugged.

Lauren laughed. "Don't think of it like homework. This is one way we learn more about God *and* ourselves. And like I said, we'll be studying this topic all summer. But for tonight … let's get back to celebrating!"

Lauren turned on the music again, pulled Mackenzie to her feet, and started to dance in front of her. Mackenzie stood awkwardly, her skinny arms at her sides, as Lauren "hit the Whoa." Sadie slid over to join in, doing a body roll as she clapped to the beat. Soon Mackenzie smirked and started to sway to the music, nodding her head. Krystal joined in, holding her giant belly as she moved from side to side. Sadie waved her hand at Tammi, who was shaking her head at them, covering a smile with her hand. She stood up, shrugged her shoulders, and started to twerk in front of Sadie. They all started cracking up, Sadie and Tammi both collapsing to the floor as they wiped away tears of laughter.

After they'd worn themselves out, Lauren turned off the lights and everyone took their spots on the floor. It wasn't long before Sadie was surrounded by the sound of soft snoring. But she couldn't sleep. Her thoughts raced, and she couldn't shake an image from her head. She kept seeing herself in front of a classroom like the one at church, but different.

Does God want me to be a teacher?

CHAPTER 41

KRYSTAL changed out of the pajamas she had worn for the last two days and ran a brush through her tangled long hair. Although she was feeling considerably better than the day before, her stomach was still a bit queasy. The doctor confirmed from her urine test that she had mild preeclampsia. Because Krystal's blood pressure was high, she would now need to bed rest until it was time to deliver the baby. She took a sip of her sports drink from the nightstand and a bite of a saltine cracker as she scanned the room for her slippers. All of her other shoes were too tight. Because of her big puffy Fred Flintstone feet and her history with bulimia, the doctor wanted to see Krystal again in a few days. In the meantime, Dr. Barnes told Krystal to continue elevating her feet as much as possible. She also said no caffeine. Ugh. No school, no track, and no coffee.

As Krystal continued to look for her slippers, Cheeto followed, rubbing against her legs, when she suddenly felt the baby kick. A sense of relief washed over her. "I'm glad you're moving around, little guy." Little guy? Now that she and Bryce had decided to raise their own child, it was time to think of a name. She wondered if Grant and Lauren had been thinking of names for their little boy. It was so awesome they had their own "little guy" to name. Krystal just hoped her bulimia hadn't caused problems for her baby. *Please no, God.*

Krystal stuffed her feet in her slippers and took the long trek downstairs, Cheeto right behind, where she met her mother's gaze. "Krystal Peterson! Get back in bed."

"Jeez! I can't stay cooped up all day. I just wanted to get more than crackers to eat."

"Well, I'll make you something. But you need to keep your feet up."

Krystal leaned her head back and stared at the ceiling. "Mom, just let me eat down here like a normal person. I'm sick of being in my room." She hoisted her bottom on the window seat of the breakfast nook and stretched her legs out. It was still her favorite spot in the house.

Mom's lips turned up slightly as she nodded and opened the fridge. "What do you feel like? There's leftover pizza with cauliflower crust, stuffed mushrooms, or my homemade minestrone soup."

"All of the above."

Mom pulled out practically the entire contents of the refrigerator and started heating things up. Krystal smiled as her Mom moved about the kitchen so intent on taking care of her daughter carrying her near-due grandson. The difference in their relationship was like night and day. They had been at odds for as long as Krystal could remember. Things escalated when Dad left and got to a tipping point with Mom's drinking and then Krystal's pregnancy. But over the past few months, they'd grown closer than they'd ever been.

"Okay, we'll start with the stuffed mushrooms and soup." Mom set two bowls of steaming hot soup and silverware on the table. Next, she grabbed sparkling waters and the rest of the smorgasbord of leftovers and placed them in the middle of the table, then sat across from Krystal.

The two sat in comfortable silence as they ate. Mom laid her spoon down and smiled at Krystal. "So, have you been thinking about names?"

"That's funny. I was just thinking about that. I haven't really until this morning." This wasn't fully true. She'd wondered about a name after the first sonogram but shoved the thought away until lately. But now … "I need to ask Bryce. He has finals all week. I guess I feel like I got off pretty easy when we explained to my teachers about being on bed rest. I only had one final. The rest of them were good with the essays and assignments I did last week. My junior year is over." Krystal slurped a spoonful of soup. "Next time I set foot on that campus, I'll be a senior … and a mom." She pushed the food around with her fork, still pondering what her infant son might look like.

"And I'll be a grandma—which makes me think of something. Shelly Williams and I have been talking. Maybe us grandmas can take turns watching little what's-his-name while you're in class?"

Krystal held the bite of stuffed mushroom in her mouth. She attempted to chew, but the thing seemed to grow bigger and bigger. Her situation was getting real. Yeah, she'd come to terms with being pregnant, but being a mother and needing childcare and all kinds of other things was overwhelming. She gulped, suddenly feeling a bit nauseous again.

"Are you okay, honey?"

"Uh, I'm not sure." Krystal set her fork down and leaned back. "I think I may have overdone it after not eating much lately."

"Maybe you should head upstairs and lay down."

Krystal scooted off the bench and stood up slowly. The room seemed to tilt sideways, so she braced her hands on the table before attempting to walk. Mom had started clearing away the dishes and didn't notice.

"Thanks, Mom. I'm going to take your advice and go to sleep for a while. Oh yeah, and Bryce said he was going to bring me dinner later. I can ask him to get sushi or something for all of us if you want." It seemed she was tired and uncomfortable all of the time.

Krystal jolted awake. She wiped the sleep from her eyes and looked around her room. How long had she been sleeping? She struggled to pushed herself up and grabbed her phone. It was five in the evening already. She texted Bryce to bring over sushi, then stood to make herself presentable before he came over. As she tugged the pajama shirt over her head, sharp cramps rolled across her lower abdomen. Krystal sucked in a breath and sat back on the bed. The cramps subsided and Krystal stood again. Like when she was in the kitchen, she felt woozy and nauseous. She gingerly pulled off the pajama bottoms and got dressed. As she took a few steps toward her door, the cramping started again. Krystal doubled over in pain, arms encircling her belly.

A black cloud of smoke hung above Krystal. Duke

Astaroth's orange, devilish eyes glowered at her from within the cloud.

"That child was unwanted and belongs to ME!"

The room was now a hellish inferno with hundreds of demons bidding the orders of the Duke. They swooped, pecked, scratched, and bit while the Duke waved its massive arms, flinging acid-like fireballs and spewing curses.

Krystal fell to the floor. She writhed in pain, rolling her head from side to side until she spotted the picture on the nightstand of her friends with the Scripture from Isaiah on the frame. "Oh, God, protect my son. I love him!"

The sound of rushing wind filled her ears and Krystal's vision blurred. She lost consciousness just as her prayer reached the heavenlies.

"It is time!" Commander Philo's voice rumbled through the sky as he plunged downward toward Earth. A legion of warrior angels followed, sparkling trails filling the sky like shooting stars.

"Stand guard and pray," the commander ordered to the company of heavenly hosts as they entered Earth's atmosphere. "Charge," he waved to his officers to follow.

Commander Philo and Silas appeared in Krystal's room with hurricane force, demons flinging left and right. Theo, Jason, and Jonathan arrived with swords drawn and the battle ensued, metal clanging and bones cracking.

Silas shouted, summoning a team of seven mighty cherubim arriving in the room like blazing comets. The massive angelic beasts covered Krystal with an unseen forcefield of protection as the battle around her continued. As quick as lightning, Silas turned and sunk his sword into Bulimia, ripping the thing's scaled hide open. The other angels jabbed and slashed, battling the rest of the demonic horde.

"Retreat!" Duke Astaroth hollered.

Silas leapt into the air as the Duke was attempting its cowardly exit. The angel jammed his sword into the great beast's side. The thing released a blood curdling shriek, its massive wings flailing as it collapsed to the floor. Silas straddled the motionless Duke. He raised his sword in both hands high above his head as Duke Astaroth snorted and swiped, claws gouging into the warrior's thigh. Silas grimaced as he plunged his sword into the beast's belly, releasing a flood of inky dark goo that oozed onto the floor then began to quickly disintegrate molecule by molecule.

Immediately, the demons zipped in dark smoky streaks in every direction. The curtains rustled and the lamp on the nightstand wiggled. Then …. silence, as though nothing had occurred. Krystal's eyelids fluttered open and she rolled to her side and tried to stand but found herself too weak. Her door opened, and she was met with Bryce's frightened stare.

"Help me," she whispered.

CHAPTER 42

MAY

MACKENZIE woke with a gasp. Was it time to get ready for school? No, it couldn't be Monday morning yet. Her room was dark and unnaturally quiet. It seemed the entire house was holding its breath along with her. Prickles sailed up her arms.

As her eyes began to adjust, an immense shadow hovered above the bed, moving lower as if it meant to swallow her up. Mackenzie wanted to scream to Jesus for help, but her mouth would not open, and her body was paralyzed. As the shadow descended, a cavernous mouth full of jagged teeth came into view. The thing was inches from her face emanating a hot rancid stench like a rotting corpse.

"I'm … going … to … EAT YOU!" The demon called Death growled, spittle dropping on Mackenzie's face.

"J-Jesus," she barely whispered.

Suddenly, at the mention of the name above all names, a sliver of light pierced the darkness and Death was forced upward, disappearing like it had been sucked into a vacuum.

"'Kenzie?" It was her father.

"Wha—"

Dad was by her bedside now. "Are you awake?" The

bed groaned when he sat down. "I'm sorry to startle you. Honey, I got a call from the hospital. I need to leave. I didn't want you to wake up and find out I'm not here."

"What's wrong?" Mackenzie asked.

Dad put his arms around her and held tight for a moment. "I'll call later."

"No. Tell me now, Dad."

He kissed the top of her head and stood. "I will as soon as I can. But I've got to get there now."

Mackenzie squinted, looking for the time. Five in the morning. "So, I need to get everyone off to school? What do I tell them?"

Dad was already to the door. "Just tell them I'm … visiting Mom."

The door shut, leaving her in the inky darkness again. Mackenzie stood up and rushed out of the bedroom and down the hall as her dad reached the front entryway.

"Dad, please wait. I'm scared."

He turned, his face pinched with pain. "I'm sorry, honey, but I've got to hurry." And with that, he shut the door.

Mackenzie wrapped her arms around herself in a hug. She was disoriented and freezing, but there was no way she was going back into the bedroom to retrieve her robe. What was that thing? Had she been dreaming? Was she awake or was she going crazy like … She shook her head, trying to clear her mind. Grabbing a jacket from the coat rack, she padded into the kitchen and sat down. She folded her arms on the table and laid her head on them.

"God," she whispered, her voice muffled by the table.

"I'm so afraid. I'm scared about Mom and I'm scared of what I just saw in my room."

Silas arrived, placing his hands upon Mackenzie's shoulders as he prayed with Scripture. "Do not fear. I have redeemed you. I know you by name, my child. My perfect love casts out all fear," he recited. "The Almighty God has sent me, dear one. You are deeply loved." Silas's throaty voice rumbled through the heavenly realm, sending the demonic creatures of all ranks and sizes into hiding as they shrieked and covered their ears.

Soon Mackenzie drifted into a peaceful sleep. Silas received an unction in his spirit to leave immediately and join his comrades at the hospital. The mighty warrior girded himself for the worst and broke into flight.

Thunder rattled the house, shaking the pictures on the walls. *BOOM!*

"I'm scared!" Del said, scooting closer to Mackenzie. "Where's Daddy?"

Mackenzie breathed heavily. "I told you already. He went to see Mom."

"That was this morning before school," Harper said. "Something is wrong. I can tell."

Mackenzie scowled at Harper and motioned to Del. Sheesh, she was going to make him even more frantic. What was wrong with her? Harper's shoulders shrank and she chewed her lip as she sat back into the sofa, arms crossed.

"Um, maybe you should call again. He's been gone

all day," Trey said. "It's starting to get dark, and now the stupid power is out." He pointed at the black screen on the TV with the remote and gave it a toss on the couch.

"I did the last time you asked me to, and he didn't pick up," Mackenzie said. "You and Harp go look for some candles and the lighter. I'll stay here with Del."

Mackenzie had a sinking feeling in the pit of her belly. *Oh God, please help.*

Trey paced the room, running his hand through his long dark bangs, then headed to the kitchen in search of candles. Bristol whimpered near the sliding glass door. Trey opened the door but stood waiting for the dog to do its business and come back. The rain splattered in sideways sheets on the concrete patio. The sky cracked with a burst of zig-zag light. Within two seconds, another rumble of thunder boomed. Bristol shoved his large body into Trey, zipped back into the house, and shook the water from his fur, dousing Trey's jeans and causing the whole room to smell like wet dog.

"Gross!" Trey said.

Del laughed. Thank God for Bristol to lighten the mood. The storm had everyone's nerves on end.

"Why is it raining so much?" Del said. "I can't go outside and play."

Harper shrugged. "It's getting dark anyway, Bud. I know it's a bummer. They say April showers bring May flowers. But it's already May and time for the rain to stop, huh?" She ruffled Del's hair and set a large three-wick candle on the kitchen table and was about to light it when the power kicked back on.

"Yay!" Del said. "Let's watch TV."

Everyone sat down in the family room to watch the Disney Channel. The lights flickered as if they would go out again, but to everyone's relief, the power remained on. Halfway through Del's favorite show, Dad walked in. Mackenzie turned and watched as he trudged closer. He didn't bother taking off his soaking wet coat. The color of his face was almost gray, darker around the jawline from his unshaven whiskers. His eyes met hers, and she knew something was terribly wrong. Once again, fear took hold and her insides began to quake.

"Daddy!" Del ran across the room and wrapped his father's legs in a hug.

Dad's face contorted as he ran his fingers through Del's messy black curls. Mackenzie looked to Harper and Trey. Their wide frightened gazes darted to her and back to Dad.

Mackenzie stood and walked toward Dad, picking up Del. "Hey, buddy. Run to your room and bring Dad that Lego masterpiece you made earlier." She set him down and he ran toward his room, feet pattering against the wood flooring. She was only buying time, hoping to help her dad and shield little Del. But what about Harper and Trey? She wished she could protect them, but knew they needed the truth just like she did.

"What happened?" she asked despite dreading his answer.

Dad's Adam's apple wobbled as he gulped. His dark eyes were ready to spill. "Let's sit down. We can wait for Del. But first, let me say that after Del goes to bed, I will talk to the three of you with more details."

Mackenzie sucked in a scant breath. A sinking feeling

overcame her. *God, please no!* She screamed in her head as she followed her dad into the living room.

Silas and Theo stood behind Mackenzie's father, the tips of their outstretched wings touching the ceiling. The two angels held out their brawny arms to brace Howard Stine, whose knees nearly buckled. They guided him into the room and prayed while he gaped at his three older children, searching for words.

Del padded carefully toward the couch, holding his Lego creation with both hands, and presented it like a prize. "Here's the wego car that Trey helped me make," Del said with his endearing lisp, causing Mackenzie to smile sadly.

Dad's lips quivered but managed to turn up slightly as Del placed the car in his lap. "Wow, this is really good. You must have worked very hard," Dad said. "I'm going to just put it here on the coffee table, okay?" Dad leaned forward and set the car down. "Come sit by me, Sport."

Del sat down next to Dad. "What's wrong, Daddy? You seem sad."

"I *am* sad. Very … sad." He paused when Del placed his chubby hand on Dad's leg. A muscle in Dad's jaw jerked as his large hand engulfed Del's and squeezed.

Every muscle tightened in Mackenzie's body. Her heart already felt like it was going to explode from seeing the anguish her sweet dad was in. She knew what he was about to say. There was nothing she could do to prepare to hear it. The lights in the room flickered again.

"There's no easy way to say this." Dad's voice wavered. "Mom went to heaven to be with Jesus last night."

Had the oxygen been sucked out of the room?

Mackenzie couldn't breathe, and she suddenly felt clammy like she was going to be sick. One thought played over and over in her brain.

Mom is dead. Mom is dead. Mom is dead.

CHAPTER 43

TAMMI waded through the cramped hallway of the music building, guitar case strapped across her back. She passed the concert band classroom. The deep *ooompah, ooompah, ooompah* of a tuba along with the flitting sounds of flutes rang out as the students started their warm-up exercises. She dodged a guy carrying a bass drum and hurried into the classical guitar classroom just as the bell rang. Tammi shrugged off the case and sank into a seat. Ah, music class. A great way to end a gloomy, rainy Monday. The late spring weather couldn't seem to make up its mind. Just a few days ago, Tammi was wearing a tank top and shorts, but today she was back to jeans and boots.

Brad Kozlowski from Bible study draped his drenched jacket over the chair next to Tammi and slid into it. He gave a quick nod and pretended to busy himself with sheet music. He'd been awkward around her since she turned him down about going out. Although she felt bad and wouldn't mind talking with Brad about music, she also knew how guys were. If you acted the slightest bit nice, they'd think you liked them. Plus, now she knew that 'Kenzie liked the guy.

The music instructor, Mr. Blaire, was engrossed in a conversation with a student at the front of the room. He'd been a little lax lately because there were only a few days left of school. Since class hadn't officially begun, Tammi pulled out a page to a song she was working on. She sensed Brad's eyes on her but didn't acknowledge him.

"Can I ask you something?" Brad asked.

Tammi kept her eyes on her paper. "Okay."

"Uh, you're close friends with Mackenzie, right?"

Tammi raised her head and squinted at Brad. "Why?"

"She wasn't at school today. We're in two classes together. I was just wondering if she's okay. I mean, she's all about keeping up her grades. We had the final in trig today. It's just weird that she'd miss it."

Maybe he does like 'Kenzie. But why'd he ask me out? Wait, 'Kenzie never answered my text. Maybe she went over to keep Krystal company? Nah, 'Kenzie would never ditch or miss a test. And come to think of it, Krystal didn't answer me either.

Tammi shrugged. "She must be sick or something. I texted her earlier, but she didn't answer. Why do you care? Do you like her?"

Brad's blue eyes widened. "Kinda—I mean, she's really smart and pretty. But I don't know what she thinks of me. I thought because you and I had music in common, maybe—" he paused. "Well, no need to revisit that."

"She's just shy," Tammi said. "Unlike me. Sorry I was so straightforward about not being interested."

"Yeah, that was pretty brutal," Brad said, squeezing the back of his neck. "So, you think I should ask her out?"

Tammi rubbed her temple. What had she gotten herself into? "Dude, I'm not playing matchmaker. If you like her, ask her out."

"Cool."

"Wait. I'm confused. Why ask me out if you actually like Mackenzie?"

Brad ran a hand through his blond hair. "I know what it looks like." His eyes rolled upward. "I kinda gave up because I didn't think I had a chance with her. I mean, I tried talking to her, but she hardly looks at me. Anyways, I knew you and I have music in common and you're cool, so—"

Tammi interrupted. "I was your second choice? Wow, I'm so honored." She placed a hand on her chest.

"Oh, man. It's not really like that."

"'Kenzie is shy. Just ask her out, you dummy." Tammi waved her arm flippantly at Brad. "And my feelings aren't hurt. So, no worries. You can stop acting all weird around me." Tammi leaned closer and stared directly into Mr. Wonderful's eyes. "But if you hurt her, you'll have to deal with me. I mean it."

"I wouldn't doubt that for a second."

The tap, tap noise from Mr. Blaire's conductor's baton on his metal music stand silenced the conversations around the room. For the duration of music class, Tammi made sure to give Brad an occasional glare to let him know she meant business—to which he'd smile and shake his head. Tammi honestly hoped things would work out with Brad and Mackenzie. He seemed like a decent guy. But would she ever find someone to love *her*?

Tammi thought about Lauren and Grant's amazing relationship. She had asked Lauren if her abuse had affected dating and how she found someone to marry. Lauren shared that like Tammi, she had been sexually promiscuous in her teen years, even the first few years after becoming a Christian. This shocked Tammi but also gave her hope. Lauren said as distorted as it seemed, she thought sex was the way to feel loved. Through counseling and growing closer to God, her thoughts began to change, and then her actions began to change. Lauren said it was when she realized how much God loved her that she was able to start loving herself. Another thing that gave Tammi hope was Lauren said she used to think she'd never find a man who could love her. Then along came Grant. She called him a man after God's own heart, saying he loved God more than anything. Their love was rock solid. And so was their faith.

Tammi hoped to find that kind of love someday.

The house was quiet and empty when Tammi got home from school to change before going to 'Kenzie's. Maybe her grandparents had gone shopping, or maybe they were visiting someone sick from church. Those two were always busy doing something for others. Stan and Thelma Gerard were like those people who take in stray animals and volunteer at the shelter, except they did it with people. Tammi knew it was the prayers of her grandparents that had contributed to where she was today. She felt so blessed to have their love and support. But for the life of her, she could not understand how in the world their son, her dad, could turn out to be such a monster. It just seemed impossible. And now that monster wasn't going to die after all. Maybe her grandparents were visiting *him* right now. She wondered if they'd given him her letter. The thought made her insides cringe.

Then it hit her. Could someone have hurt him the way he hurt her?

CHAPTER 44

SADIE rolled out a pink yoga mat and began her morning stretches before she attached the prosthetic. She sat with her legs—the normal leg and "stumpy"—in front of her and lowered her head to her knees, holding the position for thirty seconds. Before the accident last September, she would flex and point both of her feet. Now, as she flexed her right foot, pain radiated up her left leg from her stump and into her knee area. They called it phantom limb syndrome. Somehow, her body's signals got crossed and they didn't recognize the damaged part of her leg from the accident no longer existed. Even though it had been several months, sometimes out of nowhere, a wave of grief would roll over her and drag her into a swirling undertow of despair. She missed the old Sadie with both legs intact. A tiny tear trickled down her face.

I know you saved me for a reason, God. Help me not to give into this sadness. I have so many things to be thankful for.

She closed her eyes and decided to make a mental list of the good things in her life until the sorrow lifted. Her mother taught her that trick. She called it 'count your blessings.' Whoever listed the most was the winner. Sadie smiled at the memory, then opened her eyes and continued her stretches for ten more minutes before getting ready for the last day of school.

Junior year was over, and she couldn't wait to celebrate

with her friends. She sent a group text to Krystal, Mackenzie, and Tammi. Maybe they could all meet at Krystal's since she had to stay in bed.

The moment she got in the car after school, Sadie knew something was different. The music wasn't on, and the boys weren't in the back. A sick realization settled over her. There had been no response from Krystal or 'Kenzie to the group text. And Mackenzie had not answered texts or calls from either her or Tammi. Another weird thing was that Bryce wasn't at school today, and he wasn't answering his phone either. So, the plan was for Tammi to go check on 'Kenzie, and Sadie was going to ask her mom to take her to Krystal's.

"What's going on, Mom?"

Mom removed her dark designer sunglasses and tucked a strand of blonde hair behind her ear. Her usual bright-blue eyes were puffy and bloodshot. "Honey, I'm afraid I have some bad news. Mackenzie's mother passed away Monday." She reached over the armrest, grabbed Sadie's hand and squeezed it. "And Krystal is in the hospital."

"What? Oh, no!" Sadie slumped over, the air releasing from her lungs.

"Krystal and the baby are okay. But her preeclampsia is a concern. Her blood pressure got very high and she passed out. They are keeping her in the hospital to monitor her and the baby. If her condition worsens, the baby will have to come out. But for now, both are stable,"

Mom said. "I'm taking us to the church right now to meet with some others to pray. You're okay with that, right?"

Sadie frowned. Krystal was on bedrest, but she didn't expect this. *I should have gone over to check on them! But no, I was too worried about finals.*

"Oh, Mom. I feel terrible." Sadie laid her head against the seat and held her hands to her chest. "Does Krystal know about Mackenzie's mom? And what about Bryce?"

Poor Bryce! And poor Mackenzie … this is a nightmare!

"We don't want Krystal's blood pressure to spike, so we haven't told her about 'Kenzie. Her mother knows, though. Shelly Williams and Bryce are at the hospital with Krystal and her mother now." Mom rubbed Sadie's arm. "Bryce was pretty scared of course, but he's calmed down. And Tammi and her grandparents will be at the church with Grant and some others. Lauren and Pastor Dave are with the Stine family."

Sadie and her mother held hands and prayed, then left the school parking lot. Sadie sighed as she gazed out the window watching the trees, houses, and other cars whip past. She knew what it was like to lose her mother and the familiar old grief felt fresh again as she thought about her dear friend's loss. Her stomach cramped and her chest began to heave. *Please help my friends, God.*

Mom parked out front of the church. They hurried up the walk and entered the building.

"There's Thelma and Stan Gerard," Mom said.

Sadie saw them, too, but Tammi wasn't with her grandparents. She glanced around the room, and then she noticed Tammi speaking with Grant near the stage. She glided around the other clusters of people and up the aisle.

The solemn look on Grant's handsome face sent tiny prickles down Sadie's arms. "What happened to 'Kenzie's mom? How did she—" Sadie couldn't say anymore.

Tammi's gray eyes were watery, and she'd scrunched her eyebrows together as if she was in excruciating pain. "We don't know."

"Did you talk to 'Kenzie?"

Tammi shook her head. "I was on my way over there when my grandparents called and told me to come home. Once they told me, we came right over here."

Sadie remembered why Mackenzie's mom was in the mental hospital to begin with. "Oh, gosh. She didn't …"

Tammi shrugged and shook her head. "We don't know the details. But I'm really worried about 'Kenzie. She hasn't been herself for a while, ya know? But I thought things were going to be better after the sleepover with Lauren. And now this …"

Sadie looked at Grant. "You said that Lauren and Pastor Dave are with her family? What about Krystal?"

"Pastor Dave and Shirley were at the hospital with Krystal and her mother when he got the call from Mackenzie's father. Shirley stayed with the Petersons and Pastor Dave has been with the Stines. Lauren checked in on Krystal today and she's now with the Stines too."

"I don't know who to go see first," Sadie said to Tammi.

"I'll let you know when it's a good time once I have spoken with Lauren after our prayer meeting." Grant gave both girls a pat on the shoulder. "I'm going to gather everyone up front and lead us in a prayer."

Tammi looked uncomfortable. Her eyes darted to the back of the room as she quickly sat in the front row. Sadie flipped around and caught a glimpse of Jason Hughes as he meandered in the door.

"I wonder why he's here?" Tammi said.

"Yeah, that's weird. Well, maybe not. I mean, he's Lauren's brother and he probably came to pray too." Sadie saw a flicker in Tammi's eye. "Hey, he's too old for you. Remember?"

"He gave me a ticket a while back."

Sadie raised her eyebrows. She wanted to ask more, but this wasn't the time. Grant gave his brother-in-law a hug and the two headed up to the front near Sadie and Tammi. Jason's eyes flicked in Tammi's direction as he took a seat in a chair across the aisle. Grant stood at the front and called for everyone to come forward for prayer. Sadie grabbed one of Tammi's hands. It was limp and clammy. Sadie forced a smile, then bowed her head.

Unbeknownst to the churchgoers, Silas and Theo stood nearby, bright light emanating from them as they lowered their heads and prayed in the heavenly language. The girls would need holy strength to comfort their friends and encourage them in their faith.

Hundreds of demon watchers lurked throughout the church building. Yellow and orange eyes blinked from under chairs, beneath the stage, and in every available crevice. Some hissed and barred their teeth, while others cowered as another twenty of God's angels appeared.

A typical church housed numerous demons who laid in wait, ready to strike. But they weren't sure what to do about this spontaneous prayer gathering. The wretched beings had had the same orders for centuries—to block a Christian from true conviction and keep them complacent. There was no winning a Christian's soul. That deal had been sealed. So, the devil's main goal was to use his demonic minions to weaken their faith and make them ineffective. But tonight, the demons were the ones rendered ineffective as the prayers of God's angels and his people persisted.

Once the time of prayer concluded, Silas and Theo left the church to return to the Stine family. Commander Philo was keeping watch over Krystal and the baby.

Sadie picked at her chicken, taking little nibbles before pushing her plate away. There was no point. Her stomach was too upset to eat. She wanted to do something other than sit around and wait. She excused herself, went to her room, and put on workout gear. She'd missed dance practice so she wanted to at least do what she could at home. Sadie grabbed her phone in case Tammi or Lauren called, and headed for the garage to do some stretches and warm-up exercises on the barre.

She stood in a modified version of first position, arms held out in an oval shape, and sighed. Her heels couldn't touch. There was no way to even plié like a proper ballerina with her stiff prosthetic leg and foot that wouldn't turn out. When she wore her pointe leg, she was stuck in the same pointe position. And it could be years before a bionic prosthetic that she could afford would be developed. Who was she kidding? A school like Juilliard only accepted the best. It would have been a challenge to get in *before* the accident. But now …

A gaggle of demons clung upside down from the ceiling. Their deformed bat-like faces snarled as they flapped their leathery wings and chanted discouragement.

You'll never make it! Whoever heard of a handicapped ballet dancer? You're too short!

Gary didn't want you and neither will Juilliard!

Sadie rested her arms on the bar and laid her head on them. This was nothing but a pipe dream. Why were her parents and Heather encouraging it? They felt sorry for her! That had to be it. At least Heather had tried to warn her. The ragged crow called Pity landed on her back. With spindly bird legs, the thing hopped closer until it was on her shoulder. It glared at the side of her face with cold black eyes, then pecked hard against her temple with its mangled beak.

You! Peck.

Are! Peck.

Broken! Peck, peck, peck.

Sadie rubbed her throbbing head and cried out in prayer, "God, why did you save me? I thought you wanted me to dance for you." She lifted her head and focused on a poster of the cross with the names of God written within that hung on the wall. "How can I be so selfish right now when Mackenzie just lost her mom and Krystal and the baby are in danger? Oh, forgive me and please help my friends."

A loud buzz vibrated the metal tool chest where Sadie had set her phone. She quickly answered Tammi's call.

"I'm with Bryce. We're on our way over."

CHAPTER 45

KRYSTAL shifted in the hospital bed, pushing the button to raise her head. She held up the tube that ran from her irritating IV so she could grab her phone from the bedside table. She scratched at the strap around her big belly from the electronic fetal monitor that kept track of the baby. Krystal glanced at the nearby screen with a little green heart that blinked, indicating her son's heartbeat. The rhythmic sound was soothing to Krystal. As long as the heart blinked green, he was okay. If the little heart turned red, it meant he was in danger and the doctor would most likely need to get him out by cesarean section. The goal was to let the baby develop longer since she was still not due for another six weeks.

A young Chinese nurse named Alice with a cute bob haircut came in and smiled at Krystal as she picked up the paper printout that ran from beneath the machine. On the paper was a graph that showed the heartrate and the baby's pulse. Alice ran her slender fingers down the length of the printout, then quickly scribbled some notes.

"Still looking good," Alice said.

"Can I ask you something? If I had this baby now, would he be okay?"

Alice tilted her head and came a little closer.

"Well, it would be best for the baby to continue to develop in the womb. The biggest concern is the lungs.

But many babies have been born at this stage and do okay. He'd be tiny and need lots of care," Alice said. "But let's just try and stay relaxed and keep him in here—" she pointed to Krystal's belly. "—as long as possible. Are you feeling okay?"

"I was really scared. But now, I'm just bored. Any chance I can get up and walk a little? I'm really sick of this bed."

"Probably not yet. If everything still looks good, maybe the doctor will approve a small stroll in the hallway."

Alice checked Krystal's vitals and IV and flitted out of the room. Krystal sighed. Bryce and her friends had finished the last day of school, and she was stuck in the hospital. Mom had to go into work for a few hours but would return in the afternoon. Krystal hoped her friends would come and see her later. She was worried because 'Kenzie had never texted back. Sadie's text said she would check on Mackenzie. Tammi's text said they would come see her as soon as possible. Using her belly as a table for her cell phone, Krystal scrolled through TikTok and Instagram until her eyes grew heavy.

Krystal listened to the noises coming from the hallway. It seemed she never got more than an hour of sleep before waking to either a nurse checking her vitals or the sounds of a cart rolling right outside her door. She leaned forward when she heard footsteps and voices approaching. There was a baritone murmur followed by a high-pitched trill that could only belong to Sadie and

Bryce. Next came a rap on the door and in walked her friends with her mother following closely behind. Bryce held a vase of flowers, Sadie clutched a cute fuzzy stuffed bear, and Tammi carried what Krystal hoped was a chocolate shake.

Bryce set the flowers on the stand next to Krystal and bent to kiss her cheek. She breathed in his scent and threw her arms around his neck, drawing him closer. He whispered, "Uh, take it easy. We aren't alone." Krystal released her grip, and Bryce stood up, his cheeks flushed.

Sadie and Tammi approached, and Bryce stood back, making room. Sadie plopped right on the bed and shoved the stuffed animal in Krystal's face with a giggle.

Tammi set the cup she was holding on the tray. "Brought you a chocolate shake. Hope that's okay."

"Duh," Krystal said. "Hand it over." She sipped the shake and glanced around the room at her friends and mom. Where was Mackenzie? Her gaze landed back on Mom, whose eyes indicated she had something to say.

Mom took a few steps toward the bed. "Krystal—"

Krystal interrupted. "Where's 'Kenzie?" She looked from Mom to everyone else.

"She's at home with her family. She'll come to see you soon."

"What's wrong?"

A muscle in Mom's cheek shook. "Honey, Mackenzie's mother passed away Monday night. We didn't want to say anything until you and the baby were stable."

Krystal's throat tightened and she began to gasp. "Oh no! I need to see her. That's why she didn't text me back."

Bryce leaned over and wrapped her in his arms.

Krystal nuzzled her face into his shoulder and sobbed.

Krystal pulled away from Bryce. "What happened?"

"The cause of death has still not been determined," Mom said.

"I feel so helpless!"

Tammi shook her head. "We all do. There really isn't anything we can do but pray for her. And trust me, I'm sure 'Kenzie understands why you couldn't come. I think Lauren is with her right now."

"Krystal," Mom said. "I know this is hard, but you have to stay calm for the sake of your own heath and the baby's."

There was a knock on the door. Pastor Dave and Shirley entered. The caring pastor and his wife hugged each person. After a few minutes, Dave invited everyone to lay their hands on Krystal to pray over her and the baby. At the conclusion of the prayer, Tammi began to sing a song from church. Her voice rang out more beautifully than Krystal had ever heard. After the first few stanzas, Sadie joined in singing harmony. Bryce joined soon after, and then everyone was singing, including Krystal. As they sang, Krystal felt the baby kick, and she couldn't help but laugh.

"I think this little guy is going to be a musician like his daddy. Either that or a soccer player. But I think he likes the singing. He's kicking like crazy."

Bryce placed his hand on Krystal's stomach. His face lit up with a smile, and his green eyes had crinkles around the sides.

Mom extended the footrest of the ratty leather chair that sat in the corner, not far from the hospital bed. She tucked a blanket under her chin and smiled. "Night, sweetie."

"Do you have to go into work tomorrow, Mom?"

"Yep, but not 'til later." She yawned. "I'll go home to catch a shower and then go in for a few hours. I'll be back in the afternoon."

Soon Krystal heard soft snores coming from the corner. Mom must've been exhausted. Suddenly, Krystal felt a twitching in her legs and a wave of nausea washed over her. She glanced over at the fetal monitor. The little heart flashed red. She tried to prop herself up on her elbows but wasn't successful. Something wasn't right. Krystal felt for the call button nearby and pressed.

A voice crackled through a speaker. "A nurse will be right in."

Krystal wanted to cry out for her mother, but her tongue was thick and didn't work. She could only see the outline in the chair when Mom sat up straight and flew to Krystal's side. "What's going on?" Mom asked, but Krystal couldn't answer.

The door opened and light filled the room. Krystal squinted and watched an older nurse rush to the monitor. Another nurse came in and took her blood pressure. Soon a doctor was in her room. She could see his lips moving but couldn't understand what he was saying.

The next thing she knew, her bed was being wheeled out of the door and rushed through the hallway. The dark shadow of the demon called Death loomed overhead, while Silas and Theo followed closely behind, ready for battle once again.

CHAPTER 46

MACKENZIE leaned her head against the tiny window as the airplane lifted upward. Her stomach fluttered as the plane ascended higher. Harper leaned over from the middle seat to look out then quickly sat back. She grabbed Mackenzie's hand and squeezed. Trey had on his headphones and was searching for a movie on his iPad. Mackenzie watched as the trees and buildings grew smaller until the view became obscured by gigantic billows of clouds. She'd never been on an airplane before. With all of the moving around her family had done, they'd always driven.

Del was in the window seat in the row ahead of Mackenzie. Her mother's sister, Aunt Julia, sat in the middle seat next to him. Mackenzie closed her eyes. Why had Dad sent his children away with an aunt they barely knew? He said it would be good for them to have a change of scenery. "Aunt Julia has a house right near Newton Beach. You'll love it there," he'd said.

Maybe it would be a fun trip under normal circumstances. But their mother was dead, and Mackenzie never got to see her friends. Had she known that Aunt Julia was coming to take them, she wouldn't have refused to see Tammi and Sadie when they came over. Dad insisted Mackenzie and Harper talk with Lauren when she'd come to the house. Harper fell into Lauren's arms and wept uncontrollably. Mackenzie watched in frozen horror. It was as if Harper had enough tears for them both. Mackenzie had not shed even one.

Aunt Julia led them inside of her house on the hill that overlooked the ocean. Dad said Aunt Julia and her husband, Joe, were both doctors, but he didn't explain they were millionaires. The living room area was open and spacious with floor-to-ceiling windows.

"Wow!" Del said, rushing to look out.

"Let me show you to your rooms, guys," Aunt Julia said. "Boys, you'll share this room." She pointed in a doorway. Trey and Del entered, each claiming a bed.

To Mackenzie's relief, she and Harper had their own rooms with an adjoining bathroom to share. Mackenzie sat on the bed and glanced around at her personal space for the next week. The walls were a pale blue with a comforter to match. A whitewashed desk with a vase of fresh daisies sat in the corner. White shutters covered the open window, a cool salty breeze permeating the room. The entire house had a modern beach décor that was comforting.

Maybe Dad was right.

Mackenzie sat on the bed and glanced at the unanswered texts and missed calls from Tammi and Sadie. She felt a catch in her throat. She wanted to talk, but just didn't know how. There weren't any texts or calls from Krystal since the day Mackenzie's mother had died. Krystal had texted four times and called twice. She was probably angry that Mackenzie ignored her. Of all people, Mackenzie should have let Krystal know.

Mackenzie and her siblings spent the first few days at Aunt Julia and Uncle Joe's on the beach. The couple had taken time off from their medical practice to spend with the kids. One evening, her aunt called Mackenzie in her office. "Shut the door and have a seat."

Mackenzie sat in a big leather chair near the desk. Aunt Julia looked like a healthier, happier version of Mackenzie's mother, which was somehow comforting and haunting at the same time. There was a friendly glint in her obsidian eyes reminiscent of Harper's.

"I'd like to talk with you about your mother, all right?"

No, not really, Mackenzie thought but shrugged anyway.

"But first, I want you to know a few things about me. I'll start with telling you that Uncle Joe and I are both psychiatrists with our own practice. Part of the reason I took an interest in studying psychiatry was because of my sister. I wanted to help people with mental illness."

Mackenzie frowned and acid churned in her stomach. *Well, why didn't you try to help your own sister then? Now she's dead!*

Aunt Julia continued speaking about their difficult upbringing in what she called a "rigid religious home." Apparently, her mother didn't show signs of mental illness until Aunt Julia had left home for college. By the time she'd finished school, Angela and Howard had married and fled as far away from home as possible.

"I tried to have a relationship with my sister and all of you," her aunt said. "You might remember your uncle and I visiting a few times when you lived in Oklahoma?"

Mackenzie nodded to the hardwood floor.

"Your mother wasn't in a good place mentally, and your dad was in denial of how bad her illness was. We tried to help, but your family was on the move a lot and hard to keep track of. I'm so very sorry I wasn't there for my sister—for all of you," she said, her voice choked with tears.

Julia stopped talking, and the room was silent except for the distant sound of waves and night insects that floated in on the evening breeze from the open window. Mackenzie glanced up and was met with the pain-stricken face that reminded her of the last day she saw her mother. She swallowed down a hard lump, but still could not bring herself to cry. It seemed everyone had rivers to cry but her.

"I'd like to be here for you now," Aunt Julia's voice was quiet. "If you'll let me."

Another wave of anger hit Mackenzie. "Do I have a choice? I mean, we were forced to come here. I didn't even get to see my friends. I've never had friends until we moved to Arcana."

Aunt Julia came and kneeled near Mackenzie's chair. "Your dad needed to get his head straight, sweetie. It's only for a few more days. Your uncle and I will get you home for your mother's service and to see your friends. Listen, even though I'm heartbroken over my sister's untimely death, I'm hopeful for the opportunity to finally be there for your family. To get to know you. I love you and your family."

Something dislodged deep down in Mackenzie's heart—or more like what was rock-hard was now softening. "You look like her," Mackenzie said. "She was beautiful *until* …"

"I hear you're quite the artist like Angela. And you have her lovely skin."

Mackenzie looked toward the window, wishing she could somehow float away on the ocean breeze. Oh, to just leave her own skin for just a little while, to be free of the fear and depression and soar over the waves rather than drown in them. "I'm scared of—" her voice trailed off.

Aunt Julia put her hand on Mackenzie's leg. "You're worried that you might have mental issues too, right? It's okay to say it. And it's a normal concern."

Mackenzie squeezed her eyes shut and nodded.

"Well, in my professional opinion, I see no signs of that whatsoever. Not with you or your siblings. In fact, I see so much strength, and love, and faith. I also spoke briefly to Lauren and your pastor, and they say the same thing. You have carried so much for a long time as the older sister, Mackenzie." Aunt Julia's soothing words fell over her like a cozy robe in the winter. "Oh, and I want you to know that Harper told me about the cutting."

Mackenzie opened her eyes. "She *did*?" That was a big deal and a good sign.

Her aunt nodded. "Harper said she will continue seeing Lauren, and she'll talk to me via Facetime. She's going to be okay. Uncle Joe has spoken with Trey and Del. Your family has gone through a lot. But with God's help and the help you are all getting from church, you'll make it through this, sweetie." Aunt Julia opened her arms. "Come here, honey."

Mackenzie leaped forward into her aunt's arms, nearly knocking the woman over. They hugged tightly and rocked back and forth. Julia smelled sweet like Mackenzie's mother. It felt good to be held by family. Mackenzie knew she was not alone and never would be. She had God, family, and friends. How wrong she'd been to block them out.

Finally, the cleansing tears began to fall.

CHAPTER 47

DAWN chewed what was left of her thumb nail as she waited for Tammi. A middle-aged waitress with splotchy hot pink lipstick poured steaming coffee into Dawn's mug. She lifted the cup with a shaking hand and took a sip. Maybe caffeine wasn't the best idea. She checked the time … again. Dawn rehearsed in her mind how to begin the conversation. Should she start with begging Tammi's forgiveness or just get right to the point? Groveling wasn't Dawn's style. And besides, Tammi would think it was an act. But for some reason, she had to try. At this point, what did she have to lose? There was no one else who cared.

The bell on the diner door rang and Tammi strode inside, dark spiral curls blowing back gently from her face. Dawn's stomach was fluttery. She placed her hands in her lap beneath the table and dug at the skin at the sides of her nails. Tammi turned her head from side to side, eyes steely and mouth a stiff straight line.

How can I make her believe me? I could really use a friend right now.

TAMMI trudged reluctantly into Hank's diner. Hopefully she hadn't fallen into another one of Dawn's traps. She had enough to deal with at the moment without Dawn's unwelcome tricks. Mackenzie's mom was dead, and she'd skipped town without talking to her friends. And Krystal had an emergency C-section delivery of her baby who was now fighting for his little life in neonatal intensive care. At least Krystal was stable. But none of them could say they knew the same for 'Kenzie.

So, why am I here, God? Tammi prayed as she walked. *I think you want me to be here, but you know how crafty Dawn is, and I'm only seventeen. I feel like this is David and that giant Goliath dude. I need your help big time here, God.*

Tammi spotted Dawn in a booth in the far back. Dawn's narrow chin jutted up, a haughty grin on her face. Tammi breathed deeply and slid into the booth across from the little enchantress, still praying in her head. Tammi didn't speak. This was Dawn's show—let her get things rolling. She stared into the hazel eyes that had haunted her for so long. But something was different. She didn't have on the usual pound of make-up, and she wasn't wearing her usual revealing clothes. What was she up to now? Tammi glanced around the diner, twirling a straw between her fingers, waiting for Dawn to speak. Fifties' music pumped through the old-fashioned jukebox, filling the empty space between them.

"Thanks for meeting me after I stood you up," Dawn said. "I'm sorry, but I chickened out."

"Yeah, you said that in your text. So, what's this about?" Tammi noticed Dawn's dry lips were trembling. This was new too.

"I left the band."

"Why?"

"You know our manager is my uncle, right?" A muscle ticked by Dawn's right eye.

"Yeah, and?"

"Uncle Luther is evil—worse than my aunt I told you about." Dawn looked down at the table. "I mean it."

A sinking feeling threatened to pull Tammi under. No wonder Dawn acted the way she did. But Tammi could tell it wasn't an act this time. This was the real Dawn—a vulnerable girl hidden beneath the sleazy rock n' roll image. And Lord knows, Dawn would recognize true evil. Her pupils were dilated like she'd seen a ghost. The girl was frightened out of her mind.

"What did he do to you?"

"What *didn't* he do? The great apartment, nice car, awesome clothes—everything is from him. All I had to do was be whatever he wanted me to be." Dawn covered her face with shaking hands. Her nails had been bitten to the nub. "I've done so many awful things," she whispered. "But when he got into hardcore drugs and started hurting me—" She looked straight into Tammi's eyes. "He used me, and I knew it. But he never used to beat me." Her eyes were focused on the table now. "I knew that I needed out. So, this is my chance. I think I can make it on my own. I'm a pharmacy tech. I have that to fall back on. At least, I hope so. But I'll need to find a cheaper apartment."

"Will he hurt you if you leave? And what about Gary and the others?" Tammi's heart hammered in her ears.

"Gary, Gil, and Ed are mesmerized by their newfound fame and all the groupies and parties. But as for me, I've been replaced. When we were doing a gig in Vegas,

Uncle Luther lured this wanna-be-Avril Lavigne—'fresh meat' as he called her. She's a great singer—very young, beautiful, and naïve."

"I'm sorry, Dawn. Really. But what do you want from me? Seriously, I'm just a high school student."

"Well, first off, can you ever forgive me for the things I did to you and your friends? I know I've been awful." She shrugged. "I don't have a good excuse. Jealousy, maybe?"

Tammi made an audible hissing sound. "Ah, forgiveness. That word seems to follow me." She thought about the letter to her dad and the freedom she was experiencing as she was learning to forgive. "All I can say is, I will try. But I don't know if I can trust you. That, you'll have to earn."

Dawn nodded at the table and fidgeted in her seat. She looked like a small child who was being punished. "I can understand that." She looked up. "I know this will sound weird to you, but I was also was wondering if you could talk to me about—uh, *your faith*." she whispered. "I was serious when I texted you to pray for me. I've been so scared. I need a real friend."

Tammi prayed in her mind. *God, I still don't trust this girl. And I'm new at all of this Christian stuff.* Suddenly, an idea came to her.

"Okay, Dawn. But first, I have something to show you. Let's go."

Tammi and Dawn exited the elevator at the hospital where Krystal had given birth.

"This way," Tammi said, and led Dawn down the quiet white hallway with slick floors.

"Isn't this where they keep babies? I thought we were here to see your dad."

"Why?"

"Well, you wouldn't tell me, so I started trying to figure it out. He's dying of cancer, right?"

Tammi stopped in her tracks and spun toward Dawn. "No. And that's all I'll say right now. Let's go." She didn't trust Dawn and there was no way she was having *that* conversation.

They continued walking until they reached the neonatal intensive care unit. Tammi pushed a button on the wall outside of the double doors. After a moment, the doors swung open. Tammi led Dawn to the area where people could watch the babies through the enormous glass window. And there inside were Krystal and Bryce. The young couple leaned forward and stared into the clear chamber that held their tiny baby boy. The baby had tubes, tape, and wires all over his fragile body. There were five other babies in their own separate clear chambers. Some cried and flailed their little red arms and legs while others hardly seemed alive.

Standing nearby Bryce and Krystal's son was a fearsome angel with long white hair and glowing silver eyes. The angel was called Christopher and was assigned to be the child's guardian. Demons of many ranks and sizes hid in corners and crevices throughout the room. There the unholy creatures would wait until an opportunity arose to harass and torment the unsuspecting humans. The demons had their orders, but so did the angels. The spiritual battle for these young souls was only just beginning.

Dawn gasped, hands flying to her chest. She looked at Tammi with watery eyes. "Oh my gosh. Will the baby be okay?"

"I guess he's doing pretty good for being delivered six weeks early. He'll be in here for a while, though. Thank God, Krystal is doing great. They even sent her home. I know she still has pain, but she's here every day with Bryce to see the baby."

"Wow. But why did you bring me here? What does this have to do with being a Christian?" Dawn asked.

"That's the thing. It has *everything* to do with it. This has Jesus all over it."

A voice came from behind them. "Yes, it does."

The girls turned to see Pastor Dave and Lauren, both with wide grins on their faces. Tammi wanted to wrap each of them in a hug but restrained herself.

Thank you, God! I asked for help and you delivered BIG time. Who better to talk to Dawn?

"Dawn, this is Pastor Dave, and I think you remember Lauren. She's also a musician and singer."

Pastor Dave held out his arm to shake hands. Dawn raised hers reluctantly, an anxious look in her eyes. Tammi understood because she'd felt that way about church people in the past. She worried they could somehow sense all her dirty secrets. She said another quick prayer in her head, but this time not for herself—for Dawn. It was becoming a thing to pray for people she'd previously had a love/hate history with. Oh, yeah. Totally God.

"Sooo," Tammi said. "Dawn has some questions about Jesus ..."

CHAPTER 48

SADIE sat at the kitchen table cutting out shapes for a craft for Sunday school class. She'd already finished preparing the lesson based on the story about how Jesus used a little boy's lunch to feed a crowd of five thousand. She was giddy knowing the kids would love it. Lately, Sadie found herself thinking more often about her love for teaching.

A light had switched on when Claire spoke to her before the dance recital a few weeks ago. She loved dancing, and that would never change. But she could be passionate about other things too. Not that she was giving up on her dream to dance professionally, but something had shifted, and she had a whole new dream. All along, Sadie had placed her identity in becoming a dancer. The accident forced her to realize that she was way *more* than a dancer. In fact, her identity did not come from dancing at all. Dancing was only one of God's many gifts she enjoyed.

The doorbell rang and the voices of her friends filled the house. Sadie quickly picked up her lesson plan as Krystal and Tammi walked in. She looked up at her friends from the chair. It was so good to see Krystal up and around. No one would know she'd just had a baby a week ago. Sadie knew she was still feeling pain from the C-section, but you wouldn't know that either. Other than going to see the baby, Krystal had been in bed. Both of her tall friends looked especially beautiful in their dresses. Sadie had better get ready too.

"What's all this?" Krystal asked. "And you're not ready."

Tammi stuck her tongue out. "Bleh! I know what it is. Stuff for her class of runny-nosed midgets. It baffles me how you *voluntarily* do this."

Krystal laughed. "Well, it probably makes her feel like the queen of Munchkin Land!"

"Ha, ha! You guys are a riot!" Sadie flipped her long hair over her shoulder and stood. "Yikes, I lost track of time. Come upstairs with me while I get dressed." Sadie hurried out of the kitchen.

Tammi and Krystal sat on the bed thumbing through the class yearbook and snickering as Sadie slid into her pink dress.

Tammi glanced up. "Hey, that's what you're wearing? Pink? We all know it's your signature color, but aren't we supposed to wear black or like dark clothes to a funeral?" The question hung in the air then dropped with a sickening dose of reality.

They were going to the funeral for Mackenzie's mom.

Sadie looked down at herself and back at her friends, sucking in her lips. Tammi was probably right. But what about her plan she hadn't shared with her friends yet? Maybe it, too, wasn't appropriate. After all, Mackenzie had just arrived home last night. No one had even seen her yet. Sadie eyed the black and white photo of her friends and Lauren on the wall. No, Sadie knew the idea was from God.

"You're right, Tam," Sadie said. "Did you finally get to talk to 'Kenzie, Krystal?"

Krystal nodded. "She called me when she got home from the airport last night. It was awkward at first. I mean, I didn't know what to say, ya know? Oh, I'm so sorry your mom's dead—and then silence."

Sadie nodded. She swallowed down the lump in her throat and turned to change her dress. She put some lip gloss on and fluffed her curls. "Okay, I'm ready. We better get over to 'Kenzie's."

As the girls started for the door, Sadie grabbed a pink gift bag from her desk.

"Wait, what's that?" Krystal asked, pointing at the bag.

"You'll have to wait and see. I have a secret plan ..."

As Sadie predicted, both Krystal and Tammi's eyes looked up at the ceiling as they mumbled and grumbled and walked out the door. And as usual, Sadie giggled and followed behind.

Harper opened the front door with a forlorn look. Sadie was the first to step in. She quickly wrapped Harper in a hug. Although a few years younger, the sweet girl had become a friend too. Sadie released Harper, stepped back, and glanced behind, noticing Krystal and Tammi's pinched faces. Like Sadie, they were at a loss for words, and unlike Sadie, they weren't into hugs.

To everyone's relief, Harper spoke. "'Kenzie's in her room with Lauren," she said and waved for them to follow.

The girls walked behind Harper down the hall until she paused at Mackenzie's closed door. Sadie's stomach churned. They hadn't seen Mackenzie since before her mother's death. Harper knocked once and opened the door, then walked away. The three friends entered the familiar blue room with clouds on the ceiling—the artwork of Angela Stine. Lauren sat with Mackenzie on the bed. Mackenzie's eyes filled as she stood. Sadie rushed to her, Krystal and Tammi right behind. They all huddled together, their arms wrapped around Mackenzie and each other.

The soft sniffles turned to heavy sobs when Mackenzie broke free and glanced at each face. "I'm so sorry for not talking to you guys." She turned her gaze to Krystal. "Can you forgive me? I feel like a terrible best friend."

"Are you kidding? And you already said all this when we talked on the phone last night." Krystal said. "Friends until we're old and gray, remember, Gail?"

"Yeah, I remember, Helga. And you're okay to be up and around?"

Krystal nudged Mackenzie. "I'll be fine. But seriously, there's no way you could have been there. And I'm sorry I wasn't there for you too."

Tammi shook her head. "Yeah, well, you were a little busy giving birth, Helga! Not sure what's with the weird old lady names."

Everyone laughed, including Lauren, who had joined the huddle. She looked adorable with her round belly poking through her dark sleeveless sundress. "I think this would be a good time to pray together," she said.

They all held hands, and Lauren led a simple prayer asking God to strengthen the Stine family. The room radiated like the sun rising over a hill with golden beams shooting upward and outward. Silas and Theo appeared within the light. Theo's dark skin glistened in contrast with Silas's bronzed skin. Both of the angels' eyes blazed with holy white fire. The soldiers stood on either side of the girls facing one another. Their wings unfurled widely and touched tip to tip, encircling the prayer group with an impenetrable feathery covering until Lauren said amen.

Meanwhile, Commander Philo, along with a legion of warrior angels wearing full armor, stood guard outside of the house, shimmering swords drawn. It was a formidable sight in the spirit realm. There would be no demon infiltration today.

"Thanks, you guys," Mackenzie said. "I don't know how I could make it through this without you."

Sadie took a few steps back and quickly grabbed the bag she'd set down near the door. She glanced at Lauren, who was in on the plan with her. Lauren gave a nod as Sadie walked back to her friends. She reached into the bag and pulled out a glimmering silver tiara and placed it on Mackenzie's head.

"Is that, like, real?" Tammi asked. "Well, I'm sure those aren't real diamonds. What I mean is, it looks like something from The Princess Diaries."

Lauren smiled. She was now wearing one too. "It *is* real."

Krystal grabbed the side of the bag and peered inside. "What in the world? There's more of them! How did you get these?"

Sadie took out another sparkling jeweled tiara and placed it on Krystal's head. Without saying a word, she placed another on Tammi's head, and finally one on her own.

"Ballerinas always have tiaras," Sadie said.

"Huh? Come again?" Tammi said.

Sadie huffed. "I got them from the dance company."

Mackenzie walked to the mirror and looked at herself. "And we can keep these?"

"It's like the paper Lauren gave us with the warrior princess girl and the inscription on the picture frame." Sadie pointed to the picture of the friends that hung above 'Kenzie's dresser. "Yeah, we get to keep 'em, *a-a-and*, we are wearing them today to your mom's service because we need to go wearing the armor of God that Lauren has been teaching us about."

"Uh, I don't remember a crown in the armor. I think there was a helmet. But it was like stuff a Roman warrior would wear with a sword and everything. Not Ms. America," Krystal said.

Sadie sighed. Leave it to Krystal to get all technical. Ugh! She glanced toward Lauren, hoping she would bail her out.

Lauren smirked. "I'm glad you remember the helmet, Krystal. That *is* one of the pieces of armor—the helmet of salvation. But the crown is because of our identity in Christ. We are daughters of the King of kings. That makes us warrior princesses. And by the way, the Bible says we get real crowns with real jewels when we get to heaven. We will lay them at the feet of Jesus. But more on that during our summer study. Oh, but I can tell you that we receive a jewel in our crown when we lead others to Christ like you did with Dawn, Tammi."

Mackenzie's mouth dropped open in shock. "Holy cow! Dawn is a Christian now? I missed a lot in just a week. Krystal's baby and now this? You guys will have to tell me how in the world *that* happened. Unbelievable!"

"True," Lauren said. "Both are brand new lives. Both are miracles."

Tammi beamed. "It *is* a miracle about Dawn. I still can't believe it. And I'm still working on trusting her. But we can talk about that later."

Sadie chimed in. "So you see, we get armor *and* crowns!" She stuck out her tongue at Krystal.

"She's the queen of Munchkin Land," Krystal said and elbowed Sadie's ribs. Sadie gave Krystal a small shove. But Krystal lost her balance and fell into Tammi, who seemed ready to retaliate until she remembered Krystal's weakened condition.

Tammi raised her pierced brow. "Mm-hm, I'll remember that," she said half-jokingly.

Mackenzie sat on the bed with her hands in her lap and head down, unfazed by the horseplay. They needed to be more sensitive. Poor 'Kenzie. Today was her mother's funeral, for goodness' sake. Sadie felt a tug at her heart and hurried to sit next to her. Krystal sat on the other side of 'Kenzie. Lauren and Tammi drew close.

All joking aside, this was the hardest day of Mackenzie's life.

"There's been so much pain and brokenness," Mackenzie said. "I just don't know how life will ever be good again. I still can't believe she's gone."

Lauren kneeled in front of Mackenzie. "I know it's hard to see it now, but things *will* get better. God has been awakening each of you to see his great love. He can take even what was intended for evil and turn it around for our good. In fact, all of us are damaged and broken, 'Kenzie. But God—he's in the business of making things brand new." Lauren glanced at each of the girls. "Remember back when Sadie and Tammi were in the hospital and I quoted a Scripture from the book of Isaiah to you guys? It's on the frame too."

Sadie, Krystal, and Tammi nodded, but Mackenzie shook her head.

"'To all who mourn in Israel, he will give a crown of beauty for ashes, a joyous blessing instead of mourning, festive praise instead of despair,'" Lauren quoted. "God will help you push out that spirit of despair and depression, and he will replace your mourning with joy again, 'Kenzie. And we will be here through the tears *and* the joy. I promise you, joy is coming."

Sadie glanced at her wrist. "Um, guys, we've got to go."

Mackenzie swiped quickly beneath her eyes and stood. "Okay, I think I can do this." Her face contorted as she backed against the wall. "Oooh—I don't know if I can." She slid down the wall until she was sitting on the floor with her knees to her chest.

"You *can* do it, 'Kenzie," Krystal said. "I know this is the hardest thing you've ever done. But I also know how strong you are. I mean, you didn't back down through all my crap. And when you set your mind to something, you do it. You've had straight A's your whole life. Plus, we will be right there with you."

"And with Harper too," Sadie added.

"Totally," Tammi said. "She can sit next to me. I'll ask her if she wants to."

Mackenzie's lips turned up. "I know she'd like that. You guys are the best."

"You've got that right," Krystal said, and extended her hand to help Mackenzie up from the floor.

'Kenzie gave an exaggerated eye roll. She straightened her crown and gave a quick nod, then took Krystal's hand and stood. "Let's go, warrior princesses!" she said with determination, and strode toward the door.

Sadie glanced at Mackenzie and Tammi as they looked through the glass at Krystal and Bryce with their tiny son. Even though the baby still had wires and tubes, he looked a little bigger today. Sadie whispered a prayer for the health of the baby, for his parents who she hoped stayed together despite the incredible challenges ahead, for 'Kenzie who'd just buried her mother, and for Tammi to find peace and forgiveness.

"Life goes on," Mackenzie said, still looking at the young couple with their infant.

Sadie laid a hand on 'Kenzie's shoulder. "It's been a tough day. Are you okay?"

Mackenzie turned to her, dark eyes brimming. "I will be."

Tammi placed a hand on 'Kenzie's other shoulder. "I think so too."

The girls watched Krystal and Bryce leave the room behind the glass. Soon the parents were headed toward the three friends. Mackenzie took a few steps toward them and Sadie and Tammi followed.

"How's he doing?" Mackenzie asked Krystal.

Bryce answered for her. "He's great! Getting stronger every day." His smile reached his bright green eyes.

"Now that's a proud papa, right there," Tammi said.

Bryce put his arm around Krystal. "Sooo, you guys ready to get some ice cream?"

"Duh!" All four girls said in unison.

"Okay, we've got that settled," Bryce laughed. "Let's head out." He glanced at Krystal. "We can stop by and say goodnight to our son after."

Mackenzie, Tammi, and Sadie walked ahead of the lovebirds. As the friends made their way down the hallway, feet echoing on the tile, Mackenzie came to an abrupt stop, causing Bryce's sneakers to screech and everyone to halt with her. She swirled around and looked to Krystal, her dark eyes wide and wild. There was a moment of uncomfortable silence.

What was happening?

"Oh my gosh! I can't believe I didn't ask you this yet. What did you name the baby?" She cocked her head to one side. "Bryce, I bet."

"Nooo, smarty." Krystal sighed heavily, and a wide grin took over her face.

"*Isaiah* Bryce Williams!"

The End

ABOUT THE AUTHOR

BECKIE LINDSEY is an award-winning poet, author, freelancer, blogger, and the editor of Southern California Christian Voice, a division of One Christian Voice, a national news syndicating agency. She is major coffeeholic and enjoys a good book with a cat on her lap. She also loves to hike and hang out with family and friends. Beckie and her husband, Scott, have three adult children, two adorable cats and live in California.

AWAKENING STUDY QUESTIONS

SPIRITUAL WARFARE

Note: If you are not familiar with spiritual warfare, introductory teaching on this vital topic is included in *Secrets, Uninvited*, and *Daybreak*, the first three books of this series. If you do not have the books, you can purchase them online from Amazon, Barnes & Noble, or Walmart. Quantities may be ordered directly from Elk Lake Publishing, Inc.

Exposing Satan's Strategies

"Put on all of God's armor so that you will be able to stand firm against all strategies of the devil." Ephesians 6:11 NLT

Why do we experience spiritual defeats—even after salvation?

1. **Read the passage of Scripture below.**

"Stay alert! Watch out for your great enemy, the devil. He prowls around like a roaring lion, looking for someone to devour. Stand firm against him, and be strong in your faith."

1 Peter 5:8-9

Fill in the blanks using the passage above.
"_____ _____! Watch out for your great enemy, the devil. He prowls around like a _____ _____, looking for someone to devour. _____ _____ against him, and be strong

in your _____."

(Note: If you have not placed your faith in God and want to know how, please go to page 341)

2. Satan is powerful and crafty, but he is not God's equal—not even close. **Read the passage of Scripture below, then answer the question.**

"And I am convinced that nothing can ever separate us from God's love. Neither death nor life, neither angels nor demons, neither our fears for today nor our worries about tomorrow—not even the powers of hell can separate us from God's love. No power in the sky above or in the earth below—indeed, nothing in all creation will ever be able to separate us from the love of God that is revealed in Christ Jesus our Lord." Romans 8:38-39

What can separate you from God's love

_____

3. The Bible explains that we battle against three things. **Read the passage below and list the three things in bold:**

1. _____

2. _____

3. _____

*"Once you were dead because of your disobedience and your many **sins**. You used to live in sin, just like the rest of the world, obeying the **devil**—the commander of the powers in the unseen **world**. He is the spirit at work in the hearts of those who refuse to*

obey God. All of us used to live that way, following the passionate desires and inclinations of our sinful nature. By our very nature we were subject to God's anger, just like everyone else." Ephesians 2:1-3

Although Christians have the Holy Spirit living within, they also have a sinful nature that is at war with the Holy Spirit. *"But there is another power within me that is at war with my mind ... So you see how it is: In my mind I really want to obey God's law, but because of my sinful nature I am a slave to sin."* Romans 7:23;25

4. **Read the passages below and fill in the blanks with the words in bold.**

*"But you are not **controlled** by your **sinful nature**. You are controlled by **the Spirit** if you have the Spirit of God living in you. (And remember that those who do not have the Spirit of Christ living in them do not belong to him at all.) ... Therefore, dear brothers and sisters, you have no **obligation** to do what your sinful nature **urges** you to do."* Romans 8:9;12

But you are not _____ by your _____. You are controlled by _____. Therefore, dear brothers and sisters, you have no _____to do what the sinful nature _____ you to do.

5. Because God forgives us from every sin, does this mean we should go on sinning? **Read the passage below and then answer yes or no and why.**____

_____

_____

"Well then, since God's grace has set us free from the law, does that mean we can go on sinning? Of course not! Don't you realize that you become the slave of whatever you choose to obey? You can be a slave to sin, which leads to death, or you can choose to obey God, which leads to righteous living. Thank God! Once you were slaves of sin, but now you wholeheartedly obey this teaching we have given you. Now you are free from your slavery to sin, and you have become slaves to righteous living." Romans 6:15-18

Anger and Forgiveness

The Beauties from Ashes characters wrestle with anger and forgiveness. For example, Krystal is angry with her parents for separating, Mackenzie is often angry at herself for being depressed, Sadie gets angry at her parents' "no dating" rule, and Tammi is angry at her abusive father.

God gave us our emotions, including anger. Remember, we are all created in God's good image. The problem with anger is what we *do* with it.

"In your anger, do not sin. Don't let the sun go down while you are still angry, and do not give the devil a foothold." Ephesians 4:26-27

God does not tell us it is wrong to experience anger. He tells us not to sin through the expression of our anger. According to many psychologists, anger is a secondary emotion. What does this mean? Typically, one of the primary emotions like fear or sadness can be found beneath the anger.

Although Tammi is baffled by Sadie's ability to forgive her abusers, she recognizes the freedom and peace her friend demonstrates. When Tammi asked Sadie how she was able to forgive her abusers, Sadie admits that it was her continued faith in God that helped her process her anger and work on forgiveness.

Forgiveness doesn't necessarily mean that the person is not guilty of whatever they did (like Tammi and Sadie's abusers). Forgiveness also doesn't mean forgetting. Rather, forgiveness means letting go of the pain the incident(s) have caused us. As God did with Sadie, he can give us the power to not be consumed by anger. After all, God forgave us of our sins, and he calls us to forgive others.

"If you forgive those who sin against you, your heavenly Father will forgive you." Matthew 6:14

6. Are you experiencing anger toward someone? Do you think your anger is rooted in fear, sadness, or disappointment? How are you handling it?

_____

_____

_____

_____

_____

_____

Prayer is the biggest weapon we have against our anger. Here is an example of a prayer you could use.

Father, thank you for forgiving me of my sins. I want to forgive others the way you forgave me. Jesus, help me to keep my anger in check by the power of your love and Word. Show me right away when anger flares up so that I can ask for your help and not give the devil a foothold. Your Identity in Christ

With Lauren's help, the girls begin to learn that God sees them as his beloved daughters. Because God is the King of kings, this means all believers are princesses (or princes). However, the devil does not want believers to embrace who they are or who they belong to. He looks for ways to tempt us to sin and then condemns us when we do.

7. **Look up the word "condemnation" in the dictionary and write the definition below.**

_____

_____

_____

_____

8. Condemnation is one of the main strategies used against Bryce and the girls. Satan attempts the same tactic with us too. **Have you experienced this? If so, share what happened and what you did about it. __**

_____

_____

_____

_____

_____

_____

9. Read the passage of Scripture below.

"Therefore there is no condemnation for those who belong to Christ Jesus. And because you belong to him, the power of the life-giving Spirit has freed you from the power of sin that leads to death." Romans 8:1-2

Now fill in the blanks below with your name and read it aloud.

Therefore there is no condemnation for _____ who belongs to Christ Jesus. And because _____ belongs to him, the power of the life-giving Spirit has freed _____ from the power of sin that leads to death.

The antidote for condemnation is the truth of God's Word.

It is important to know what the Bible says about those who belong to Christ.

10. A) Pick three Scriptures from "Who I Am in Christ" to read each day. B) Write your favorites on notecards, and work on memorizing one verse each week. C) Add your name to your favorite Scriptures.

Who I Am In Christ

I am treasured. (Deuteronomy 7:6; 14:2; 26:18; 1 Peter 2:9-10)

I am loved beyond comparison. (1 John 4:19; 4:10; 3:16; Romans 5:8; 8:34-39)

I am God's special possession. (1 Peter 2:9;

Deuteronomy 14:2)**I am God's child.** (1 John 3:1; Galatians 3:26)**I am wonderfully created by God.** (Psalm 139:13-14)

I am worth dying for. (1 John 3:16; Romans 5:7-9)

I am forgiven. (Ephesians 1:7; 1 John 1:9; Romans 8:1, 33-39)

I am secure for all eternity. (2 Corinthians 1:22; John 10:28-29)**I am seated with Jesus Christ in the heavenly realm.** (Ephesians 2:6)

I am set free. (Romans 6:18; Galatians 5:1)

I am precious to Him. (Isaiah 43:4)

I am set apart. (John 15:16,19; 1 Peter 2:9)

I can do everything through Christ who gives me strength. (Philippians 4:13)

I am a princess (or prince) in God's kingdom. (John 1:12; 1 Timothy 6:15)

I have the mind of Christ. (1 Corinthians 2:16)

I am God's co-worker. (2 Corinthians 6:1; 1 Corinthians 3:9)

I am a friend of God. (John 15:15)

11. **Extra credit! Read Romans chapters 6-8 and journal what you learn.**

How You Can Become a Christian
A—ADMIT

Admit to God that you are a sinner (Romans 3:23; Romans 6:23). Repent, which means to turn away from your sin (Acts 3:19).

B—BELIEVE

Believe that Jesus is God's Son and accept God's gift of forgiveness of sin (Romans 5:8; Acts 4:12; John 3:16; John 14:6).

C—CHOOSE

Choose to follow Jesus as your Lord and Savior (Romans 10:9-10, 13).

Now, say a simple prayer like this:

God, I know I have sinned, and that sin has separated me from you. I believe you sent your Son, Jesus, as the only way back to you. I believe Jesus died on the cross, rose again, and is alive. Please forgive me. I ask Jesus to come into my life as my Lord and Savior. I will obey you and live for you the rest of my life.

Resources:

1. If you are feeling suicidal, lonely, or depressed, please reach out for help.**Samaritan's Hope offers 24/7 crisis services. 1-877- 870-HOPE (4673) | Call or text 24/7.**

2. If you are pregnant and need assistance or if you are considering abortion, please talk to a trusted adult or counselor before you take any action.
Heartbeat International offers assistance. 24/7 helpline (1-800-712-HELP).

3. For anyone affected by abuse and needing support, you are not alone.

National Domestic Violence Hotline offers crisis support 24/7 (1-800-799-7233).

4. Are you struggling with an eating disorder? Please do not suffer alone.

Center for Discovery Eating Disorder Treatment. (1-855-399-1186).

Appendix:

Anderson, N. (2001) *Who I am in Christ.* Bloomington, Minnesota. Bethany House Publishers

Shirer, P. (2015) *Armor of God.* Nashville, TN. LifeWay Press

OTHER BOOKS BY BECKIE LINDSEY

Beauty From Ashes Series
Secrets
Uninvited
Daybreak
Awakening